T0160764

GUTTER BOYS

Also by Alvin Orloff

I Married An Earthling

GUTTER BOYS

A Novel

by

Alvin Orloff

Manic D Press
San Francisco

© 2004 Alvin Orloff. All rights reserved. Published by Manic D Press. No part of this book may be used or reproduced in any manner whatsoever without written permission of the publisher except in the case of brief quotations embodied in critical articles or reviews. For information, address Manic D Press, Box 410804, San Francisco, California 94141. www.manicdpress.com

Cover design: Scott Idleman/Blink

Library of Congress Cataloging-in-Publication Data

Orloff, Alvin, 1961-
Gutter boys : a novel / by Alvin Orloff.
p. cm.
ISBN 0-916397-93-9 (trade pbk. original : alk. paper)
1. Gay youth—Fiction. 2. Young men—Fiction. 3. Sex customs—Fiction. 4. New wave music—Fiction. 5. Manhattan (New York, N.Y.)—Fiction. 6. San Francisco (Calif.)—Fiction. I. Title.
PS3565.R5795G88 2004
813'.54—dc22
2004008760

"We are all of us in the gutter,
but some of us are looking at the stars."
— Oscar Wilde

This book is dedicated to my favorite stargazer,
Tony Vaguely

Prologue

Americans, as everyone knows, are a forward-looking people. This has some wonderful consequences (an amazing capacity for self-reinvention and a disinclination to hold grudges) but also some drawbacks, chief among them an ignorance of history and a tendency to romanticize the past as a better, simpler and/or more vital time. Nostalgic visions bump historical facts and personal memories right out of our heads. Hence, I have taken the liberty of providing a brief synopsis, a social snapshot if you will, of the years 1981 and 1982. Without further ado, please follow me back, back, back through the mists of time to the dawn of the '80s...

You do not need to check your email, because there are no personal computers and there is no internet. Banish from your mind any thoughts of driving down the street in your SUV while talking on your cell phone, because they too have yet to be invented. While you're at it, forget about Palm Pilots, Cuisinarts, DVDs, or digital anything. No call-waiting. The newest technological wonder is the ATM. Should you be one of the lucky few with access to this innovation, your banking no longer need be done on weekdays between the hours of ten and three.

The word "Yuppie" hasn't been coined yet but "Preppies" are everywhere, advocating a return to the values and styles of the East Coast WASP aristocracy. Thanks to their influence there has been a huge revival for formerly passé phenomena like the penny loafer and the Republican Party.

Synthpop is sweeping the charts, bringing with it a gender-bending aesthetic that instantly makes it the music of choice amongst young homosexuals. While women like Annie Lennox cross-dress, men and straight stars slather their faces in makeup like Duran Duran. A host of flamboyantly, if not openly, gay male performers attain superstardom including members of The B-52s, Culture Club, The Associates, Klaus Nomi, Dead or Alive, Pete Shelley, and Soft Cell.

Unemployment is nearing 10% and for the first time since the 1930s, homelessness and begging are found beyond the confines of skid row, shocking and shaming the nation.

A spunky punky young group of London designers is turning the fashion world upside-down by flinging rubber kink, the pirate look, and all manner of multi-culti madness onto the runways. Those who still favor the more conservative looks of Milan and Paris suddenly look like Eurotrash.

Far from being today's chainstore-ridden, overpriced, and sanitized playground for plutocrats, Manhattan is the nation's foremost example of urban decay. Nineteenth century squalor—tenements and trash, exotic accents and unsanitary conditions—is shockingly common. The poor and wealthy alike are forced into daily contact with decrepitude and danger.

Fruit does not come with little labels stuck on it. It is only fruit.

Hippies, though greatly diminished in numbers since their heyday in the late '60s and early '70s, are still common as mud. They hate synthpop because it's, like, so artificial, man.

Outside San Francisco, the few existing gay anti-discrimination laws have been repealed under pressure from Anita Bryant and the Moral Majority. The success of gay lib in the '70s seems like a brief anomaly, now ending. There are no open homosexuals in Congress, big business, religion, professional sports, or even Hollywood.

A new and strangely addictive video game called Pac Man is captivating the nation's youth, replacing pinball machines as the arcade game of choice.

President Reagan, while pushing the usual Robin Hood in reverse agenda of the right wing, distinguishes himself with an over-the-top loopiness. He avers that trees cause pollution, fails to recognize the sole African-American member of his cabinet, and relates transparently fabricated anecdotes about welfare queens buying vodka with food stamps. All this is done with a sly wink to the camera and a cloying air of simulated folksiness. He is massively popular. Leftists, irked that The People have forsaken them, become cynical and cranky.

Only the wealthy have VCRs, cable TV, or telephone answering machines.

The Cold War death match between the United States and the Soviet Union is dragging into its fourth decade. While the latter nominally seems a Communist super-power, it is in fact a crumbling, old-style European empire run by geriatric white men. Most of the left has abandoned it as a source of political inspiration (turning instead to Red China or literary theory) but a few stalwarts still believe, despite all evidence, it is humanity's greatest hope.

Abuse and family dysfunction have not yet been pathologized in popular culture. The nuclear family is imagined as both the foundation of a healthy society and a peaceful haven from life's turmoil instead of the roiling cauldron of sadism and sexual intrigue those of us familiar with modern TV talk shows now know it to be.

Inspired by Dada and surrealism, retro Futurism, swinging London, Andy Warhol, and punk rock, a scene known simply as "Downtown" is springing up in Lower Manhattan. Equally eclectic, iconoclastic, and whimsical, among the participants in this new underground are painters Keith Haring, Kenny Scharf and Jean-Michel Basquiat, performers Jon Sex, Ann Magnussen and Joey Arias, fashion designer Stephen Sprouse, literary lioness Tama Janowitz, and musical act Kid Creole & The Coconuts.

TV evangelists, some of them actually wearing polyester suits and pinky rings, become hugely popular, bilking hundreds of millions of dollars out of gullible Christians while spreading hatred of homosexuality and liberalism. This unexpected upsurge of fundamentalism creates a feeling disorientation and anxiety among secular types.

Punk, originally the province of intellectuals, hairdressers, eccentrics, and art students, is increasingly popular with macho teenage boys. They hate synthpop because it's, like, so artificial, dude.

The war on drugs has not yet been declared and the study of addiction is in its infancy. Urban sophisticates consider the recovery movement to be square, if not reactionary, and hard narcotics nothing more than a bit of naughty fun.

A new subculture soon to be called Hip Hop (as of yet, not distinguished by misogyny, conspicuous consumption, or gangsta thuggery) is taking New York by storm. The subways are covered in shockingly beautiful graffiti art, superhumanly talented break-dancers perform on street corners, and the innovative sounds of rappin', scratchin', and samplin' are wafting from the outer boroughs into the chic nightclubs of Manhattan.

The scourge of AIDS is as yet undiscovered. Countless bathhouses, movie theaters, sex clubs, public restrooms, bars, discos, parks, abandoned buildings, cars, and private homes in America's gay ghettos play host to a protracted sexual debauchery, the likes of which has not been seen since the days of the ancient Roman emperors.

Stranger In The Night

I'm sweating and deliriously happy, pogoing to the hyper-bombastic strains of "Carcass" by Siouxsie and the Banshees. The tiny dance floor in the back of the Stud has turned into a pinball machine with boys for balls. We're all of us bouncing around like crazy, knocking into each other, the walls, passersby. When two boys collide there's sometimes a little groping, which is as close as I've ever come in all my nineteen years to making out with another human being. As I hurtle past the door to the bathroom I notice a tall bleached blond with luminously white skin and the features of an impossibly handsome leprechaun. He's wearing a ratty black vinyl jacket held together with silver electrical tape and leaning against the back wall scrutinizing the crowd, almost scowling. When the song ends, I lean against the wall a few feet away from him and try not to look like I'm staring. To my amazement, the beauty's pale blue eyes give me the once over and as my usual social anxiety reflex kicks in (run, run, run!), he introduces himself.

"Hey, I'm Colin. Didn't I see you at the Mabuhay Gardens the other night? When the Captivations played?" His voice is deep and his eyes look right into mine as he speaks, making my spine tingle. "I love that Farfisa organ, it's so '60s."

I'm shocked someone so perfect would notice me. "Yeah, I was there. I'm Jeremy. I write lyrics for them." The band did two songs of mine, a cabaret-style number about being an unpopular shut-in and a plea for human cloning so I could be my own lover and escape a life of loneliness. "Lizzie, the lead singer, she's my roommate."

"Cool. What do you drink?"

Before my brain can think, my mouth answers, "I don't."

He sneers, "You'll learn," and walks off. I feel idiotic as I watch him disappear into the crowd. I've said the most utterly wrong thing possible. Or was it just that Colin, a tall, blond, all-American Apollo, wasn't all that interested in me, a tiny guy with spotty skin, a huge nose, and unruly black hair that sticks up like a cartoon person being electrocuted? I feel a wave of despair. The sexual revolution has been in full swing for years now, but somehow I've remained in the Bastille of virginity. Ever since I went through puberty, six unspeakably long years ago, I've watched my peers discover spin-the-bottle, necking, sex, sex in hot tubs, sex with older men, three-ways, one night stands, bathhouses, and orgies. And through it all I've lacked the nerve to do anything but stand on the sidelines ogling.

To work off the mountains of nervous energy accumulated during my brief failed encounter I start flailing around to the hypnotically danceable "Dirty Back Road" by the B-52s. Two songs later I'm astonished when Colin taps me on the shoulder. I follow him to the edge of the dance floor where he hands me a glass of murky brown liquid.

"Rum and Coke," he says. "Drink it." I'm so flattered by his attention that I forget I hate liquor (previous attempts to imbibe have resulted in nausea and vomiting) and take a huge sip. It's disgusting.

We talk scene talk: bands and clubs and clothes. I learn Colin is from back east but recently came out here to S.F. at the request of a world-famous actor whose name he's not at liberty to divulge and with whom he's having an affair. Suddenly it's two and the bar is closing. Half the patrons stand around outside chatting or negotiating, while the tired, the hopeless, and the already paired off vanish into the foggy night. Colin turns to me, hugs his thin jacket to his thin body.

"It's freezing out here! Unless a Saint Bernard with a little barrel of hooch around its neck comes by, I think we should go to your place."

Awed by my good fortune, though not exactly sure what's going to be expected of me, I instantaneously agree. Colin is about six inches taller than me and walks so quickly I have to jog a little to keep up. As we cross Market Street, a car full of guys stops to hoot and wolf-whistle at him. My suspicion is confirmed: I'm walking home with the cutest boy who's ever trod the face of the Earth.

In no time we arrive at the crumbling Victorian flat on Octavia Street where I live in cheerful squalor with my pal Lizzie. As Colin and I step into the living room Lizzie looks up from her friend Sheila's nails, upon which she's been meticulously painting little Union Jacks, and lets out a low whistle. "Hubba, hubba! Where'd Jeremy find you?"

"The gutter," says Colin quickly.

"And what does your father do?" asks Sheila in a nasal imitation of an upper-crust matron interrogating her child's prom date.

"Papa?" Colin pronounces the word in the French manner as he drapes himself on the mattress we use for a living room couch. "Business of some sort I should imagine. Mama is of course always busy with her charity balls."

"Balls, balls... yes, I see," says Lizzie. "And yourself?"

"One barely has time for anything at all between fittings and French lessons, but one tries to do what one can," whispers Colin breathily.

Sheila takes her turn. "And where did you find that divine jacket! It's simply too, too."

"Gift of the Countess Capriccio... or was it something the stable boy left? I really can't recall!" says Colin with a tinkly debutante laugh. He gets up and puts an arm on my shoulder. "Now, which way to your boudoir?"

As we enter my room I turn on the light. Colin instantly turns it off so that we're illuminated only by the street lamp outside my window, which is actually pretty bright. He crouches and begins going through the records I keep in a stack on the floor. After a minute, during which I babble about albums, he puts on *Ziggy Stardust*. Then he stands and looks right at me. That he has to bend down for a kiss somehow makes it extra romantic.

Moments later I find myself naked on my unmade single bed lying under Colin's rockstar-thin body. The crown of my head tingles—I feel so strange I want to jab myself with a safety pin to see if I'm dreaming. We begin trying to insert part A into slot B and so forth, but nothing quite fits anywhere. From what little I know about sex it doesn't seem to be going too well. After a few minutes Colin pulls away from me.

"Wait," he says. For what? I wonder. He lies down beside me; his eyes fixed on the ceiling. Have I done something wrong? Before I can say anything stupid or needy or desperate, he begins to speak.

"I grew up in New England, but it wasn't pretty. A mill town. Deadly dull. My dad worked night shift at the plant and my mom was a checkout clerk at the supermarket. I have two brothers and three sisters." I relax. He's not rejecting me. He's telling a story.

"That's a lot of kids," I say.

"Irish Catholic," he explains. "Mom was miscast as a mother. She tried, but she just didn't know how to keep up." He gets up from the bed and removes a pint of Wild Turkey from the pocket of his jacket, which he's left lying on the floor. After taking a huge swig he offers me one. As the liquor burns my throat he gets back under the covers. "Once Mom just lost it and my sister Millie had to take me to my uncle's house on a bus in the middle of the night. She'd been drinking and spanking me and drinking and spanking and drinking and spanking. It was winter, really cold and snowing, and I didn't understand what was going on. Millie kept saying Mom was a witch. I thought she meant like with the black hat and a broom and a cauldron and everything so I kept saying, "No, she's not. No, she's not."

"That's horrible!" I commiserate. "My parents never spanked me."

Colin gives me a funny little look and continues. "I was the youngest so I was pretty lucky. Mom mostly just ignored me, like she was just tired of kids by the time I came along. And all my brothers and sisters took care of me, too. Especially Jack. He's a big New York show queen, a dancer type. He'd take me to see summer stock plays and give me all his *After Dark* magazines when he was done with them. By the time I was twelve I was a big Sondheim queen." He laughs. "I'd volunteer for all the community theater productions and hang out with the small-town closet cases. My first affair was with this kid who was playing Oliver. God, what a monster. Every kid who ever played Oliver always turns into an egomaniac. That play is a monster-making machine." He takes another huge swig of Wild Turkey.

"Then," Colin continues, "I went Glam Rock. I dyed my hair scarlet and got a Bowie-style shag. All the jocks decided to kill me, so for about a year I had to crawl home from school behind rows of shrubbery and cut through people's yards. A few times they caught me and roughed me up, but I always got away before they did any major damage. Then Jack moved to New York and I got to go visit him. His friends thought I was cute and they'd flirt with me, but he'd keep telling them, "Remember, he's only a kid!" Of course I was already having affairs with my drama coach and two of my cousins." He turns his head to face mine. "But I didn't have any friends till I met Nick. He was so pretty he could stop traffic. I mean, he would just walk into a McDonald's and whole families would stop chewing their Big Macs and stare. He hated it though. He just wanted to be a regular guy, but the regular guys hated him. Like, he'd go to their houses and their sisters and even their moms would be flirting with him. By senior year he didn't have any friends but me. We did everything together, played basketball, hitchhiked to Boston to see shows, traded clothes... until he... slit his wrists... and then..." There are suddenly tears in Colin's eyes. Tears inches away from my face. Desperately wanting to comfort him, I put my arm on his but he brushes it away.

"I'm sorry," I say, both about trying to touch him, as well as his friend. The first side of the record ends and Colin, sniffling and wiping tears out of his eyes, gets up and turns it over. After another gargantuan swig of booze he crawls back into bed, takes a deep breath and, his composure regained, starts talking again.

He's visibly drunk now and shocking facts come rapidly in a slurred, mixed-up tumble. After graduating high school, Colin stayed with his brother in New York and secretly became a hustler while pretending he worked as a waiter in a crêperie he'd actually been fired from after two days. Colin met the rich famous actor who fell madly in love with him at first sight. Colin heard Patti Smith and decided to write poetry. Colin is twenty-three. Colin's brother found out he was turning tricks and told him to get out, so he came to San Francisco. Colin sometimes plays basketball at the Marina with teen idol Robby Benson. Colin loves to spend rainy afternoons at the library researching art history and reading great literature. Colin lives at The National, a residence hotel on the sleazy part of Market Street, and works at Le Salon, a porno store in North Beach.

By the time Colin tells me that the first trick he turned in San Francisco was with a drunk conventioneer who sang, "San Francisco, open your Golden Gate..." as he sodomized Colin, he's laughing. I'm glad he's happy again, but shocked at the cavalier attitude he has towards his life's seedy dramas.

Eventually Colin pauses, mumbles, shifts his body onto his side and falls asleep. I don't have quite enough room to lie on my back, the way I usually do, and I'm too excited to sleep anyway, so I just lie on my side and stare at Colin for what seems like ages, marveling. Sometime around dawn, when I'm finally sleepy, I mold my body against his and drift off, imagining that I'm melting into him.

Some hours later the feeble sunlight of a foggy morning rouses me. I sit up and blink my eyes, then focus on Colin. I now feel an attraction toward him that might be love but feels more like gravity, a simple, taken-for-granted, and entirely irresistible physical force. This attraction is now as much a part of me as yearning for vintage clothes or wanting to be famous. *Colin, Colin, Colin.*

Leaving him to sleep I throw on some underpants and lope into the kitchen to fix English muffins with peanut butter. I bring a tray back to my bed in which Colin — perfect, beautiful Colin — is still sleeping. I shake him and he opens his eyes.

"Whu...?"

"Breakfast!"

"Ougheohwoh," says Colin. He sits up and after a bleary-eyed moment, takes a bite of food. "Stop staring at me like that," he commands sharply, mouth full of muffin.

"Huh?" I had no idea I was staring. "Sorry."

"Look, last night was... fun, but we're just going to be friends, all right?"

Devastation.

"But, Colin..." I'm about to tell him he's the only boy I'll ever love till the day I die, that I can't... won't... live without him, but even with my limited (well, actually nonexistent) experience with men, I know that'll just scare him away. Then I concoct The Plan. Just like in *His Girl Friday* or any number of other old Hollywood screwball comedies, I'll become Colin's best pal, a wisecracking sidekick. During a series of hilarious hijinks and wacky shenanigans we'll become an inseparable team. Then, just before he marries the beautiful society deb he *thinks* he's in love with, Colin will realize I'm the man for him and rush into my arms. We live happily ever after. The end. Simple.

"Sure," I say to Colin with a smile. "Whatever you say. Just pals."

Colin collapses out of bed and starts dressing. "I have some things I have to do... meet someone." He takes another bite of muffin.

"Let me give you my phone number," I say, scribbling it on a scrap of paper. "I'll be at art history and astronomy this afternoon. I go to S.F. State. Did I tell you that? But I'll be home tonight."

"Yeah, OK," he says. I try to read his face. What's he thinking? He's thinking, where is my other sock? In a flash he's dressed. I wrap a sheet over my underpants-clad body like an ill-fitting toga and walk him down the long, cold, dark hallway to the front door. "Call me tonight, OK?"

"I'll try," he says. For a moment he looks at my face as if wondering where to plant a good-bye kiss. "Later," he says, and he's out the door. Unkissed and hating it, I run to the kitchen where Lizzie is sipping tea and tell her everything.

"He said he'll try to call you but didn't give you his number? Sounds like a brush-off. Sure is pretty though. Those cheekbones, they're like wings on a plane!"

I'm not disturbed by her prediction in the least. "He probably doesn't have a number because he lives at a residence hotel. He's going to call. And that's not all he's going to do."

I retreat to my room where I discover my Gramma Bea. How do I explain this so I don't sound crazy? Gramma Bea lived next door to my family while I was growing up. She always seemed magical because she was from England, land of Mary Poppins and the Beatles, and spoke with the hint of a lovely accent. Although she was rather strict about manners and morals, she also had a way of turning everything into a game that I just loved. If I came home from school bruised and belittled (which happened more frequently than I'd have liked), she could always cheer me up with a game of twenty questions, a look through her postcard collection, or an invitation to watch TV: *Hollywood Squares*, Merv

Griffin, or what have you. She passed away when I was eleven, but then every so often started manifesting herself to me, slightly transparent but otherwise no worse for wear.

Now she's standing in front of me with her perfect posture wearing her dignified skirt suit, tall, thin as a reed, her hair in a frosted set of curls. She's put out, I can tell, her arms are folded and she's frowning. "Jeremy, your behavior last night was atrocious. Really, drinking straight out of the bottle!"

This is a damning transgression, but I have a loophole. "I only did it because my guest was drinking out of the bottle and I wanted to make him feel at home, just like you told me Queen Victoria drank out of her fingerbowl because one of her dinner guests did."

"You could have gotten him a glass, dear," she says only slightly mollified.

"I will next time," I promise.

"You're growing up," says Gramma Bea as she gives me a little hug that I can't feel because she's only ectoplasm, not flesh. "Try not to get too attached to this Colin. I grant you he's handsome as the sun, and I know he's your first beau and that's always special, but there's something a bit dodgy about him. Promise me you'll be careful?"

"Sure," I say.

"Fine then," she whispers, and with that, fades.

I'm not off the hook yet. In her place appears my Nana Leah. When I was growing up, Nana Leah was only an occasional visitor. Every few years she'd show up bearing gifts of Russian candy and *Sputnik* magazines. She was always very serious and prone to making weird pronouncements like, "I just want I should live long enough to see the revolution come to America."

"But Nana Leah, we already had the American Revolution!" I said, amazed that an adult wouldn't know that.

"She means a different one," explained my dad.

I'd vaguely understood that we were talking politics. "I wrote President Nixon a letter asking him to outlaw pollution."

"You'll be a great revolutionary some day," she said, with a noble faraway look in her eye. I felt like she was bestowing a special fate on me, like kids in storybooks who are prophesied for greatness. She died around the same time as Gramma Bea and has been haunting me, if you want to call it that, with equal vigor.

"Jeremy, what's the meaning of this?" Nana asks, looking disheveled in her shabby floral dress and sensible shoes. Unlike Gramma Bea, she doesn't bother with makeup or old lady hairdos. "You're turning into a *faygeleh*?"

I've never heard the word *faygeleh* before, but I can guess what it means. "I'm gay, Nana. We're an oppressed minority group, too."

"What are you talking about? It's a mental illness."

I've been ready for this argument for a long time. "Actually, there have been lots of homosexuals involved in labor and socialist movements since the 19th century; in England there was Edward Carpenter..."

"Well," interrupts Nana Leah, "at least this Colin is working class."

"That reminds me, I have to go or I'll be late for class," I say, gathering up my books and papers.

"I'm sure this is just a phase," says Nana Leah as she vanishes. "You'll find yourself a nice... girl." I suspect she had to force herself not specify Jewish. Even a *shikseh* would be better than a man.

All day long, while everyone I know is wishing and praying for the demise of President Reagan (who has just been shot by a Jody Foster-worshipping maniac), I imagine waves of pure will emanating from my brain commanding Colin to call. At eight o'clock as I'm sitting in my room doing homework I hear the phone ring and dash to the living room. "I'll get it! I'll get it! I'll get it!" I scream as I dive for the receiver, knocking Lizzie into the wall. My telepathic prowess is proven. It's Colin.

"Hi Jeremy, it's me." Lounging on the mattress, I settle in for a long chat, kicking my legs up and twirling the cord around my finger, imitating the photo of '60s TV teen princess Patty Duke that Lizzie taped to our refrigerator.

"Oh, hi Colin. How've you been? Do anything exciting today?"

"I spent the day reading Rilke," he says.

"What?"

"Not what, who. Rainer Maria Rilke? The German poet?"

"Is he the one that wrote *All Quiet on the Western Front*?" I ask.

"No, that was Erich Maria Remarque."

"Oh right, him," I bluff.

"Well, Tennessee Williams was influenced by Rilke so I wanted to read him," says Colin.

"Tennessee Williams wrote plays, right?" I ask.

"You don't know Tennessee Williams?" Colin is shocked and saddened.

I feel like a simpleton. "I've heard of him."

"*Cat on a Hot Tin Roof? Streetcar Named Desire? Suddenly Last Summer?*"

"I haven't seen them," I admit, "but I've heard of them."

I can almost hear Colin's eyes rolling heavenward. "Well, you've got to see them. All."

"OK, sure," I agree. "I will."

"Tennessee Williams is not only the best American playwright ever, he wrote incredible short stories and came out of the closet before just about anyone." Colin spends the next hour telling me about Tennessee Williams' life and work, then expands his lecture into a survey of twentieth century gay American writers with a special emphasis on their sexual habits. Sometime around midnight he pauses. "Wow, look at the time. Hey, I'll call you tomorrow. G'night."

"I'll be here. Don't forget. Call tomorrow." I'm hysterically happy, even if I now know for a total fact that I'm an ignoramus.

A few hours later I fall asleep with my pillow doing a poor impersonation of Colin's body.

Colin phones the next day, and the next, spending hours on the phone each time. It becomes an issue with Lizzie, how I tie up the phone all the time. Tensions escalate, our friendship hangs in the balance, but I could no more put down the phone when I'm speaking to Colin than I could cut out my own appendix and eat it. When Lizzie gets too insistent I tell Colin, "Wait right there, don't move!" and run the eight blocks from my house to his tiny, threadbare hotel room. There's one little wooden chair but neither of us sits on it. He lies on his bed while I curl up at his feet like a dog or a hot water bottle. When the room gets too claustrophobic we walk for hours to nowhere in particular.

Colin is always lecturing me on literature, pornography, European cinema, booze, politics, Broadway, existentialism, whatever topic flits into his head. Radical opinions flow out of his thin red lips with unstudied eloquence, revealing a mind that begrudges the slightest concession to privilege, conformity, or tradition. A militant iconoclast and leveler, his sympathy for underdogs and outcasts is all the more endearing in that he has absolutely no self-pity despite having grown up in seemingly abject poverty. "A real man of the people," says Nana Leah approvingly. "Even if he is a *faygeleh*."

Most of the time we think alike, but on the few occasions we discover a disagreement we'll argue till we reach an accord, no matter how long it takes. He's a good debater—witty, stubborn, and articulate—with a Jesuit's love of dogma (though as a Catholic he's lapsed as can be). Coming from a family of Jewish lefties (for whom arguing is as much an art form as oil painting was to the Renaissance Italians), I'm not one to give in easily. When I offhandedly remark that I don't see what's so hot about Franz Marc and his paintings of blue horses (which I've just learned about in my art history class) he launches into a three-day crusade to convince me of their importance. He explains how the horse symbolizes power and blue symbolizes passivity. The paintings reveal that the two can be reconciled—an important lesson for brutish Americans. I'm flattered that he takes my opinions seriously enough to try to change them, and by the time he's done, I love Franz Marc... sort of.

Colin, like me (and most of the "blank generation") venerates pop culture with a mix of sincerity and satire that inclines us to take everything from Disneyland to Frank Sinatra to cowboy hats *very* seriously. We debate whether the Monkees or the Archies (bubblegum bands that hippies hated for their lack of authenticity and that we love for the same reason) were better. "The Monkees spread counterculture ideals to suburbia," Colin says in the same professorial tone he uses when discussing Jean Paul Sartre or Hannah Arendt. "And they had a lot of very talented people writing their songs. The Archies sanitized contemporary musical and clothing fashions by removing them from their countercultural context. The Archies lived with their families in suburbia while the Monkees lived together communally without any authority figures. And the Monkees could lead kids into liking the Beatles. The Archies were more likely to get kids into the Carpenters."

"Sure," I admit, "but "Sugar, Sugar" always makes me want to dance."

The only argument we can't finish is about American involvement in World War II. Colin thinks all war is unconditionally wrong, while I get hysterical and start looking for blunt objects and projectiles whenever the word "Nazi" is mentioned.

"We couldn't just let the Germans take over the world! Are you crazy? What about the Holocaust? Pardon me, but I don't think a lampshade made with my acne-ridden skin would look very pretty." I've used the line before, but I make it come out like I'd just thought of it.

Colin remains maddeningly calm. "Violence never solves anything."

"If I were to write that statement on a school paper, the professor would take out a red marker and write 'Prove' in the margin. You just don't care about the Nazis because you're not..."

"Jewish?" fills in Colin. "Not that you are either. Have you ever celebrated even one Jewish holiday?"

"My family wasn't religious, but the Nazis would've killed us anyway. Being pacifist and letting people like that commit genocide is not humanitarian."

"War," Colin quotes slowly from the ubiquitous '60s posters we both remember from childhood, "is not healthy... for children... and other... living... things." I can't figure out how to respond to his statement. The way he says it, it's both a camp zinger and his real sentiment, so I just sigh and silently vow to win the argument later.

The discussion reminds me of the first time my dead grandmothers appeared.

I'd been leaning against a fence during recess with my friend David having a typical 5th grade conversation about the best stuff to have on a moon base. I'd wanted underground hydroponic farms but he insisted we could just have food tablets shipped from Earth. Without warning, a tough kid named Mickey came over eyeing us with a menacing look.

"Hey, Rabinowitz!" barked Mickey, his chin jutting forward aggressively. "You see *Star Trek* the other night? With all those brains in the... whaddyacallem, petri dishes?"

"Yeah," I said.

"I bet you weaklings'll be the first one they do that to. They'll take your brains out and hook 'em up by wires to some computer and throw your bodies away!" He laughed and socked my arm. Womp!

"Punch him back," said a voice over my left shoulder. "Give that little tin Hitler what for!"

I looked up and screamed. It was Nana Leah. I knew right away she was a ghost because I could see through her a little bit, plus she'd died three weeks ago.

Mickey hit David, who got all stiff and snooty. "I don't believe in fighting."

"Petit bourgeois utopian pacifists... you can't count on them," said Nana Leah with a shake of her head.

I was thankful that David and Mickey didn't seem to see or hear her, but I already felt alienated from my peers and realized that this supernatural intrusion could only set me apart further.

"Nana, go away!" I pleaded.

"I'm not your *Nana*," said Mickey.

"Nana, why are you here?" I asked, just thinking it this time.

"Where should I be?" asked Nana. "Can't a grandmother look after her grandson? Is that such a crime?"

Mickey shoved me.

"Just ignore him, dear," sniffed Gramma Bea from my right. I screamed all over again, even louder because I'd been to her funeral and had seen her dead body with my own eyes. "There's no need to indulge in common brawling," she added.

"Common brawler," I said to Mickey, my voice sounding a little like Gramma Bea's, all English and high-class. He hit my arm again in the same place so it would hurt more.

Nana Leah shook her tiny transparent fist at Mickey in anger. "The oppressor of the international proletariat and disadvantaged ethnic minorities always scapegoats the intelligentsia," she said.

"Dirty hippies," said Mickey as he socked David's arm again.

David started freaking out. "Leave us alone, leave us alone, leave us alone," he said rocking his body back and forth. "Leave us alone, leave us alone, leave us alone." Once I'd overheard his mother say that David was high-strung.

"Notify the appropriate authorities," ordered Gramma Bea. "You'll be doing Mickey a favor by turning him in. It's not as if he's challenged you to a fair fight in an honorable fashion. Hooligans need to be firmly reprimanded and disciplined."

It was like on TV when someone has to make a decision and a little devil, red-skinned with a tail and pitchfork, appears on one shoulder and a little angel in a white robe with wings and a halo appears on the other. Only I got grandmas.

"Dirty Jew bastards," spat Mickey. David forgot he didn't believe in fighting and pushed Mickey, although he was so scared he looked away while he did it. Mickey pushed David back so hard he fell down.

"Don't let his vulgar anti-Semitism bother you," advised Gramma Bea. "Disraeli was of Jewish extraction and he was a great statesman and a faithful servant of Queen Victoria."

"Help!" I screamed, far more terrified of my grandmothers than of Mickey.

David was sobbing by that point. "This is just like Viet Nam!"

The gym coach heard me and began slowly walking across the playing field.

"Better not tell, you little pansies," snarled Mickey as he jogged off.

"It'd serve you right if we did," I called out after him.

As the coach arrived Nana Leah and Gramma Bea vanished into the ether. David was sniveling and my arm really, really hurt. Maybe being a brain in a petri dish wouldn't be so bad.

Colin starts tagging along when Lizzie and I make our excursions to scour the thrift shops for goofy knickknacks, trashy novels, and clothes from the '50s and '60s. Purple Heart and Salvation Army are not only magic consumer wonderlands (what Macy's and Sears are to suburban people), but social hotspots where we're sure to run into friends from the clubs. More than once I've had a panic attack trying to figure out what to wear to Thriftown. Colin's forte is switching the price tags on items so you can get that $5 mohair sweater when you only have $3.50. "It's not like stealing," he rationalizes, "they're still getting money for the charities. All this stuff is donated anyway."

Lizzie and I are always going to see bands and on the rare occasion we don't invite Colin along we generally run into him at the show. He and I are always dancing up a storm and leaving clubs soaked with perspiration, risking a chill in the eternally freezing San Francisco night. Then, if there's no party afterwards, Lizzie will go off with whatever hot rockboy she's snagged (Jealous? Why, yes I am...) and Colin and I will traipse off alone in search of cheap restaurants with out-of-date décor: gleaming chrome Art Deco soda fountains! Orange molded plastic lamps in disturbing biomorphic shapes! Powder blue linoleum countertops with overlapping gold boomerang designs! If we're not feeling sleepy then we'll walk till dawn through the Tenderloin's slummy streets or the empty warehouse district, always talking, talking, talking.

Everybody loves Colin: he's so enthusiastic, always has a bottle in his pocket, and is game for anything. He happily joins Lizzie, me, and a few pals when we decide to make a high camp pilgrimage to Haight Street, that dingy boulevard of broken pipe dreams. Rifling through the enormous horde of thrift store '60s junk lying around the apartment, we try to approximate Carnaby Street psychedelic drag. I wind up in a pair of striped bellbottoms, a fringed vest, and neckerchief, resembling an extra from a community college production of *Hair* who's lost his wig. Lizzie doesn't look much better with her granny dress, square-toed boots, and short spiky hair, but Colin looks pretty realistic in a purple puff-sleeved shirt, flared faux denim trousers, white vinyl hat, and wire-rimmed, rectangular, rose-colored sunglasses. We stroll till we find a grimy burger joint with a jukebox that hasn't changed its selection in a dozen years, put on "Plastic Fantastic Lover" for six songs straight, and do pretend acid freakout dancing while real hippie burn-outs watch in horror.

When I'm not with Colin, my life seems as dry and colorless as stale Saltine crackers. While studying at school, hanging around with friends, or shoveling popcorn at my movie theater candy counter job, I'm only thinking of how I'll describe these actions to Colin later and guessing how he'll interpret them. Everything I say and do is calculated to create discussion topics or amusing anecdotes for him. Nothing seems real to me as it's happening, events only take on shape and color when I tell Colin about them later. The only things I don't compulsively discuss with him are my grandmothers. He doesn't believe in ghosts.

Sometimes Colin will vanish for a day or two and later tell me he's been with his world-famous actor. As we spend more and more time together though, these disappearances become less frequent and finally he claims the actor has gone back east. Then, in a dramatic scene in a seedy Chinatown basement restaurant, after I've begged and begged for him to reveal his lover's secret identity, he tells me the shocking truth: there is no actor. There's never been any actor. At first I'm not sure what to think, so I don't think anything. I just chew my pan-fried noodles and scrutinize Colin's face for signs of embarrassment, of which there are none.

"So why'd you make up the story?"

"Just because."

"Did you really have a friend... what was his name... Nick... who killed himself?"

He looks pained. "I'd rather not talk about that."

"So you're not seeing anyone now. You could..." as my mouth jabbers away I stare at my food, suddenly noticing how the green of the broccoli spears is almost neon, "...be my boyfriend, if you wanted to."

"What did I tell you about that the very first morning after I met you?" His voice is cold, schoolmarmish.

Argh! I've loused up The Plan, made my pitch too soon. "You said we were just going to be friends. I just thought..."

"You thought we might just have sex anyway, like I'd forget that I'm not interested in you because you're interested in me."

"No, no, I didn't mean..."

"Get this through your head," the schoolmarm has been replaced by an army drill sergeant. "You're not having sex with me. Now or ever." The way he says "sex" makes it sound dirty, the very opposite of making love.

"Do you have a boyfriend?" I ask for no real reason. I don't see how he can since he spends every night talking to me either on the phone or in person.

"That's actually none of your business," he snaps.

"Single as a blade of grass," whispers a disembodied Gramma Bea.

The next day, Colin invites me to keep him company at work. Walking in the door of the porno shop my eyes are assaulted by naked females on hundreds of magazines and 'marital aids', all of them cooing seductively, posing, pouting, and staring straight at me. I try to avert my eyes but every which way I look there are more chicks, ladies, gals, bimbos, and broads. Here and there, naked men pop out as well. Some of them hairy-chested straight men with gold chains around their necks; others, radiant examples of ephebic beauty, are clearly gay.

Like many New Wavers, I'm prone to wearing skinny ties and pointy shoes, relics from the repressed post-war populuxe era that seems as distant here in freaky, groovy, laidback California as the Middle Ages. Like a few especially campy types, I've even adopted some antiquated speech patterns, resurrecting such lost words as darn and golly to use as expletives in place of the more common synonyms for feces and intercourse. I am fairly unique, however, in having adopted in earnest much of the era's squelching morality, which strikes me as both irresistibly funny and oddly reassuring. The upshot is I have never before seen smut.

Colin, seeing me avert my gaze towards the linoleum floor, smirks. "Sit down and relax," he commands, pointing to a chair next to the register. As I do, I force myself to look up at Colin, though I can feel the warmth of a blush on my cheeks.

"I like your sweater," I say, just to be saying something. The vertically striped blue and white cardigan really is fab. My comment to Colin launches him on a monologue about mod fashion. I can barely listen I'm so fascinated by all the sailors, tourists, college boys, and swingers who come in to ogle the porn.

The waxy yellow fluorescent light (or is it a corporeal manifestation of sin?) imbues them all a sinister glow. Whether laughing and clowning or businesslike, they don't seem aware of their lurid appearance. How can they all be so at ease in this tawdry atmosphere of plastic love dolls and Swedish erotica?

"I can't believe it's not just dirty old men who come in here," I say in the middle of Colin's discourse on Mary Quant.

"All men are like dogs, get used to it." The way he says "dogs" is somewhere between indifference and admiration.

"Not all men," I say, thinking of my father. And maybe, I hope, myself.

He looks right at me and speaks extra slowly to make sure I absorb this important lesson. "They may hide it, put on an act about how holy or above it all they are, but you're gonna learn sooner or later: all men are dirty old men."

Colin calls and says he's hungry and would I bring him some fresh plums? Minutes later I'm saying Hi to Irma, the 400-lb. leather dyke at the front desk of the National Hotel. She looks especially dressed up today, sporting handcuffs, a studded belt, chaps, a vest, and a policeman's cap. "Hot date?" I ask. I'm not shy around girls; it's only boys who turn me into a blushing mute.

"You know it, honey," she says with a wink. "There's a little lady I know who needs some interrogation."

I walk down the hall, which smells sickeningly of both mold and disinfectant, to Colin's room. "Mmmm, plums!" As he starts eating I notice a shoebox full of photos.

"What're these?"

"Brontosaurus eggs."

"They're photos!" I start poring through images of Colin and his family. Meaty-faced Mom and Dad, mangy dog, kid after kid after kid. One photo of Colin at about eighteen particularly entrances me. With long, curly hair, he sits on a low hanging tree branch looking up at the sun with a beatific, luminous smile of pure innocence and love. I can't take my eyes off the image, which reminds me slightly of a painting of Saint Francis preaching to the birds that I saw in art history class.

"I ain't no square with my corkscrew hair," sings Colin, quoting the T-Rex lyric, as he looks over my shoulder, his mouth full of plum. "I look better in this one." He pulls out a shot of him with his Bowie 'do.

"Nice," I say, though the other photo is still holding my consciousness hostage. Colin starts handing me various images of him in theater productions, with his family, at school. "Our home," he says, pointing to a dilapidated row house in front of which a ten-year-old Colin, dressed as a cowboy, plays in the dirt.

"All of you, six kids and your parents, lived in that little place?"

"Sure."

Did you have your own room?"

"Shared one with my brothers."

"Wow." When I leave, hours later, I'm still thinking of the teenage Colin with his long, long hair, looking up at the sun with that big, big smile.

On New Year's Day the telephone wakes me out of a deep sleep. I'm much the worse for the preceding night's debauch, suffering from cottonmouth, pounding head, and sour stomach. It's Colin. "So... I'm leaving. I've got a plane to New York tonight."

"What?"

"My New Year's resolution is I'm moving to Manhattan."

This is most definitely not in The Plan. "Hold on, I'll be right over." In a panic I dress and run to Colin's hotel. Sweating and frantic I knock on his door, hoping this will be some game or test. But when the door opens, I see that his walls are bare and a suitcase full of his bright '60s cardigan sweaters and black peg-leg jeans is sitting on his bed.

Colin looks tired. "Hi, c'mon in."

I don't bother with hello. "Why?"

Colin sighs and lies down on his bed. "It's time to move on," he says neutrally.

"What does that mean? What will you do in New York? Where will you live?" I notice that a crack on his wall vaguely resembles the Mississippi River.

"It means I'm bored with San Francisco."

Several uncomfortable moments of silence. Every day for months I've spent hours talking to this person, thinking about him, dreaming about him, and now he's just going to disappear.

"What... about... me?" I ask, staring up at him and imagining that my eyes are huge, lovable and puppylike.

"What... about... me?" mimics Colin expertly, making me sound like a mewling lap dog magically endowed with a human voice. "Look, I have to catch my plane. I'll write or call or something." I can feel myself rigid with anxiety. My reason for living is leaving. Colin gets up and closes his suitcase. "I need to finish up. You'd better go." He opens the door.

I stand in the doorway. "Promise you'll call me from New York?"

"Sure." He follows as I trudge down the hall like a condemned man going to the gallows.

"You can come back, too. If you don't like New York."

"Sure."

I walk onto the street and turn to face Colin as he stands in the hotel doorway. "I could join you there later. I've always wanted to live in New York."

Colin looks me right in the eye then kisses me on the cheek. "Bye." Colin never touches people in a friendly way. He doesn't even shake hands. So that kiss is actually good news. Plus that "bye" didn't sound so completely, totally final. Did it?

I begin a sad march homewards. "It was probably for the best, dear," says Gramma Bea, materializing beside me. "He was amusing, I'll grant you, but... and I know Americans hate this expression... not of your class." She bestows a kindly, apologetic smile on me. "You need to get back to college and study for a career instead of spending all your time gallivanting about."

This strikes me as absurd. Even in my desolation I can feel every cell in my body itching for adventure, booze, romance, dancing, drama, glamour, action, danger, and sex. "Gee, Gramma, I don't know. I like to go out."

"Perhaps you could find someone who's more down to Earth," she suggests, using a metaphor that truly speaks to me since the sidewalk does feel like it's dropping away beneath my feet. "Someone who thinks a bit more about his future and..." She peers at my face and sighs her surrender. "You'll get over him, Jeremy, honestly you will. If you'll accept an old cliché from your dear grandmother, time heals all wounds."

"But Gramma, he's The One."

"You can't make someone love you," she chides. "Not someone like that anyway."

"Maybe you can," I say, too upset to think anymore. "We'll see."

Gramma Bea vanishes and I continue on my trek.

Weeks later, sick of watching me mope around the kitchen with a long face, Lizzie sets me up on a date with James, an art student she knows from one of her classes at State. He shows up at the door in a rat pack style sharkskin suit with a white shirt and skinny black tie. Acceptable, if uninspired, gear. Good-looking, I think as I gaze at his delicate features, pale skin, and jet-black hair that's parted in the middle and greased back '20s style... but no Colin. James, speaking in a voice so whispery it sounds like a put-on, suggests we go to an Antonioni film at The Strand. It's a long, long movie. Maybe the longest I've ever seen. Afterwards as we walk slowly back to my place I tell him I thought the film was boring.

"I thought it was brilliant," he says in his little mouse voice.

"Come on! Empires could rise and fall in the time it took that woman to walk down that hallway with all the doors. What was so great about it?"

He's quiet for a moment, thinking. "I don't want to argue," he says quietly. Strike one. We arrive at my door. He crushes his body against mine and kisses me on the lips. "I'll call you," he says.

On our second date I suggest Chinatown for dinner, but James is against it. "I don't eat, I smoke." Instead I get a sandwich and spend the evening at his clean, minimally furnished apartment in North Beach watching him make collages using 1950s advertising images of babies and housewives set in wastelands of animal skulls, tanks, automobiles, and raw meat. Afterwards we sink into his bed for a tepid, joyless, make-out session.

I screw up my courage. "Maybe we should try..." performing the act would be less embarrassing than naming it, "going, you know, all the way."

"Fucking?" he asks incredulously. "Don't be disgusting." Strike two.

We see each other every few days for the next several weeks, always for artsy movies or coffee. Lizzie starts referring to us as boyfriends. I don't contradict her. Neither of us likes the other, but then neither of us has anyone else to date. There are hardly any gay boys on the punk and New Wave scene, and romance with disco-loving vulgarians or hippie-dippy leftovers would be unthinkable.

One day after a miserable afternoon of listening to James issue snippy put-downs of everyone and everything he finds unsophisticated: The Captivations, non-smokers, the Democratic Party, Germans, Hamburger Mary's, people who don't get at least some of their laundry done professionally... I'm fed up.

"What a bourgeois parasite," I say to Nana Leah, expecting her to agree and tell me to dump him. To my infinite surprise and irritation, she comes to his defense.

"I think his art shows the devastation being brought about by decadent Western consumerism."

"Does not!" I shriek. "Everyone is doing '50s ads and post-apocalyptic landscapes. It's trite."

"It exposes the aggression being waged against the peace-loving people of the Soviet Union by the capitalist war machine," she responds gullibly.

Exasperated, I turn to Gramma Bea, who's ambivalent. "James certainly does have breeding, and I dare say he's quite handsome in his way, but if he doesn't make your heart sing... Well, it's ungentlemanly to lead someone on."

James invites me to see his favorite band, Modus Vivendi, an atonal quartet famous for making outfits out of Saran Wrap and day-glo cardboard. After a seven-minute song consisting of the same three notes repeated on a synthesizer while the band members strike karate poses and shout something in Japanese, he turns to me with a look of rapt wonder on his face. "They are sooo brilliant," he whispers. Strike three. On the way home I tell him I don't think we should date anymore and he just sighs with relief.

I'm moping worse than ever so Lizzie drags me to a beer-soaked party at the loft of beloved local band, the Mutants. I immediately gravitate to the kitchen area where I clown around with girls and Cheez Whiz while in the living room area a band plays and people dance or make out. Hours later I climb out the window onto the fire escape where a few party guests are sitting with their legs dangling over the side and calling out rude comments to the people milling around on the sidewalk two stories below. Billy, the extremely butch lead singer for The Berets, is sitting next to me dressed in a dull green '50s gas station attendant jumpsuit with the name "Lou" on a patch above the front pocket. More than once I've swooned while watching him on stage, his sweat-soaked body doing the rock star thing, exuding sexual charisma. Up close I'm even more dazzled. He has high, wide cheekbones, gorgeously greasy black rockabilly hair, and perfect olive skin. As usual in such situations I lose my ability to speak, but for once in my life someone desirable takes the initiative.

"You look like one of the Dave Clark 5," says Billy in an approving tone. In fact, I am dressed just like them: black Chelsea boots, white peg leg jeans, black suit jacket, white shirt, skinny black tie, and little mod black hat.

"Wow, you got it!" I say, honestly impressed. I tell him all about an interview album of theirs Lizzie found in which they're referred to as "One of the better looking bands coming out of England today!" by the interviewer so often that it starts coming out as one word, "oneofthebetterlookingbandscomingoutof Englandtoday!" Without knowing exactly how, I find myself in a broom closet with Billy. As he holds me in his strong arms and thrusts his tongue down my throat I momentarily forget Colin. All I can think about is the taut, tattooed flesh of Billy Beret. *Billy, Billy, Billy.* His hand forces my head down to his nether regions and in a minute or two, it's all over. Afterwards he demands I swear an oath of secrecy and under no circumstances tell anyone what we've done, then dashes off without a goodbye. Several hours later I wickedly induce convulsions of laughter in Lizzie and several of her pals as I imitate Billy's cowardly plea, "Don't tell anyone!"

From time to time postcards arrive from Colin. He claims to be happy, has found work at a porno theater on West Street, likes the weather, the scene. I spend more of my meager salary than I can afford on long distance (calling him at the theater because the room he lets doesn't have a phone) just so I can hear his voice and know there's someone somewhere who understands me. He invariably chirps away for a few minutes about how New Yorkers are so much smarter and more sophisticated than the pretentious hicks in California, then has to run off to meet some friends at a bar or a nightclub. It sounds like he's having a blast.

Despite my weekly pilgrimages to the Stud, Colin remains the first and last person to ever take me home. Occasionally I venture into the twilight netherworld of the Polk or Castro bars, but invariably end up sitting in a corner, hating the disco, annoyed by the stench of poppers, and completely unnoticed by the clientele who all have mustaches anyway. I'm probably about as attracted to men in mustaches as a straight boy, I think, secretly proud of my one similarity to the masters of the universe.

Lizzie tries to cheer me up by being companionable but I'm getting bored hanging out at shows where just about everyone's straight. I lose interest in the tepid friendships I have with school chums. Colin dominates my thoughts all day and keeps me company in my dreams all night. Nobody else would ever spend so much time analyzing me, educating me, listening to me. Nobody else could make doing laundry fun or walking empty streets into an adventure. Colin will still fall in love with me. The Plan just didn't have enough time to work. With less thought than a yo-yo requires to spool up to a finger, I buy a plane ticket.

Colin doesn't protest when I call to tell him I'll be arriving shortly and even offers to let me stay with him till I find a place. Lizzie, predictably, thinks I'm crazy to move to a city I've never even visited to moon over a guy who's already rejected me, but I don't care in the least. The world outside of Colin has ceased to matter. When I tell my parents I'll be abandoning college at the end of the semester and running off to New York City they respond with the expected fuss (to which I pay no attention), but my grandmothers, for once putting up a united front, are less easily ignored. They're of the mind that by dropping out of school I'm being, as Gramma Bea puts it, "improvident." After I look up the word, I tell them, I'm only nineteen. I have plenty of time to prepare for the future.

Decadence

"The scientific reason that the plane is going down now is that it's landing," says the tiny boy seated next to me. His mother smiles proudly and half glances over to see if I've noticed how marvelously precocious her child is. I ignore her and stare out my window through the hazy smog at the flat gray New Jersey suburbs that stretch out as far as the eye can see. Then the plane turns and I get a good view of Manhattan in all its vertical glory, reminding me of a picture I once saw of a medieval castle city surrounded by moat. Wow.

The process of deplaning, picking up my luggage, bussing to the Port Authority, and catching a cab (for a journey that turns out to be all of five blocks) seems endless. By the time I'm standing in front of 4B, Colin's door, I feel like a nine-year-old on Christmas morning. "Colin?" The door opens immediately revealing a minuscule room, half of which is taken up by an unmade bed and the other half of which is taken up by Colin. He's unchanged except that his hair, formerly the pale yellow of unsalted butter, is now arctic white — a startling contrast to his eyebrows which he's dyed jet black. Seeing him for the first time in four months I feel like I've stepped into one of those elevators that goes down faster than your stomach.

"Welcome to my Easy-Bake Oven," says Colin, taking a seat on the bed. I step into the airless, sweltering, unspeakably hot room. It smells of Colin, making me want to swoon, fall into his arms, smother him with kisses and merge my body into his so that we can be one forever and ever and ever and ever. Instead I give a little wave as I set down my battered, bulky suitcase and sit next to him. Colin smiles and surprises me with a friendly kiss on the cheek. "You'll be glad you came to New York. The heat makes everyone incredibly sexual and all the Puerto Rican boys run around with their shirts off."

"Oh?" I say, noticing that Colin's jeans have been strategically torn at the crotch, revealing his white underpants.

"And the pizza here is about a thousand times better than S.F. And there's always something to do..." He plays civic booster for a while, now and then questioning me about friends back in California, but not listening to my answers. After a while the strangeness of our being together eases and I wilt onto the bed, exhausted with excitement, and doze off.

Colin is shaking me awake. "C'mon, nap time's over. We're going out."

I feel braindead. "What time is it? Where are we going? What should I wear?" I sit up, open my suitcase and stare blankly at the mass of clothes. If only I knew how to fold things properly. As Colin dresses I put on a pair of navy blue slacks and a plaid short-sleeved shirt.

"Too Beaver Cleaver," says Colin. "Dressing like a child from the 1950s is not sexy."

"OK," I say, wanting to be agreeable. I change into a pair of skintight black peg-leg jeans and a Ramones tee shirt.

"No," says Colin with a little shake of the head.

"Well, what should I wear?" I ask, flattered that someone so worldly and beautiful cares enough to make sure I'm wearing the right thing.

Colin begins digging through my suitcase. "This is cute," he says, holding up a faux Western belt with colored beads spelling out San Francisco.

"I got it at Woolworth's," I say.

He puts it back. "But not right for tonight. Let me see you in these Levis." The jeans are so tight I have to jump up and down several times and wriggle around like a fish out of water to get into them. "Those'll do," says Colin. "And here..." He takes out a plain black tee shirt and, using his teeth, makes a small incision, then rips off several inches of fabric so it will bare my midriff. "Put this on."

I pull the skimpy rag over my head. "I'm not sure this looks right," I protest, staring at my naked stomach in his full-length mirror. "I look like some trampy guy you'd see in *In Touch* magazine."

"Well, you do look kind of sexy," says Colin. Sexy to whom? I wonder. Him? "But not that good," he adds.

Without warning or prelude, Colin casually says, "You know, you don't have to start looking for a place of your own, really. You could stay here with me in The Oven if you shared the rent. I know it's small, but we could manage. Could you get a hundred an' twenty-five dollars... right away?"

"Sure," I say. "But is this tiny place really $250 a month? I only paid $120 back in S.F. for a room three times this big."

"Yeah, but that's cheap for New York," explains Colin. He really wants the money *right away* so I walk the three blocks to the Port Authority to exchange some traveler's checks. Where will I sleep? I wonder. There really isn't anywhere except his bed.

Night is falling as I make my way back. Clumps of rough-looking Black and Hispanic guys loiter on street corners for Lord-only-knows-what nefarious purposes and I get a tiny rush of fear that I find exciting, even pleasant. "Wanna date, Sugar?" asks a tall, cocoa-colored woman in a lurid pink micro-mini dress. I shake my head, no. "Faggot," she mutters, half-weary, half-nasty. I'm so happy to be living with the love of my life in a big grimy city that this doesn't disturb me in the slightest.

I find Colin waiting for me in the shabby little lobby of his building. He snaps his fingers. "Moolah? moolah?"

I hand him the cash, which he stuffs in the front pocket of his slightly obscene blue jeans. "Thanks," he says bolting out the door into the broiling hot night. "I know we won't have much room, but you're really lucky to find any place at all. New York's not like California. Living out there is like floating in Jell-O." He wrinkles his nose to show his distaste for easy living.

I disagree. "Jell-O is brightly colored, it's always gray in San Francisco. I say it's more like floating in oatmeal."

"Maybe it's more like butternut ice cream," he says, "it's always so cold." As we head downtown, chatting away as if Colin had never abandoned me, I stare with awe at the fallen majesty of Manhattan. A stunning Beaux Arts facade is defaced by a cheap plastic martini glass advertising cocktail hour from three to seven. People on the street talk in loud New Yawk voices and rudely push past without even a muttered "Excuse me." An old neon sign on a fancy Art Deco hotel illuminates a garbage-strewn alleyway in which I see an actual rat. Cars honk ineffectually at arrogant pedestrians. The patina of soot and indifference lends an anything-goes aura to all the chaos that has my spine tingling with excitement.

When we finally descend into the foul-smelling bowels of the subway system the train is graffitied with an odd duck-like cartoon character and what looks like startlingly beautiful, unreadable, day-glo Mayan hieroglyphic. The car is packed with glazed-eyed commuters, weary shoppers, and listless teenage hoodlums. How can they not be excited in the most important city on Earth? Colin is quiet but as the train jiggles and lurches I hear Nana Leah. "The Moscow subway is clean and has beautiful oil paintings for the masses to enjoy while they commute to work." She's shown me pictures from her trip to the Soviet Union and the Moscow subway does indeed resemble an art museum. Unfortunately, it doesn't connect Times Square with the West Village.

When we emerge onto the streets, Colin tells me all about Manhattan's amazing sexual possibilities. "You can sleep with a different guy every night, or go to the baths and have as many as you want all at once." I'm shocked. As a rule, Colin and I avoided the bars (except the Stud on New Wave night) and bathhouses in San Francisco as a sort of unofficial protest against the gay ghetto's slavish devotion to disco music. Evidently this policy is void in the state of New York.

We hit bar after bar as Colin plays tourguide. "This is an S&M bar, leather guys into sadism and masochism," or "This is an S&M bar, pretty boys into standing and modeling." Everywhere we go heads turn to ogle Colin, who ignores the stares with the grace of royalty. He can have his pick of anyone, I think, and there are a heck of a lot of anyones around here. How can I compete with an entire city full of gorgeous men? But I love him and they don't, I remind myself, and love conquers all. Everybody always says so.

By four, after we close out The Ninth Circle and head back to our(!) room, I'm in a state of barely contained frenzy from all the talk of sex, all the beer, and all the Colin. Stumbling into The Oven, Colin turns on a little fan in the little window and collapses on his narrow bed. Looped enough to feel lucky, I throw myself down next to him, my bare arm touching his. "Too hot," he says, rising wearily to help me make a pallet out of blankets. Lulled by the fan's whir, I fall asleep on the sliver of floor between the bed and the wall, my new home.

The next day Colin takes off for work and I roam around Midtown taking in the sights and forgetting plans to send postcards back home. It's so hot all I can eat is a slice of pizza. Colin is right. It's absolutely delicious, unlike its California equivalent, which tastes like ketchup on mushed down Wonder Bread. On the other hand, in California you can walk into the middle of traffic and cars will stop, the driver cheerfully waving you across the street. Here the cars seem to actually try to hit you and I only narrowly escape death on several occasions. Pedestrians also display this sort of malicious purposefulness, bowling me right over with their determined strides.

"I lived here for thirty-two years but I never liked this city," says Nana Leah, popping up behind me as I'm waiting for the light to change so I can cross Fifth Avenue.

"It's not pretty like San Francisco, but you've got to admit it's exciting," I counter.

She gestures towards a huge pile of rotting garbage sitting by the gutter. "Dirty, expensive, noisy and overcrowded... this is exciting? Tenements and sweatshops are exciting? Crooked cops and millionaire exploiters of the working class are exciting?"

"Sure, there's all that, Nana, but there's other stuff too: theaters, museums, people from everywhere, artists, writers. The whole world is right here. I mean, weren't you excited when you first saw New York?"

"I was terrified!" says Nana Leah. "Before I arrived the biggest city I'd ever been in was Minsk, which, let me tell you, was no great metropolis. The big advantage to New York was you didn't have to hide from the Black Hundreds."

"The who?" I ask.

Nana's face darkens. "The *chernosotentsy*. Back in Russia the Czar's police organized the reactionary elements to kill Jews and revolutionaries. People were thrown from windows. People were trampled by horses. We didn't just decide to make a revolution, you know. We had to."

I imagine Nana as a young woman: a petite fireball with voluminous black hair tied in a kerchief, waving a revolutionary banner in the face of saber-wielding Cossacks. "Tell me more," I plead.

She shrugs, her anger dissipated. "What's to tell? Things got worse. I moved to America. I had your father. He had you. The end."

"I still like New York," I say.

"Fine, like New York," says Nana Leah, mopping her brow with a white hankie. "It's too hot to argue." She fades away. It's always seemed odd to me that ghosts are susceptible to weather, but then I'm never sure I believe they're real anyway.

Once night falls I return to Colin's room, switch on the fan and lie on the bed fantasizing about our marriage. I decide we'd be wed on the traffic island in the middle of Time Square. I can see us there in tuxedos with ruffled shirts kissing for all the world to see... tossing the bouquet... getting showered with orange blossoms by our legions of friends... proud parents waving as we get into a convertible with huge fins and shoes tied on back. Before I can get to the honeymoon, a tired and grumpy Colin barges into the room.

"Eaugh," he says in greeting as he rips his clothing off, wraps a towel around his nether regions and heads down the hall for a shower. Forty-three minutes later he returns, smiling and perky. "You gotta lend me twenty dollars." His towel falls to the floor and he opens the tiny armoire at the end of his bed that holds all his worldly possessions. I try not to stare at his trim, freckled body as he pulls on a pair of jeans and a striped tee shirt that's three sizes too small for him.

"Sure, sure." I find my wallet and hand him the cash without a second (or even a first) thought. If my head, genitals, or right hand was detachable and he'd asked for any of them instead, it would be no different.

"We're going out. I get paid tomorrow. I'll pay you back then. Now make yourself pretty. Put on those jeans from last night and this tank top and... do you have any boots?"

"No."

He wrinkles his nose with distaste. "Just sneakers?"

"I have some pointy '60s dress shoes with buckles on the side."

"Nah," he says, "Do you have black Converse?"

"Sure," I say.

"Wear those," he commands.

"How come?" I ask. "Where are we going?"

Colin's face hides a smile. "You'll see."

Half an hour later Colin turns to me with a smile. "Here we are," he says. The way he says "here" makes it sound like we should be somewhere interesting or important instead of standing on a deserted street of warehouses devoted to light industrial enterprises.

"And where is here?" I venture to ask.

Colin points to a nondescript door.

"What's in there?"

Colin opens the door. A long, narrow flight of steep stairs leads to another door guarded by a burly middle-aged man sitting at a little booth, the side of which has a sheet of paper with a list of No's. No cologne. No dress shirts. No dress slacks. No white sneakers. The man looks us up and down, nods, then Colin and I hand him our money and the door swings open. But for the music (some sort of stripped down, throbbing, wordless essence-of-disco) the place could be a disreputable 19th century seaside tavern. It's barely lit, the ceiling is perilously low, the benches and tables are made of dark wood, and at least half of the all-male crowd is sporting mutton chop sideburns or walrus mustaches. Ahoy, mateys!

"Dress codes are fascist," I declare as I follow Colin to the bar where he orders us beers from a bartender wearing an outfit not unlike that of a Civil War infantryman.

Colin turns snippy. "I think there should be more dress codes. They keep things distinct. Wouldn't it be nice to keep bell-bottoms out of New Wave clubs?"

"Hhhmmmm... maybe," I allow.

"And the theater is more fun when all the men are wearing ties and the ladies are in their best frocks. Dressing up makes it special. And nobody ever, under absolutely any circumstances, should be allowed to leave the house wearing socks with sandals."

"People should be educated stylistically so they don't want to wear bad clothing," I counter. "Forbidding people to do stuff just makes them want to do it more."

"Nobody here wants to dress femme," Colin says, waving with his mug of beer at all the manly men surrounding us. He has a point. The clientele look like bikers or prospectors (except that nobody has a beer belly). It suddenly hits me that I'm the youngest person present by five or ten years, except, no, there are a few other boys around, but they've camouflaged themselves as men. This desperate machismo strikes me as unforgivably bad taste, totally un-New Wave. I consider asking Colin why we're here again but he's standing up and gesturing for me to follow him through a dark doorway. I set my mug on a cigarette machine and follow him into the stygian gloom. Once my eyes have adjusted, I see a bunch of nude and semi-nude guys all tangled up as if they were playing a game of strip Twister. Never having seen such a thing outside of a porn magazine, I step over to take a closer look. A hand reaches out and tentatively pets me as if I was a strange and possibly vicious dog. I step away to follow Colin who's moved into another darkened sex room.

"The usual," remarks Colin airily as we pass a hooded man chained to a wall. I half expect a torch-carrying hunchbacked dwarf or perhaps Vampira to appear and flog him with a cat-o-nine-tails, so closely does the scene resemble that of a low budget horror film.

"Piss on the faggot, yeah, that's right, piss on the faggot," rasps a hairy-chested guy lying in a bathtub as several men oblige him.

"What a ham," whispers Colin. "Probably an aging chorus boy."

As we pass rooms full of slings and sodomy, bondage and blowjobs, my mind whirls. I'm not the least interested in the cheap theatrics but there are some cute guys, and for the first time in my life they're giving me the once over, lusting after me. One guy even grabs my ass. Nobody, however, dares touch Colin—I assume because he's too perfect and desirable. It would be like pawing Kim Novak at a studio-sponsored charity ball.

We make it back to the front room, which no longer seems so dark. As I reclaim my beer mug I become conscious of hundreds of eyes roaming over my body like ants over food at a picnic. It even sort of tickles. "Have you been here before?" I ask Colin.

"Do you like this place? Why are we here?" By way of response Colin pulls his shirt off and sets off for the back rooms. "Have fun!" he says over his shoulder. I watch with panic as he disappears into the dark.

"Colin, wait," I say. He does not wait. "Colin," I call out, a bit louder. "*Colin!*"

What am I supposed to do now? A he-man sits down next to me and casually rests his hand on my crotch without so much as a "How do you do?" He isn't even looking at me. "Pardon me," I say, "I have to find my friend." I gingerly remove his hairy paw and head after Colin. Meat to the lions. I'm instantly immobilized, flat against a wall being disrobed and ravished by half a dozen men. Colin is nowhere in sight. I reflect that The Plan calls for me to feign indifference to Colin. How better to do that than by joining him in his debauchery? I gently push away anyone elderly or with too much facial hair and let the rest do as they please. A few guys try to pry me away from the wall to get at my rear, but with great resolve I stay put. They give up and content themselves with frontal ravishment, pulling down my pants, then my underpants, then...

I remember the last time I was naked around a lot of men, right before I quit going to gym class forever in tenth grade. Images flash before me: a crush of sweaty adolescents pushing and jostling into a locker room. Lean bodies emerge from sweaty clothes. Ever alert to the potential for humiliation, I emulate the super-speed of The Flash as I change, but to no avail. Boys grab my clothing and hide it from me. Clad only in a towel, I scream bloody murder. Then my towel is ripped from my waist and my naked, chubby body is laughed at by one and all.

My disturbing memory is quickly displaced by waves of intense physical pleasure. Half a dozen men are pawing my no-longer-chubby body. The edges of my flesh dissolve and I'm part of a mass of sensation floating like some alien entity composed of pure energy on *Star Trek*, a shimmering formless presence depicted by special effects; blurry, distorted camera lens; pink, chartreuse, and lavender lighting; eerie angelic harmonies. When finally, after untold hours, I'm satisfied, my essence coalesces into a single human form and my mind verbalizes again. Gosh, I think, public sex isn't creepy or weird like I thought it would be. It's fun!

The next day my body is still tingling all over as I'm staring out the window of a pizzeria on St. Mark's Place. There are so many drop dead gorgeous, ultra-trendy people rushing around it's making my head spin. Then I see Lizzie's friend Sheila from San Francisco walking by. From tip to toe Sheila goes like this: a mass of curly black hair (big on top, short on the sides and back), a pair of gigantic eyebrows perpetually raised in wonder and excitement, a large nose-beak with a tiny silver ring on the left nostril, huge blue lipsticked lips, a red leather jacket (despite the heat) barely concealing bosoms out to here, black peg leg pants barely concealing hips out to there, small calves, and tiny feet daintily thrust into pointy little black elf boots. Pizza in hand, I run onto the street and call out, "Sheila!"

"Oh my God! Jeremy!" she screams. "What're you doing in New York? Have you heard this yet?" She holds aloft an album. Sheila's not one of those girls who thinks apologizing for how fat she is or telling you about her day is conversation. She's like a gigantic computer that decides what's cool and what's not and broadcasts this information to the world in the loudest and most emphatic possible tones.

I look at the album she's holding which has a strange line drawing of two guys on the cover. "Soft Cell," I read. "What's that?" I take a bite of my pizza. "I live here now."

"It's the best ever. I'm just a couple of blocks away. You have to come over right now and hear this." I agree, happy to see someone I know and have someone to talk to whom I'm not madly, hopelessly, in love with. Sheila's tiny room is just as it was in San Francisco, knee deep in clothes, records and magazines, every inch of wall covered in posters. As I scarf my pizza she gabs away about how she's applying to work at the Fiorucci store and has all these great new albums. When she puts Soft Cell on her hi-fi I'm immediately transfixed. "Tainted Love" and "Where Did Our Love Go," two unutterably fabulous old Motown songs, are set to an electronic beat with distinctively theatrical but heartfelt vocals.

"Gay as a goose," says Sheila, holding up a magazine photo of the mischievously smiling lead singer, a dazzlingly cute waif dressed all in black with fetish jewelry and enough eyeliner for a dozen drag queens. I lean in to read the name, Marc Almond.

"He is obviously the most perfect, happening, now creature on the planet," I say. When Sheila and I get going we tend to speak like over-exuberant liner notes or the more hysterical teenybopper magazines.

We spend the rest of the afternoon together, listening to Depeche Mode's brilliant new album, *Speak and Spell*, while reading *The Face* and *Flexipop*. We fantasize about living in London, which we know from these magazines is a city where any queen with an ounce of hairspray and a synthesizer can form a New Wave band and hit the big time. There, even more than New York, the punk Do It Yourself ethic has migrated into the worlds of dance music, fashion, art, and design, unleashing heaps of new talent. The New Wave sound — danceable synthesizer beats and vocals that can do anything from shriek to croon — is wildly sophisticated and fun. Best of all, New Wave guys wear gobs of make-up and sing about other boys.

I'm staring at Colin's reflection in the glass of the subway door. His hair is gelled up into a flat top and he's exuding retro '50s style, all-American, freshly scrubbed wholesomeness. This is a perverted façade, an act designed to enhance his sex appeal to quasi-pederasts. Next to him I look positively immigrant-like and seedy, a huddled mass yearning to breathe free. Would he like me if I were taller, fairer, and had more delicate features? If I were less Jewish looking? Television and movies have tipped me off to the unpleasant fact that Jews are considered smart and funny, not handsome and sexy. Even complaining about this is such a cliché that I never stopped to think if it could be true. If handsomeness came on a scale of one to a hundred, and you could trade I.Q. points for beauty points, how many of the former would I be willing to trade for the latter?

My inane calculations are interrupted by Colin who starts telling me about his job at Man's World, a dirty movie theater down by the docks, where I've agreed to spend the day with him. "I only make five an hour, but we all take 'tips' from the register." He rubs his fingers together in the universal symbol for cash. I wonder about the wisdom of admitting to thievery in public. We're mashed into a throng of commuters, any one of whom could overhear us. "My boss is wild, a lot of fun. He used to hang out with the Beats and the Warhol crowd till he had to stop doing drugs because he went blind from too much speed."

Just then the subway lurches to a halt and a frail, gray old man crashes into a pregnant woman seated in front of me. "God! What's wrong with you!" she screams as the man gets up, apologizing profusely and making nervous little appeasing gestures with his hands.

A woman next to me turns around and it's Gramma Bea. "We all knew God was blond," she begins, her eyes getting a faraway look, "back in Yorkshire. We thought he'd wear a white robe and sit on a big throne and be very, very handsome with light blue eyes and curly hair." She laughs gaily at her little reminiscence, letting me know she knows better than to believe in such fairytales now. "I drew a picture of him once and my uncle said he didn't think God would be quite so very pretty." She laughs again and vanishes. She's inaudible and invisible to Colin who talks right through her anecdote. I wonder for the zillionth time if I'm crazy or just especially sensitive to otherworldly vibrations.

"Have you ever seen a ghost?" I blurt out.

"No. What makes you ask?"

I've changed the subject too quickly, aroused suspicion. "No reason," I say.

It's only just noon when we leave the subway but already there are guys cruising Christopher Street: sitting on cars, window shopping, leaning against walls, wearing next to nothing. I love the heat and fervently wish it was always a hundred and two degrees out, but Colin looks drained, though perhaps it's only because he's on his way to work. When we finally leave the burning sidewalk to enter the theater we're assaulted by the frosty air-conditioned coolness. It's so chilly I wish I'd brought a jacket. Colin's shift started two hours ago, but he's not the least bit concerned. He's late every day, often by several hours, but doesn't get fired because all his co-workers are always late too. They all cover for each other, sometimes working twelve, fourteen, or even sixteen hours straight.

I'm surprised that the Man's World lobby looks just like that of a regular movie theater. The only difference is the lube and poppers for sale alongside the candy and popcorn. That, and on the wall to the left there's a giant poster of a leather man lying ass up in a sling. Colin introduces me to his co-worker, Ralph, who's just getting off. He wears the skimpy, skintight clothes so many gays do, but on him they look ridiculous. He's hefty, balding (though young), and has a self-conscious smile that's so submissive, so defeated, he might as well wear a sign around his neck saying, "Kick me!" I was fat till just a year ago. Did I look like that? Ralph shakes my hand and gives me a guiltily lust-ridden smile as he says, "Pleased ta meetchya," in nasal New Yawkese.

After he leaves, Colin gives me the dish. "He lives with his mother in Queens, one of those old broads who float around in a caftan and too much jewelry drinking highballs and crying over the soap operas. You know, he's only twenty-one but he's dating some guy in his forties. Poor thing. Hey, lemme give you a quick tour."

Man's World turns out to be nothing more than two tiny rooms, one with a maze full of glory holes and one with a few rows of ramshackle theater seats in front of a small screen showing smutty movies. The place is empty except for a couple of closety types lurking in the shadows, examining each other with cold, dead fish eyes.

"See," says Colin as we go back to the front desk. "Less than exhilarating." I make myself at home on the lobby sofa as he sits behind the register with a copy of the *East Village Eye*. "Hey, look," he says after a minute's perusing. "There's a review of the San Francisco music scene and they mention The Offs. They say they're the best of the bands to come out of 'that cultural backwater.'"

"I always liked The Offs," I admit. "Except that one song about hustlers, "You Fascinate Me"."

Colin peeks at me over the top of the paper. "Only because you wanted Don Vinyl to be fascinated by you and he wasn't." Colin knows me so well.

"Don is cute as far as lead singers go, but not the only cute lead singer from San Francisco," I say coyly.

"The only gay one," says Colin.

"Not exactly," I say. "Remember the Berets? Remember Billy?"

"The one with the poufy hair? What about him?" asks Colin, lifting his eyebrows sardonically.

"His hair is not poufy!" I say with more emphasis than the point requires. "Anyway, we had a little affair in a broom closet, though he made me promise not to tell anyone afterwards."

"A broom closet? At least you didn't have to look at his hair while you did it," says Colin. "God, he needs conditioner, or at least more pomade."

"His hair looked great."

"How could you see in the broom closet?"

"I saw it before I went into the broom closet!"

Colin is dispassionately surprised. "No split ends, nothing?"

"No!"

"I think maybe he over-processed it," conjectures Colin. "You know, dyed it black one time too many."

52

"He looked really, really cute!"

"I mean, you'd think being a lead singer and all he wouldn't walk around with the hair of a middle-aged lesbian school teacher from Santa Fe."

"He looked great," I growl.

Colin backs off. "So how'd you nab him?"

"It was his idea," I say, trying not to sound like I'm bragging.

"That's cool." The way Colin says *cool* makes it sound like, "I can't believe you had sex with someone with such terrible hair," so I drop the subject.

As the afternoon drones on, Colin reads aloud from a huge article about El Salvador where the U.S.-backed, right wing death squads have recently taken time out from slaughtering and terrorizing the peasantry to murder several American nuns. "God, you know, I hate nuns too," says Colin. "But murder, that's a bit *de trop*, wouldn't you say?

"How come you hate nuns?" I ask.

"I went to Catholic school for half a year, and I've never met a meaner bunch of..." Colin shakes his head like it's too unpleasant to continue. "Hey, look at this," he holds up the paper so I can see a small ad with a drawing of a waitress with an elongated musical note covering her eyes.

"Danceteria," I read.

"We're going there tonight," announces Colin, "It's the funnest club ever."

An hour later, Colin and I are still lazing around Man's World when a boy even shorter than me with a cute monkey face and a sun-browned, compact little body bursts into the lobby.

"You could fry a egg on a bald man's head out dere. Hotter than fuck," he announces as he removes his mirrored aviator sunglasses and takes a seat behind the counter. I love his thick Dead End Kid accent, so much sexier than the relaxed, middle-class blandness of Californian speech.

"Thanks for showing up... now that your shift is almost over," says Colin. "I had to work here all alone. Eddie, this is Jeremy and vice versa."

"Hey," says Eddie. As he gives me a little smile and a wave he bats his long eyelashes at me flirtatiously.

"Hi," I say, involuntarily imagining the two of us in a debauched orgiastic frenzy.

Eddie turns back to Colin and starts whining. "Jeez, dere wasn't nobody out dere. Didn't turn one trick all afternoon. Hope something with cash comes in here." He doesn't look hopeful as he fans his perspiring face with a copy of *Honcho*. "I gotta get some money for the operation." He turns to me to explain. "I gotta get this operation on my ass. Y'know how guys get carried away, dey just want to crawl right up in dere."

"Dat sucks," I say, trying to throw a little New Yawk into my accent and failing miserably. My middle class background (or was it all the *Masterpiece Theater* I watched with Gramma Bea?) has permanently saddled me with good diction and a formality of speech I feel to be both less than sexy and somewhat at odds with my plebian countenance.

As Eddie and Colin gossip about work we're joined by a rail-thin transvestite dressed in a bizarre black spandex outfit. "Honey, you know it's hot when there ain't nobody out there lookin' for boy pussy," she announces as she bursts through the door to sit on the sofa next to me. "Hello, I'm Varlena." She pronounces it Var-lay'-na, sophisticated and European rather than countrified or Southern.

"My roommate," explains Eddie as I nod hello.

"I just finished sewing this, what do you think?" Varlena stands up and twirls around. Though I don't know quite what to think, I politely join Eddie and Colin in fawning over her strange get-up. Varlena then treats us to a lengthy explanation of how the garment was conceived and executed, where she's going to wear it, and who it's going to allow her to have sex with for how much money. As she yammers on I try to decide if she's ugly or not. After a while I conclude that if you don't mind a few missing teeth, she is in fact pretty. Her cheekbones are enormous and her mauve-tinted lips rather large and kissable. It turns me off, though, that she moves with the exaggerated histrionics of Gloria Swanson in *Sunset Boulevard.* That, and I can't say I care for the red spandex headband holding her long crimped hair in place. Too disco.

Just as the discussion of the outfit is growing unendurable, a standard mustachioed gay clone type arrives to start his shift. "Hallooo one and all," he says with a frighteningly manic intensity. "Mama's here, and she's got deliveries for her little babies!" He hands Colin and Eddie each a bulging white envelope.

Colin stuffs the envelope in his pocket. "Thanks, Mama. Hey, you don't mind if I split now?"

"Not at all, my dear," says Mama, his eyes strangely aglitter.

"I wanna get outta here too," says Eddie who hasn't done anything remotely resembling work since he's arrived.

Mama begins energetically dusting the countertop, though it doesn't need it. "By all means, take off. Enjoy the day. Enjoy, enjoy." As Colin, Eddie, Varlena, and I push through the door I hear him chattering to himself. "The boys may work from sun to sun, but Mama's work is never done."

We all walk together up Christopher Street, which is still liberally strewn with lazy, sexy, and half-naked male bodies. "Man, I wanna find a date with air conditionin'," says Eddie. "I don't care if he ain't got no money, I just want air conditionin'."

An expensively dressed man in an alligator shirt and penny loafers sashaying down the street with a tiny, prissy dog glares at Varlena as he passes. "Street trash," he hisses to himself.

"What did you say?" shrieks Varlena. The man doesn't stop but Varlena isn't going to let it go. "What did you say?!" No response. She runs around in front of him to block his way. Her back arches, her eyes shoot fire, and somehow she seems to physically grow, assuming gargantuan, inhuman proportions. "I'll get you yet, my little pretty! And your little dog too! Ah, hah, hah,

hah!" she cackles. As the man flees in mortal terror I see a look of triumph on Varlena's face.

"Asswipe preppy bastard," says Eddie as Varlena rejoins us. "If it were ten degrees cooler I woulda knocked his block off."

Varlena and Eddie leave us at the subway stop, heading off for an early evening beer. "So, they're like your friends?" I ask as neutrally as possible.

"Yeah," says Colin. "They're a lot of fun, even if they're not clued in about music or clothing."

"I'll say," I murmur.

Colin glares at me, his eyes slit-like and hard. "At least they're not nice, safe, pampered, repressed little suburbanites who think they're better than anyone who hasn't jumped on the latest trend. They've both been on their own since they were like thirteen or fourteen years old. They didn't have parents who read to them or paid their tuition at State University. So no, they might not be completely up on the latest import album or the novel everybody is reading or the proper way to make yourself sound clever and clued in." I turn my head away, ashamed of my snobbery. Colin softens his tone and unslits his eyes. "It's pretty incredible actually, to see them in action. Hustling, I mean. They can turn tricks anywhere. I've seen Eddie do it on the subway."

Suddenly I remember the envelope. "What was that Mama gave you?"

"You'll see," say Colin.

"Tell me!" I plead.

"You'll see."

"Tell me, tell me, tell me!"

Colin just smiles.

After eating our deli sandwiches Colin pulls out the envelope. "Mama gets drugs delivered like normal people get the paper or milk. All us guys at the theater put in weekly orders for black beauties, pot, acid, or whatever we want."

"Oh?" I don't know what to think. Lizzie always made a big show of wanting drugs, any kind of drugs, but she never seemed to actually do any, at least not while I was around. I don't recall Colin ever mentioning them before except when Wilson, a gorgeous junkie boy Lizzie dated briefly, insisted that William Burroughs wrote the best drug literature and Colin, Lizzie, and I threw him into an apoplectic frenzy by insisting Jackie Susann's *Valley of the Dolls* was better.

"Here, take this," Colin says, handing me a small black pill and swallowing one of his own with chocolate milk.

I pop my pill. "I don't feel anything."

"It takes a while to work," he explains. "Now, it's time to get pretty." He opens a little jar of Queen Helene's Mint Julep Facial Mask and we slather our faces with green goo. For the next half-hour we weave rapturous fantasies about Queen Helene, whom we imagine as a spectacularly beautiful dethroned Eastern European monarch who's gone quite mad. When not busy sleeping with her chauffeur, footman, or stable boy, she creates beauty products based on her favorite cocktails.

"Dahlink, you zimply muzt try my new Martini Viss Olive Unter Eye Cream."

"And zen you muzt do zometink for your coiffure. Try uzink my Scotch On Ze Rocks conditioner."

As I'm washing off my face I notice that I'm in an unusually good mood, and by the time I finish dressing I feel an extreme euphoria compounded with a wave of energy so strong I can't remember what being tired was ever like. I look at myself in the mirror and for once I think I look OK, maybe sexy even. The club is twenty-two blocks south and three avenues over, but we're so amped we decide to walk, which turns out to be so much fun I can't imagine why anyone ever takes the subway or rides in cars. Could anything be more fun than walking? *Fun, fun, fun!*

Danceteria is a huge place, full of the cutest kids I've ever seen and the best music I've ever heard: the darkly catchy "Love Cascade" by Leisure Process, the jarringly off-kilter "Janitor" by the Suburban Lawns, the wildly danceable "Kiss Me" by Tin Tin, the daringly drippy "Love Plus One" by Haircut 100. Colin and I dervish around the floor all night, drenching our bodies with sweat. Like bees that do a dance in their hive to tell their comrades the location of some good pollen, we communicate through movements and gestures. Though we don't speak for hours, we each know when the other finds a vocal pretentious, a beat infectious, a synth-wash irritating, or a nearby dancer cute. Though it's daybreak when we leave, neither of us is tired, so we decide to walk home.

Somewhere around Thirty-third Street Colin announces, "Chocolate milk time," and heads toward a deli. As the electric door opens automatically and we leave behind the golden light of dawn for a harshly artificial fluorescent glare, we hear strange computerized sounds coming from the radio. "Eech, nee, san, shee," calls out a chipmunk voice. "Adeen, dva, tre," responds a robot voice, "Planet Rock, don't stop." Colin points to our image on a TV monitor behind the counter. "Future is now," he says. And he's right.

Colin tells me about an East Village bathhouse he knows of that's always looking for new employees. I show up and sure enough, the manager, a badly aging queen named Allen with hair dyed the color of cheddar cheese, puts me right to work. "Welcome to the team," he says as he firmly shakes my hand. He calls Jaime, a superhumanly beautiful Puerto Rican boy, over to get me started. First, Jaime shows me how to clean the tiny sex cubicles, each just big enough for a bed and nightstand. Between guests the sheets are changed and any stray items or mysterious substances (ick!) are removed. Then we fish gunk out of the hot tub. "Don't ever go in there," Jaime warns with a serious look on his exquisite face. Finally, we wash huge hampers of sheets and towels in the tiny, sweltering laundry room. Along the way I'm introduced to a couple of co-workers: sassy, gum chewing, tough cookie types who remind me of Eddie.

Although the pay is lousy, I discover a fringe benefit midway through the afternoon when Jaime finds a *Playboy* magazine under a chair in the "social" room. His eyes light up and he drags me by the hand into the nearest cubicle and we make out while he flips through the pages. "Oh, she's verrry seeexy, no?" he asks pointing to a blonde woman with breasts the size of beach balls. "Uh, yeah. Sure," I say. An hour later an Italian boy with the compellingly broken nose of a boxer comes through the front door and makes goo-goo eyes at me. After he changes into a towel in the locker room (while I try to look inconspicuous wiping and re-wiping the sinks) he beckons me into his cubicle.

On my way home in a subway car full of bedraggled worker bees, I marvel at my new career. I got lucky twice in one day... and I didn't even start work till after lunch.

I'm standing outside Man's World waiting for Colin to get off. A couple of scantily dressed she-male hookers are parading slowly up the street. Every time a car approaches they manically turn to face the vehicle, flip their hair, thrust out their hips, and sling their purses over their backs like fashion models.

Colin emerges accompanied by Eddie. We say our hellos and start walking towards the subway. "Hey, see that, see that?" whispers Eddie. He jerks his head towards a newish mini-van with darkened windows slowly cruising up West Street. "I think dat's da gang of chickenhawk leather queens, y'know, da ones dat drive around an' pick up young boys, dope 'em, and use 'em in S&M sex scenes."

"Well, who'd get in a van full of strange men?" I wonder.

Eddie sidles up next to me to whisper his answer. He's so close I can smell his pizza breath. "Dey don't exactly extend an invitation. Sometimes it's just a bonk on da head. Varlena knew dis guy once said it happened to him. He was out workin' when a van pulls up and dis guy in chaps and a vest starts talkin' to him. Next thing he knows he's wandering da streets two days later wit a headache and welts on his ass."

"Did he describe the van?" asks Colin.

"He was on acid and 'ludes when dey picked him up. Alls he could remembuh is a room wit candles and a buncha guys. Rumor is, once da guys in da van got ahold of dis guy who dey knew was a queerbasher and starred him in a snuff film."

"That's barbaric!" I blurt out. "What about trial by jury? And two wrongs don't make a right!"

"You forgot 'might doesn't make right' in your list of tired clichés," says Colin.

"Well, dis was some goon dat really fucked up a lot of people," says Eddie, eying the van nervously.

Colin keeps an eye on the van too, but has a hard look on his face. "Maybe it'll take some creepy snuff queens being 'barbaric' before people learn to leave gays alone. I mean, we're not safe anywhere. Just last year a crazy Biblethumper went on a rampage and killed two men inside the Ramrod."

"Fuckin' shit-for-brains asshole bastard oughta fry," says Eddie.

I feel myself turning willowy and feminine. "But if we become just as violent as they are then what do we really accomplish?"

Colin sighs. "The ability to walk around without getting beaten or shot by idiot homophobes. I say, go snuff queens." This from the pacifist who would've stayed out of World War II.

I try to see into the windows of the van. It's tinted pretty heavily but I can just make out shapes moving inside. People? Orangutans? I really can't tell. "So you're saying it's a jungle out there and we shouldn't bother with moral codes and due process and all that?"

Colin looks at his feet, then the sky. "Of course not. But I'm not gonna cry any bitter tears for queer-bashers. Karma, y'know?"

"Well, how do we know they even got the right guy? Did they have fingerprints? It's not like they're the police."

Eddie leans back his head and emits a loud "Ha!" that makes him sound like a wild bird of some sort. "Da police! Dat's cute," he says patronizingly. "Dis one's cute," he says to Colin in case he missed it.

Colin turns and looks me right in the eye. "You really have to be careful in this city. I mean, sooner or later everyone gets their gay knocks, but, well, just be careful."

Even though we haven't been walking fast (Colin slows down for Eddie and other people, it's only when alone or with me that he walks like he's in a race), we catch up with the slow, slow van. A shiver runs up my spine. I see Colin's face freeze in nervousness and Eddie looks queasy. I know I should be wary too, but growing up in the unnatural safety of suburbia has made it impossible for me to really believe anywhere could be so lawless that people are kidnapped by sexual psychopaths in broad daylight. New York apparently is that kind of place.

Colin and I go out every night. We're always whispering, giggling, and talking together, even in cruisy situations when everyone else is silent and still as a mannequin. Though I'm too shy to make the first move, being nineteen means I can always get picked up by someone a bit older. It's fun going to strange men's homes (the lack of privacy makes our place off limits) and getting to know them a little. A rail-thin writer explains all about his macrobiotic diet. A guy with a purple refrigerator tells me about his past as a glam rock roadie. A chef who lives with his extended family (there might even be a wife in there somewhere) in an elegant East Side flat takes me home, where I stand behind him as he talks to his mother who ignores me as if I'm invisible. The highlight of each encounter comes when I describe it to Colin. He also tells me about his, which makes me not jealous (now that I've experienced instant gratification I wouldn't begrudge it to anyone) but frustrated. Why them and not me? Am I ugly?

It's three a.m. and I'm standing on the edge of a dance floor peering at the mad, swirling crowd of astonishingly attractive club-hoppers. Along the walls, out of the glare of disco lights, guys are lined up, eyeing the dance floor, chatting, drinking and making out. "Go talk to that cute boy over there," says Colin, pointing at a luscious lad lurking behind a pillar. "He looks like your type."

"You know I can't do that," I whisper.

"Why?" asks Colin, his voice brittle with exasperation.

"Maybe he'll come over here and say hi to me," I suggest.

"And maybe he won't, so why don't you say hi to him?"

I'm getting angry that Colin is making me spell this out. "Because he'll just reject me and then I'd feel bad."

"Go," says Colin. He gives me The Look, a thin-lipped, eyebrow furrowed, prelude to anger, so I go. The boy is still standing statue-like by the pillar. My feet start moving towards him but they feel like lead. When I finally reach him, I squeak out a small "Hi" and try not to flinch.

"Hi," says the boy in a disturbingly flat tone.

"Good music tonight, huh?" I comment, just as the song changes from the über-cool "Collapsing New People" by Fad Gadget to the more pedestrian (though still wonderful) "Call Me" by Blondie.

The boy shoots me a withering glance. "Golly gee, sure is," he says in a bitterly mocking hick accent. Before I can react he walks away. I manage, just barely, to summon the strength to return to Colin.

"He... he..."

"I heard," says Colin. "It was only two yards away. But it's his loss, not yours. I mean, you're not the richest person here, and not the prettiest, and not even the youngest. You're not the smartest or the funniest or the most sincere. Someone in here is definitely more talented, someone is more hardworking, and someone is luckier. But, look!" He drags me by the hand to the bathroom. It's brightly lit inside so I whip out my wraparound sunglasses. Colin takes me by the shoulders and turns me to face the mirror. "What do you see?"

"A nineteen-year-old with a big nose and spotty skin."

"What's he wearing?" asks Colin.

"A sleeveless day-glo pink tee shirt with askew purple triangles."

"And?" he prods.

"A dangly earring made out of a glittery chartreuse plastic fishing lure."

"And what has this person done with his hair?" sing-songs Colin merrily.

"Dyed it Clairol blue-black and sprayed it up to add six inches of much needed height."

"And the rest?"

"Pants made out of parachute material with a side zipper..."

"All of it," coaxes Colin.

"Black Converse high-tops, day-glo green socks, and two bracelets consisting of a black leather cockring with metal studs and a turquoise blue kitty collar with rhinestones."

Colin lets go of my shoulders and I turn from the mirror. He looks me straight in the eye. "Nobody, but nobody, at this club is more New Wave than you are." This really shouldn't make me feel better, but it does.

We're standing in front of the Mudd Club where an intimidatingly trendy doorman behind a velvet rope is choosing who gets admitted and who's banished into the night. As we make our way through the thin crowd of people trying not to look desperate, I wonder if we're going to make the grade. Colin, reading my face, reassures me. "The whole door thing is just to keep dorky straight guys from flooding the clubs. The door people practically never stop girls or gay guys. The clubs are like an inversion of the power structure, an extension of '60s radicalism, really."

Nana Leah manifests, shaking her finger angrily at Colin. "Clubs are not protests. How are you going to change the world by dancing or watching shows?" I relay her concerns to Colin. He stands aside from the people who want in to the nightclub and faces me so he can deliver a lecture.

"Emma Goldman was dancing once..." he begins.

"Who?" I ask.

He sighs. "Only one of the most famous anarchists from the turn of the century. Emma Goldman was dancing once and somebody asked her how she could dance when so many people were suffering and she said, 'If I can't dance, then I don't want any part of your revolution.' Or something like that. Anyway, it's hard to change people's minds with picket signs and boycotts. When people are nightclubbing their defenses aren't up so they're more receptive to new ideas and more willing to cross boundaries.

"For instance, blacks and whites didn't hang out together till jazz and the Harlem renaissance came along. Then, once all the hipsters and trendy people started interracial partying, segregation became passé, déclassé even. After that it was just a matter of time till it was repealed. And now with New Wave and the Downtown scene, gays and trendy straights are partying together. In twenty years homophobia will be so un-hip even suburbanites will support gay rights just so they don't look like bumpkins."

"I don't know what he's talking about, and I bet he doesn't either," whispers Nana Leah.

"And you've heard of Cafe Society?" asks Colin, still waxing pedantic.

I shake my head no.

"It used to be that rich people would only socialize with each other, so the people running things lived in their own private world walled off from outside influences and new ideas. Then, starting in the twenties, Cafe Society came along and everyone started mixing: the nouveau riche, whores, aristocrats, intellectuals, politicians, journalists, artists, entertainers, writers, everyone. Well, the new club scene is like Cafe Society only it's even more democratic because it includes drag queens and punks and radicals and teenagers, and everybody gets their fifteen minutes of fame. It's not enough to redistribute wealth. You have to redistribute fame, too. Let everybody be a celebrity. That's cultural democracy."

"Sounds reasonable," I admit. Then I think of a hole in Colin's argument. "But you do see un-hip people in clubs all the time."

"You have to let some of them in to keep the clubs profitable, just not so many that it become uncomfortable for fabulous people," he says. "It's actually great they're there because it gives them a chance to mix with people they'd never see on TV. Plus, in clubland you can't be anonymous and passive like a TV viewer, you're forced to interact with strangers and have a personality. Leaving the suburbs and TV behind to become a clubhopper is a giant existential step towards personhood."

I hear Nana Leah's voice, "Bah! You don't start a revolution by drinking cocktails in nightclubs. It's just a pastime for the idle rich."

Then, as if to prove her wrong, I'm treated to a display of magically fabulous reverse discrimination when a gaggle of suits from a limousine is turned away from the door and Colin and I are waved in.

While nightclubbing we sometimes run into celebrities, and from Colin's example I learn the proper way to act when you spot them. To stare, even for a millisecond, instantly marks one as a gawker, a suburban nobody. The Downtown thing to do is play it casual, act like you're a celebrity too, though perhaps one whom the media is too boorish to focus on. Colin is expert at this, making idle chit-chat with everyone from Alexis Smith to Billy Idol. I never get to see if he could keep cool with his hero, Andy Warhol, but I do run into my own paragon of fabulousness.

I've just finished reapplying the smudgy black eyeliner (without which I feel stark naked) in the bathroom mirror of a small East Village club when Marc Almond, lead singer of Soft Cell (the only human being, aside from Colin, I'd consider marrying) appears. He faces the mirror and starts froofing his hair, a curly mop of black curls with purple roots. "Did you have to bleach the roots but not the ends to do that?" I ask, outwardly cool as a Sno-cone despite the electrifying, white-hot mania I feel inside.

"No, I have naturally light hair. I just waited till the dyed part grew out and put violet over the whole thing," Marc says in the melodious voice I've swooned to a thousand times.

"Nice," I say as I leave the bathroom. I want to stay, but simply don't dare. Even offstage he radiates a seedy glamour that intimidates as much as enthralls. Outside I gasp for air, lurk in a corner, and watch with awe as he walks away, taking care to note every aspect of his clothing and manner so I can relate his miraculous appearance to Sheila in minutest detail.

I glean from Colin's unspoken attitudes that the staged spectacles of nightlife (people eating dinner behind glass plates like a museum diorama or deranged Germans in auto mechanic jumpsuits banging on hubcaps) may be amusing diversions but are not to be taken too seriously. The important thing is what you do yourself, even if it's just schmoozing and dancing. Colin loves to pump people for information, find out what ticks them off, tickles them pink, and makes them tick. People are always confiding in him, spilling secrets about their sex lives, political views, and family histories within moments of "hello," and "how do you do." Even though New York is enormous, we see many of the same faces over and over. Weirdly, Colin loses interest in people once he has their story. He has no close friends besides me.

I may be too shy to schmooze well (I just stand six inches behind Colin and occasionally supply a *bon mot*), but I absolutely live to dance. From watching others I develop a style all my own that's midway between a parody of the hyper-energetic styles found on '60s TV dance shows and modern New Wave dance styles. I flail, shimmy, skank, twirl, twist and make robot arms at an alarmingly rapid pace. Every time someone says I dance well it's like one nasty insult I received while growing up is magically erased. I'll often spend four, six, even eight hours on the dance floor in absolute bliss.

Our favorite club is The Anvil on Tuesday nights. In addition to a basement orgy room where cute guys pack in as tight as subway commuters, they play all the new groups from England before anyone else: the Au Pairs, ABC, O.M.D.

There's also a show in which demented drags do lip sync. One night a giant, histrionic Black queen in a green sequined dress does "Tainted Love," not the Soft Cell cover that's topping the charts, but the original haunting soul version by Gloria Jones. It's like all the pain of all the mismatched love from the moment the first stone age man clubbed the first stone age woman over the head and dragged her back to his cave has been stored up for this one harrowing song. The performer is a true drama queen and emotes as if not just her love, but she herself, her lover, her child, and maybe the world itself are all dying. Then, at the finale, just when I think every bit of emotional mileage has been wrenched out of the song, she literally bursts into flame: fire shooting up a foot or two from her arms and wig. After gasping as one, the audience bursts into a round of wild applause for this slightly insane display of pyrotechnics. My spine tingles uncontrollably and despite the warmth I experience a shiver of fear, not at the sight of the flames, which are put out instantly, but at the thought that Colin and I might be destined for a tainted love flambé.

"You know, she does the fire bit every time she performs," whispers a man behind me to his friend. "But it never gets old."

Debauchery

I ask Colin where we're going but he just says, "You'll see."
See what? I wonder. We've been walking and walking but for
blocks there's been nothing but meatpacking plants, red brick
warehouses, rundown storefronts. It's a blindingly sunny late
afternoon and sweltering hot; the air is so humid it feels like
something you could swim through. Still, Colin tramps along at
his usual breakneck pace. I actually have to jog to keep up with
him. As we turn onto West Street, there are half a dozen young
guys leaning against a brick building looking sultry, smoking,
talking, each keeping one eye on the road in front of them. They
remind me of the bad kids who hung around the parking lot
outside high school getting stoned instead of going to classes:
slightly feral.

Suddenly I see a dirty white economy car driven by a balding
middle-aged man pull to the curb a few yards ahead. A skinny
kid wearing cutoff shorts and a tank top saunters up to its open
window, leans down, and starts chatting. After a moment he gets
in and the car drives away. They're turning tricks, I think, a bit
shocked, even though I've read all about this in John Rechy's *City
of Night*.

"Victims of bourgeois decadence," intones Nana Leah, shaking her head sadly while fanning herself with a copy of Engels' *Origin of the Family, Private Property and The State.*

Gramma Bea is right next to her. "They're tarts!" she warns with some concern. She can tell I thought the boy was handsome.

"Bourgeois moralizing," sniffs Nana Leah. "They're doing what they have to do to survive under capitalism. You'd rather they starve?"

"Of course not," says Gramma Bea, "but I don't think Jeremy needs to be exposed to this sordidness. He's at an impressionable age."

"Well, he'd certainly be better off organizing industrial laborers," says Nana Leah. "These lumpen-proles are useless."

"No human being is useless," admonishes Gramma Bea, breathing hard with the effort of keeping up with Colin and me as we barrel down the street.

"Useless to the revolution," clarifies Nana Leah, huffing and puffing a bit herself.

Gramma Bea's hefty body slumps to an exhausted halt. "You will be careful, won't you? Jeremy, darling?"

"And stay out of trouble," adds Nana Leah.

"Of course," I agree.

My grandmothers vanish in a puff of ectoplasmic evaporation.

As Colin and I pass the hustlers, I'm half-afraid they'll say something mean, but they ignore us. A block further on we pass a bar, from which I can hear the faint strains of manic High N-R-G Disco—*doo da doo da doo dooo menergy, doo da doo da doo doo menergy, talkin' bout men-er-gy!* emanating from within. "That's the Cockring," explains Colin. "A famous leather bar." There's no sign but I'm still a bit shocked that a public establishment can have such a raunchy name. Then Colin leads me across the street under an elevated highway and through a parking lot to a huge abandoned warehouse with broken windows and peeling industrial gray paint. It sits on a pier jutting into the Hudson.

We enter through a partially unhinged screen door as Colin, also partially unhinged from a few belts of Wild Turkey, tells about the place. The warehouse is not only cruised by gay men, but home to packs of transvestite hookers who sleep on filthy mattresses and eke out a living by servicing the erotic needs of suburban closet-cases they pick up in the parking lot out front. He speaks quietly so as not to break the eerie silence prevailing inside, as if we'd just entered a cathedral instead of a drive-in whorehouse. I look around for the transvestites but only see a few standard-issue horny homos prowling amidst the rubble and debris of the gigantic airplane hangar-like space. Bits of the walls and roof have disintegrated so it's nicely ventilated and you can see the sky that, just this moment, is a stunning shade of sapphire.

Like a baby duck following its mother, I walk right behind Colin, exploring nooks, crannies, and hidden rooms, occasionally climbing over chunks of broken concrete, splintery wood, or rusted metal beams. Here and there I spy men engaged in furtive sex or displaying their bodies just so; hips thrust forward, lips in a half sneer/half pout, eyes staring ahead blankly saying, "Go ahead, make the first move." Through a doorless exit we find a walkway surrounding the warehouse and sit for a moment, dangling our legs over the edge of the pier. Looking out over the brown/green Hudson at a hazy New Jersey, I inhale the luscious smell of salt water and decaying wood. Colin is completely silent which is thrillingly unusual. I don't know what to expect and I like it that way.

After a few minutes Colin motions for me to follow him back inside and up a stairway leading to an old office still containing the dilapidated remnants of a desk, a couple of broken file cabinets, and a moldy rug. The walls are covered with insane graffiti. Scribbled in pencil or magic marker are crudely drawn genitalia, elaborate advertisements for peculiar sexual needs, phone numbers. There's something that looks like a bedroll in the corner. "We better keep out of here," advises Colin. Stepping over a hole in the floor (how do people get around in here at night?), I'm spotted by a wandering leatherman in full regalia: boots, harness, chaps, and police cap. He gives me an unmistakable look. I'd ignore him and keep moving, but Colin stops in his tracks, so I do too. The leatherman, through gestures, lets it be known that he wants my hot teenage ass. I look at Colin who indicates wordlessly for me to bend over.

I hesitate (after all, I'm basically a virgin) but obey. If this is what Colin wants, then this is what The Plan calls for. This is my destiny. I place both hands on a wall in front of me and thrust out my rear. He must be thirty if he's a day, I think with distaste as the leatherman pulls down my jeans, then my underpants. Then a region in my body where I didn't know it was possible to feel pain suddenly reminds me of the Johnny Cash line about "a burning ring of fire."

Ouch! George Washington, ouch! John Adams, ouch! Thomas Jefferson, ouch! During the dull routine of being queerbashed in school I learned to dissociate from bodily pain through recitation: the Gettysburg Address, French verbs, presidents, whatever. James Madison, ouch! James Monroe, ouch! Guys are gathering around to watch. John Quincy Adams, ouch! It's almost too much to bear, but I can see Colin beaming with pride at the spectacle he's orchestrated. Andrew Jackson, ouch! Between the thrill of pleasing him, the subtle excitement of being the center of attention, and the pain, I forget to be shy. Martin Van Buren, ouch! So this is sex.

After the leatherman finishes he slaps me on my ass (affectionately? who can say?) and strides off stiffly into the congealing gloom of early evening. I feel as if my internal organs might just slide out of my body. All around men are still staring at me, waiting, hoping, as I pull up my pants. Colin approaches.

"Never again," I whisper, feeling like the veteran of some bizarre war.

"C'mon," says Colin, leading me downstairs where there are now a fair number of guys lurking and skulking about. "After-work crowd," he whispers. Seconds later Colin starts making out with a handsome Italian boy. I stand for a second, made slightly leery by my recent experience, but then get drawn into an alcove by the stare of a floppy-haired waif. He's wearing torn, trendy black clothing and his natural sweetness quickly restores my faith in the magic of homosexuality. As we finish our puppyish interaction I ask his name but he just smiles, kisses me softly on the lips and wanders away. It's dark as Colin and I leave the pier, but thanks to a hundred million electric lights there are no stars above. That's all right, I don't miss them. The sexual compulsives of lower Manhattan have plenty enough star power for me.

Colin often tells me, "Variety is the spice of sex!" I would find this evidence of a coarse and vulgar nature if his search for variety weren't so baroquely fanciful. Colin isn't one of those queens who discuss whether they're in the mood for Italian or Asian as though he were deciding where to have dinner instead of the ethnicity of his next sexual conquest. No, Colin has developed a set of highly peculiar fetishes.

For example, Colin has a mania for the younger male employees of pizzerias, "pizza boys." He explains that the repressed, macho working class Italian environment (and perhaps also all that spicy tomato sauce) inflames their passion so that if you so much as put your hand on their ass they'll go crazy like wild stallions. Colin also obsesses over suburban American kids so smitten with the glamour of British pop they become "fake English accent boys." He finds their pretentiousness cute and insists that they're terrific in bed. Then there are "science guys" who are so busy thinking about neutrinos or microbes or what have you that they're completely innocent. Not only do they not realize it when they're cute, they sometimes don't even notice they're gay and will be incredibly grateful if you point it out.

At the apex of Colin's list of love objects is the "mama's boy." Colin positively swoons whenever he sees a boy wearing clothes so dorky that "only his mother" could have chosen them. The mama's boy is not especially handsome or good in bed, but presents the thrilling challenge of defilement. Colin tells me about his escapades with one mama's boy. "We strip down to just our underwear and stand a few feet apart and just look. We don't touch each other, at all, ever. He's real small and he wears kid's underwear with choo-choo trains on them."

Though I go home with all sorts, my preferred type is the New Wave boy. Unlike S.F. where the macho clone look still prevails, New York overflows with cruising boys wearing pointy shoes, retro shirts, peg-leg jeans, studded belts and bracelets, dayglo socks, and gravity-defying hair in unnatural hues. These trendy clothes are as erotically charged to me as leather, muscles, or military-camouflage are to regular gays, and I happily indulge myself with their owners whenever I can. Though etiquette requires exchanging phone numbers after all but the most cursory of back room encounter, any interest I have in a second date melts like ice cream in the sun with the slightest reminder of Colin.

"Aren't you ever going to settle down with one boy?" I ask him one day, apropos of nothing.

"I would if I fell in love," says Colin.

"You fall in love three times a week," I point out.

"I want to have as much fun as possible till I meet Mr. Right." Colin's eyes get a little bit starry. "When I finally find love with a capital L, then I'll settle down. Sexual promiscuity's not so much fun when you're old anyway."

"So how old is old?" I ask, wondering how long I'll have to wait till Colin is ready to pair bond.

"I dunno," says Colin. "Fifty? Sixty?"

It's a glorious day, warm and saturated with sunlight the color of honey. Colin and I are walking down Broadway when he shrieks and points to a wall of posters for the new Village People album, *Renaissance*. Instead of epitomizing the '70s gay clone culture we so passionately hate, now they've tried to jump on the bandwagon for the next trend and become gender-bending new romantics. Their über-macho bodies are no longer clad in cop,

Indian, leatherman, or cowboy drag, but adorned in tight leather pants and metallic sequined toreador jackets. Better yet, their square-jawed Tom of Finland faces are covered in full mime-style makeup with raccoon eyes and multiple beauty marks. One even has tiny braided hair extensions. It's the most deliciously wrong thing imaginable; perhaps the most deliciously wrong thing in all of recorded human history. We convulse with shrill uncontrollable laughter causing several passersby to stare at us, quite a feat in mind-your-own-business Manhattan.

We're still giggling minutes later when we reach Washington Square and settle on a park bench. The sun beats down furiously, pummeling us really, and before long it's uncomfortably hot. "We need beer," announces Colin. Walking through the Village I'm amazed for the thousandth time at the resilience and lushness of New York's vegetation, the strange twisted weeds pushing up through the pavement's cracks. A perfect metaphor for the vitality of the life force in this incredible city, I would think, were I the sort of person who thought like that.

Soon we're tucked away into the comforting darkness of Boots & Saddles. Colin takes his shirt off and instructs me to do the same. As if by magic, a slightly older guy (30? 40?) comes over to us and says hello. He's sporting an unforgivable pink Izod shirt, its little alligator emblem broadcasting his allegiance to preppiedom, but he's thoughtfully brought a beer for each of us, so we overlook this transgression. We're dehydrated and drink thirstily while making idle chit-chat with our benefactor, who turns out to be a contractor, whatever that is. As he yammers on about his house on Fire Island he stares up and down our torsos, his eyes gleaming with lust. When we've finished our beers Colin says we have to be going. The man's face falls while his smile stays put through force of will, an ugly thing to behold.

"Trolls," explains Colin as we walk down Christopher Street, "will always buy you beers."

"What's a troll?" I ask, trotting to keep up with him.

"A dirty old man... no wait..." He suddenly thinks of a better definition and smiles slyly. "A troll is someone who wants you more than you want them."

We spend the remainder of the afternoon, all of the evening, and half of the night wandering from bar to bar getting trolls to buy us beers, flirting, and carrying on. "What a couple of floozies!" whispers Gramma Bea, reproachful but half-amused in spite of herself. Nana Leah makes a brief appearance to sit tight-lipped and disapproving as I bombastically demonstrate the Watusi to an amused older gentleman before disappearing without a word. By the time Colin and I begin weaving our way towards the subway to go home we're staggering around like cartoon drunks. Turning a corner onto Sixth Avenue we're surrounded by a swarm of Puerto Rican preteens, giggling and bouncing around as if they were at a birthday party.

"Gimme yer money!" shouts a boy of about twelve with a smile right out of a toothpaste commercial. My first thought is that it's two in the morning on a school night and these kids really ought to be home in bed.

"Or we fuck you up!" says another with a peal of childish laughter. Can this be serious?

"Ohhhh, we're being muuuuged," slurs Colin, simultaneously digging around in his pocket for some cash and staring lustily at a cute gay boy walking on the other side of the street.

"You guys are fags!" declares a boy, who in about two years will be a real heartbreaker.

"Yeees, yeeees, you hit the nail right on the hammer... the head," says Colin as he finds a crumpled $5 bill, stares at it with confusion then thrusts it into the hands of a chubby girl with too much makeup on. She holds the bill up for her friends to see and lets out a super-high pitched squeal of delight. "Shush!" commands Colin sternly. "There's babies sleeping." He points to the windows all around us as the kids laugh and laugh.

"More!" commands the heartbreaker.

"Yeah," agrees his friend with the bright smile. "Lots more!"

"C'mon," I say, trying to pull Colin away by the arm. "Let's get out of here." There are six of them and two of us, but they're wee little things without even so much in the way of a weapon as a rat-tailed teasing comb, so I'm not afraid. A cab turns the corner and I run into the street. "Taxi! Taxi! Colin, come on!"

"Wait!" he commands, still looking for money. "We're beeeeing mugged."

Our pint-sized assailants all think this is the funniest thing they've ever heard and while they crack up, literally clutching their sides in pain from laughing so hard, I pull Colin into the waiting cab. He stares back at the kids with glazed eyes as I give our address. Though the driver speeds like a demon, the ride uptown seems to take forever. My stomach lurches this way and that from an overabundance of alcohol, and Colin looks even worse than I feel. The grizzled driver turns around as we wait at a stoplight.

"Ya buddy's pretty soused. He ain't gonna upchuck in my car, is he?"

"Of course not," I snap, though naturally I have no idea what Colin will do. When the taxi finally pulls to a stop outside our door I wonder if the driver will help me get Colin to the door as he might with a rich lady's luggage, but he speeds off the second I manage to pull Colin onto the pavement. Colin's too heavy to lift, so I pinch his arm... hard.

"Oww!" It works. He's awake enough to walk into the building and up the stairs with only the minor assist of my shoulder to lean on. Once inside The Oven, Colin falls on his bed with a thud. I turn on the light. "Off!" he commands. I obey and we're lit only by the streetlamp outside the window. Just like the first night we were together, I think. "Clothes off me," Colin commands. It's not easy, especially since he can barely sit up and I'm pretty drunk and exhausted myself, but the thrill of touching his flesh gives me energy. So much energy that when he's finally naked I strip off my own clothes and fall on top of him, kissing every part of his body.

"Uh-uh," says Colin.

"I love you, I love you, I love you," I explain, kissing him again. Colin's flesh is warm to my lips, his smell more potent than any drug. My head is spinning from alcohol and I can only maintain my balance by keeping one hand on the wall. Gramma Bea takes this inopportune moment to pay a visit. I can sort of see her sitting where a pile of clothes in the corner sat just a moment ago, arms folded and brow furrowed with disapproval.

"A gentleman does not press his advantage," she says curtly. I agree, but my body is on autopilot. My hands read Colin's body like Braille; my tongue samples him like a judge at a cooking competition. "Are you listening to me?" demands Gramma Bea. I don't respond and she disappears, clicking her tongue.

"Are we shtill being mugged?" asks Colin.

Blowjobs, I think. Men like blowjobs. I set to work, deriving no pleasure from the task. Why do people like this? I wonder. Where is it supposed to feel good, your mouth? I remember the agony of the leatherman at the piers. Oh my god, I must be a top. Who knew?

Colin is instantly hard and I feel that I've made progress. Then he mumbles, "Not you," and rolls on his side. I want to scream. Colin's body wants me, but his mind, even in this drunken state, is dead set against me.

I whisper, "But I love you."

"Don't," says Colin.

Dizzy and depressed, I give up and lie next to him, clinging like a drowning man holding onto a bit of wood in the midst of a stormy ocean. In my drunken state the bed really does feel like the surface of a stormy ocean, everything spinning and swirling. I can nearly see the waves cresting and crashing, hear the roar and feel the undertow. Colin is the only thing keeping me from being pulled down to the bottom of the sea by watery demons.

"Self-dramatizing," declares Gramma Bea, reappearing to stare down at me with pity and disgust. I hadn't expected her back and I'm shocked into near sobriety, then angered.

"Go away, Gramma!"

"Respect your elders! A bit of fun is one thing, but you've gone quite too far with this." I close my eyes and keep them shut as she lectures me on and on about duty and fair play. I know she's right about everything.

"OK, OK, OK!" I say finally. "I stopped, I stopped."

It's silent so I open my eyes. She's gone. "Leggo of me," says Colin, giving me a mild, utterly ineffectual shove. Feeling absolutely hopeless I crawl onto the blankets next to the bed and mercifully pass out.

I awake the next morning when the cruel sun assaults my eyes. I instinctively pull on some shorts and rush down the hall to bathroom. One of the other tenants is in there and taking his sweet time so I'm dancing around like a Hollywood Indian at a rain dance before I can finally get in to pee. Once relieved I take a long drink of the funny-tasting sink water and splash my face. The previous night appears in my mind's eye. How could I be so stupid as to jeopardize The Plan that way? Stumbling back into The Oven I see Colin lying naked, face down on the bed, absolutely still and fear the worst. Then I see him breathe. Relief. Without thinking I sit beside him and gingerly put my hand on his back, then run it down to his buttocks, feeling his smooth skin.

Colin's voice creaks out with what sounds like great difficulty, "Isn't it enough that you raped me last night?"

I freeze, then remove my hand. "That wasn't ever rape."

"I said didn't want to and you just kept going." Colin, with great effort, pulls himself up and assumes a sitting position. "Rape." His face is hard: steely eyes, lips set into a thin, tense line. It's The Look, but times ten. He stands and wraps a towel around his middle. "Now I need a long, hot shower." He quietly walks out the door.

I'm devastated. Will Colin kick me out? Call the police? Am I really a rapist? Impossible. Rapists are like war criminals or murderers, only dirtier and creepier. Colin isn't hurt; it can't be rape. Or can it? I did stop. Eventually. Then I remember Gramma

Bea and know without a doubt that I'm a monster. I hunch myself into the corner as hot tears run down my face and await my fate as if it were a firing squad.

After a hundred thousand billion eternities Colin stomps back into the room. "Get dressed," he orders in a too-calm voice. As we pull on our clothes I keep my eyes glued to his face for signs of anger, forgiveness, anything, but it's unreadable. I hope he can tell I've been crying, I think as my heart races with panic and my mind churns with guilt. I hope he knows how wretched I am.

"I'm sorry, I was drunk."

"I'm sorry, I was drunk," he mimics perfectly. "Drunkenness is a wife-beater's excuse."

I shut up and will the tears back to my face. Crocodile tears? I'm so confused I don't really know. No matter, my eyes stay dry.

"We're going to the Empire Diner for breakfast," Colin says flatly. Jubilation! I won't be banished from his life. Still, Colin is unusually—ominously—quiet as we walk down the street through a scene so happy it looks like it was drawn in crayon by an eight-year-old. The sun shines, birds flitter about the lushly green trees, and the New Yorkers seem slightly less harassed than usual. Even the car horns sound exuberantly impatient rather than angry.

At the sight of the Art Deco diner my spirits lift. One of the things Colin and I love most about New York is that, unlike the rest of America, it still has diners instead of Burger Kings and McDonalds. If I died and went to heaven, I wouldn't be at all surprised to be greeted at the pearly gates by a lady chewing gum and wearing a starched blue uniform with a white apron who'd lead me onto a chrome swivel stool in front of a long Formica bar with a breakfast special on it. Inside it's not crowded so we sit at a booth. "I'll be back," says Colin, heading towards the bathrooms.

"Don't worry, I have this figured out," says Nana Leah, sidling in next to me. "Rape is an instrument of patriarchal oppression used by men to maintain their hegemony over women, whom they regard as their property, mere instruments of social reproduction," she's reading this from one of her little red books.

"What you did last night had nothing to do with oppressing women so it can't be rape," she concludes, not sounding very convinced.

"Nana, I've got to deal with this myself."

Despite her devout atheism, Nana Leah turns her face upwards and addresses the heavens. "Boys he likes! From a boy I'm going to get a grandchild?" On TV when old Jewish people do this it's supposed to be funny, but I don't feel like laughing.

Colin and the waitress arrive simultaneously and Nana Leah vanishes. After we order, Colin leafs through *The Voice* while I stare miserably out the window at the perfect day. Colin is the first to speak.

"Reagan's going to mess everything up, cutting taxes for the wealthy and getting rid of the safety net and all that. The rich and the poor won't be able to mix socially. The rich will be afraid of getting ripped off or asked for money and the poor won't be able to afford to hang out in the same places anyway. Society's going to be divided by class and instead of expressing themselves, people are going to spend all their time advertising their status. It'll be shallow, like the Eisenhower era. Parties will suck."

Forgiveness! Only my dimly remembered sense of propriety and the remains of a hangover prevent me from jumping up on the counter and tap dancing. I'm also impressed. This is an unusually subtle point, one that Nana Leah would never get. She just wants to divvy up the wealth evenly and doesn't care about free expression or good parties. *Colin is so smart.*

I run out for a copy of *The Post* and *The Times* and we spend the rest of the meal reading aloud to each other, sharing tidbits that will tickle our fancies or reaffirm our worldviews. While sipping my orange juice I catch sight of my reflection in the window. I have a gaping, idiotic grin on my face. I try to suppress it and look cool, but I'm physically unable. At the end of the meal Colin hands me the check.

"Two seventy-five each, with tip," I figure.

Colin gives me a hard look. "I didn't bring any money." I'm so relieved he doesn't hate me for raping him, so happy after our perfect breakfast in this perfect diner on this perfect day that I'm delighted to pay the bill.

I get a raise at my bathhouse job and decide I need a new outfit to celebrate. Unlike S.F., Manhattan lacks super-cheap thriftstores so we have to shop at "vintage" stores where the clothing is only slightly cheaper than new. We hit several on and around St. Mark's Place and finally find one where the prices aren't too outrageous. It even has that old clothing smell that I've grown to love wafting from piles of unsorted, unfolded rags in the bargain bins. I immediately find a pair of nifty low-waisted blue slacks, while Colin discovers a polyester tee shirt with a weird pattern consisting of smears of color and not quite shapes.

"Put this on," he commands, handing me the shirt.

"Why? It's polyester." I crinkle my nose in disapproval of what I consider to be a disco fabric.

"The pattern is evocative of Wassily Kandinsky's early work," says Colin, shaking the shirt in my face.

"Who?"

"You should have paid more attention in art history. Put it on."

"But I don't want it," I whine.

"You're not being fun." The cold fury with which he speaks these words makes it clear that this is not a just a misdemeanor, not a mere felony, but a capital offense. I slip into a changing booth and try on the shirt, which is too small for me.

"That looks great. Get that," says Colin.

"It's not my size and it's ugly," I protest.

Colin is incredulous. "Why would I want to hang around someone who isn't any fun? Why would anyone want to hang around someone who isn't any fun?"

"It isn't any fun wearing a shirt that's not only polyester which makes me sweat like a pig, but that's way too small for me. Look!"

I lift my arms sideways, causing the shirt to ride up over my stomach.

"Listen to me, just get the shirt," he says. His eyes and mouth narrow into furious slits. The Look, which I dread the way most people dread doctors' shots or drinking sour milk, frightens me into going up to the counter. Before I can make my purchase though, some unconscious instinct compels me to place the tee shirt on a pile of clothes and start rummaging for something else. Colin observes this willful disobedience in silence and walks out of the store. What should I do? I follow him. He doesn't turn to look at me, just strides up the street as I trot along behind him wondering why he's so mad. Finally he turns into a deli and orders toasted onion bagel with a shmear. Feeling idiotic, I order the same. Without warning Colin breaks the silence. "Why are you following me?" He sounds completely calm, but his mouth is still a tight little line.

"I though we were out shopping."

"Well, we're done," says Colin.

"What're we gonna do now?" I ask.

"I don't know or care what you're going to do, but I'm going to have a bagel."

"Gee, so am I."

"Can't you think for yourself? I get a bagel. You get a bagel. You want to be independent? Go do something by yourself." His crystal clear blue eyes are looking right through me with fearsome intensity.

"OK," I say. After a silent moment we're both served. Leaving the store I walk north and he walks south. It doesn't take long before I'm bored by my own company. I call Sheila but she doesn't answer and I spend rest of the afternoon chastising myself for being disagreeable. The stupid shirt was only three dollars, I could have just bought it and thrown it away. Exiting the subway on 42nd Street I hear a low rumble of thunder and my face is splashed with a gargantuan teardrop of rain. I run to The Oven, getting soggy in what I can tell is only the beginning of a torrential downpour. I open the door hoping Colin will be inside but the room is empty. I decide, for the first time in New York, to turn in early and read. As a huge electrical storm rages outside, I sit on Colin's bed reading his copy of *Our Lady of the Flowers,* though I'd prefer something a little lighter. Hours later I fall into a fitful sleep. At eight the next morning the alarm wakes me, still lying on Colin's bed. Obviously he hasn't come home. I don't have time to worry about this because I have to rush off to work.

I arrive to find that Allen is upset and has called a meeting. Half a dozen of the other indifferent, drugged-out, sexaholic employees and I stand around his fastidiously clean desk as he folds his hands, leans forward, and looks each of us in the eye as if he were about to give the annual report at a stockholders meeting. "This is a *man's* club, where *men* come to have sex with other *men*," he explains, as if we hadn't noticed. "I have heard some of the staff referring to each other, and even the customers, as "she." This will not be tolerated." The lecture goes on and on as my co-workers and I shoot each other little looks of incredulity. For the rest of the day all employees, managers, customers, and inanimate objects are feminized.

The cash register jams. "She's stuck."

Point to a trashcan. "Miss Thing needs emptying."

"Girl, you do it."

When I get home I can tell Colin hasn't been in; the bed is unrumpled, there's no clothing on the floor, no garbage in the can, no empty food containers on the windowsill. This is so unlike him I'm worried enough to call Man's World. I get Mama who tells me, "No my dear, Mama hasn't seen Colin. You sound worried. Perhaps you'd like to come on down and wait for him. You're welcome to sit on Mama's lap if it'll make you feel better." I politely decline.

I wonder, has Colin met with an accident? Should I call the hospitals? Could Colin have been kidnapped by the scary guys in the van Eddie pointed out? Probably not, he said they specialized in young boys and Colin's already in his twenties. Then I remember the story about the Ramrod. Could Colin have been slaughtered by a rampaging Christian lunatic? I run out to a payphone and call the police.

"No, there's been no fanatical anti-gay murders," says an amused officer.

"Could I file a missing person report?" I ask.

"Why don't you wait? Maybe he just went for a walk," says the officer in a jolly tone.

"But I haven't seen him since yesterday!" I protest.

"Maybe it was a long walk."

I go back to The Oven and try to read. It's still storming and thanks to the steady patter of rain on the window I'm able, eventually, to fall into a fitful sleep. I wake up the next day exhausted and with an inchoate sense of terror. I only recall its source when I open my eyes and see Colin's empty bed. There's nothing to do but go to work. Midway through the afternoon I fake a stomachache so I can leave early. Back at The Oven there's still no sign of Colin.

I jog down to the Port Authority, find a luxurious sit-down phone booth and start calling local hospitals to ask about emergency admissions. I'm variously put on hold for twenty minutes, told to try earlier in the day when things aren't so busy, and told nobody of that description has been admitted. There are plenty more hospitals to call but I give up and go back home to wait. I start to pace. The room is so small I can only take three small steps before I have to turn around which makes for very unsatisfying pacing. Clearly The Oven is no place to hold a vigil so I head onto the street.

First, I find myself walking with no apparent goal. Then I find myself in a sleazy bar drinking a beer amidst the after-work cruisers. Suddenly I find myself in the back room, for the first time ever without Colin. A sinewy boy with sandy blond hair gives me the eye and in moments we're making out. I try to pull off his shirt (the more of a boy I can drink in with my eyes the better) but he tugs it down. I try again until I catch sight of some nasty yellowy-purple bruises and decide to let him keep it on. When we're finished my mind instantly returns to the hideous reality that Colin *is missing* and I run back to The Oven.

"Where've you been?" asks Colin, sprawled on his bed reading page six of *The Post*.

"I've been looking everywhere for you!" I scream.

"You called my work looking for me. I could have gotten fired. I told them I was at my grandmother's funeral and they didn't believe me because they said you'd called to ask where I was. I had to tell them I forget to tell you I was going away."

"You could have told me where you were! Where were you?"

"It's none of your business." His mouth is beginning to set into that thin line that precedes The Look, so I let it drop.

"OK, sorry. That was stupid of me. To call your work like that."

"Jeez, you shouldn't worry about me," he says in a conciliatory tone.

"But you could have been..."

He cuts me short. "Here," he says, tossing a postcard to me.

It's shows strange wafts of color floating on (in?) a depthless field. I look at it for a full minute (briefly falling into a vivid, abstract alternate universe where form follows not function but some other alien, inscrutable logic) before I deliver my verdict. "That's strange... pretty... *beautiful*."

"That," he says flatly, "is Wassily Kandinsky."

Colin and I are sitting on his bed eating watermelon and blueberries. It's so beastly hot out that anything but fruit would sink to the bottom of our stomachs and just sit there making a huge fuss. As we eat, Colin reads aloud from an exposé in The *Voice* about the resurgent Republicans. We're horrified, sure, but the corruption, mendacity, and sadism is so over-the-top, out-of-control, and crazy that it's become hugely entertaining as well. Ronald Reagan more closely resembles a super-villain from a comic book or a James Bond movie than a politician.

Colin absentmindedly glances out the window. "Hey, look. Liz's limo's here."

"Huh?"

"You know Liz Taylor is doing Lillian Hellman's *Little Foxes* at the theater down the street?"

"So?" I ask.

"You're being entirely too cavalier about this." He stands up, scattering blueberries across his already stained bedspread. "It's Liz Taylor! C'mon. If we hurry we can see her up close. She doesn't walk fast." Before I know it we're running down the three flights of stairs to the street. "We've got to see her!" he says over and over, "We've got to see Liz!" *Liz, Liz, Liz!*

By the time we're plunging through the heavy traffic of 45th Street I'm as semi-ironically starstruck as he is. I have to see not just Liz, but the brazen hussy who stole Debbie's guy. I have to see the queen of Egypt. I have to see Martha! "Make way!" I shout at a woman blocking my path, "We gotta see Liz!" We reach the edge of the small crowd of rubberneckers just in time to see our beloved legend, looking dazed but glamorous underneath huge, spiked, jet-black hair. She's absolutely beautiful in a mannequinish way. Makeup put on with a trowel, gown of white sequins, minuscule lap dog. The superhumanly regular pace at which her head turns from right to left and back again suggests a Disneyland style audio-animatronic exhibit, and her tight little smile seems to come from another world. We push through to the front of the crowd just as she enters the stage door.

"Damn," says Colin. "I wanted to see her eyes. I wanted to see if they were really violet." Our own tiny *Day of the Locust* over, we walk back to the apartment to finish dinner.

There are so many different ways for gay men to be ugly. Insecure or nervous types get the "service with a smile" look reminiscent of overly solicitous male flight attendants. Some deeply disappointed souls (invariably clutching a cigarette and cocktail regardless of the hour) get "bitchy, swishy, sour face," a shade of nastiness you can spot at nine yards. The less ghettoized succumb to "hearty, wholesome luggishness" and sit around discussing their sexual perversions like traveling salesmen engaging in shop talk. Virtually too common to even notice are the "over-coiffed, pseudo-Euro models," whose insipidness and vanity ooze from every pore.

I stare into the bathroom mirror. Having a big nose, acne craters and a weak chin, it's all the more important that my hair is really perfect. If I tease it just right, use just enough spray, I can get my forelock to curl over my forehead just right without it getting too stiff and looking weird. While I'm performing this delicate task (which has taken half an hour so far, and could easily take half an hour more) there's a knock at the door. "Jeremy! C'mon, I need to shower." I let Colin in. "I have a date tonight with Cliff," he explains, shucking off his clothes.

"Cliff?"

"The handsomest boy on Earth." Colin isn't given to superlatives and his standards of beauty are higher than anyone I've ever known. Cliff must really be a knockout.

"How long have you known this Cliff?" I ask.

Colin hops into the shower. "We met at the docks last night and he gave me a blowjob by moonlight. Très romantic. When he smiles he has these amazing dimples. Today I visited him where he works selling bongs and sunglasses and knickknacks at this table in the Village. He took a break and we got stoned in the bathroom, then when I was leaving he kissed me right on the street in front of all these tourists."

Cliff. A pretty-boy name if ever there was one. Has anyone named Cliff ever been less than stunningly handsome? I suspect not. "So I suppose you're going steady with this Cliff person," I say. I'm making only the mildest effort to keep the bitterness out of my voice despite my conviction that The Plan requires me to transcend jealousy.

"Nah. He has a boyfriend—some older guy named Barry—who he's sworn never to leave. I guess the guy took him in off the streets when he was young and showed him the ropes and stuff. But he fools around all the time."

"So you're two-timing."

"No, Cliff is two-timing."

"But you admit what you're doing is wrong."

Colin hops out of the shower and begins vigorously toweling himself. "Don't be such a prig. He's the cutest boy who ever lived. He's gorgeous. And he's picking me up in just a few minutes. We're going to the movies."

I feel like screaming but instead I run back to our room and throw on my sexiest outfit: the tight Levi's with the sleeveless tee shirt Colin ripped at the midriff. Or does it make me look too cheap? I'm about to change again but Colin walks into the room and begins to dress while humming to himself so I just sit on my blankets pretending to read and moping.

Knock, knock! I steel myself as Colin opens the door. I see a skinny guy in a black trench coat (it's raining), with ratty, white Converse sneakers and a '60s clear plastic umbrella like girls used to carry in grade school. There's nothing commercial about his looks, you'd never see his type in a porn film or a jeans advertisement, but he's stunning—pale, almost bluish skin, bushy eyebrows that meet in the middle (what Colin calls "a unibrow"), enormous lips, smoldering brown eyes with lashes so long they look fake, and a shaggy mop of brownish black hair evoking the Beatles circa *Rubber Soul*, and yes, a pair of world-class dimples. Though he must be at least twenty-two, his impish grin makes you think of a ten-year-old caught leafing through Dad's *Playboys*.

Colin pulls on his coat while he introduces us. "Cliff, Jeremy... Jeremy, Cliff."

I shake Cliff's hand, which is soft and makes me think of sex. "Pleased to meet you," I lie.

"You comin' too?" he asks in a squeaky-cute New Yawk accent.

"No," answers Colin.

Cliff sees the music magazine I'm holding. "Hey, Eno!" He looks me right in the eye and gives me a thumbs-up sign. "*Here*

Come the Warm Jets is, like, my favorite album." I want to hate him but find it completely impossible. He's friendly, dresses well, and shares my taste in music. I surreptitiously scan his person looking for flaws. No luck. He's perfect in every way.

"C'mon, we'll be late," says Colin, walking out the door.

"See ya," says Cliff with a little wave and a goofy (flirtatious?) grin. As he follows Colin into the hall I notice he walks with a slight limp in his left leg that's completely endearing.

Alone again (naturally), all I can do is stare into space, devastated. I'd fall for Cliff myself given half, or even a quarter, of a chance.

"Guess what!?" Colin is ecstatic.

"What?" I ask, shielding my eyes from the light and groggily staring up at him from the hard floor where I had, moments ago, been fast asleep.

"Cliff's lover, Barry, manages a building on West 14th Street by 8th Avenue. It's gonna be renovated next year, but right now he's renting it out to all his friends for cheap."

"So?"

"There's a vacancy and Cliff said he talked to Barry and we could move in."

"I take it your date went well."

Colin just smiles.

"So we'd be living in the same building as Cliff and Barry?" I ask.

"Right next door. It's a loft with a loft bed and a kitchenette, and it's only four hundred a month!"

"So I could have a bed?" If I must lose Colin to Cliff, at least I'd like a mattress to lie on as I cry myself to death.

"Absolutely."

"And we only share the bathroom with Cliff, Barry, and one other guy! The only thing is we need first, last, and a security deposit to move in." He looks at me questioningly, appraisingly. "And we need it right away."

"Yeah," I say to the unasked question about money.

"We can look at the apartment tomorrow. I'll meet you outside work when you get off."

I close my eyes. "OK, whatever you want. Just shut off the light."

I do not sleep easily.

Barry opens the door to the old building that might, I think, be a brownstone. He has a long, sad bassethound face that contrasts with his colorful kimono. "Hey, y'all, welcome!" he says in a warm Southern drawl as he leads us though the dark hallway to the first door on the right. Colin claims Barry has no idea he and Cliff are having an affair, but I wonder. He looks at Colin rather strangely. "This here's the loft," Barry says, opening the door and gesturing with courtly politeness to what, in California, would just be a medium-sized room with a high ceiling. Half the room is taken up by a loft bed platform under which is the kitchenette area. There's a small cabinet that's been used as a cutting board, a hot plate, and a half-sized fridge that smells strongly of old cabbage. The rest of the room is empty but for a tiny dresser, and dark as there's only one small window facing a tiny trash-filled yard. "One of you can sleep up there," says Barry pointing to the loft.

I get up on the dresser and skibble up onto the loft. There's not quite enough room to stand, but I immediately love it because it feels like a tree fort.

Barry says, "In a year they're remodeling and these walls'll be torn down to make bigger apartments for rich folks." He looks wistful. "I don't know where we're all gonna go when that happens. This area may be slummy now, but the way things are going I wouldn't be surprised if twenty years from now there's not a poor person left in Manhattan. It'll be a city of millionaires."

I jump down to the ground. Near where I land I notice a smeary, spooky makeup impression of a face on the wall. "What's this?" I ask.

Barry walks over to examine my find. "Last people who lived here were these two drag queens. Nice folks but they drank too much. Looks like one them got the idea to press her face on the wall. You can paint in here any way you want though."

Compared to The Oven the place is palatial. Colin and I don't even have to confer. We both know we'll do anything to get it.

Barry and Colin talk business as I look out the window at a smashed stroller, a rotting carcass of something, and what looks like, but couldn't be, an airplane tail. In the middle of this dump there's a gorgeous old maple tree. Colin comes to stand beside me. "Can you get six hundred dollars by next Tuesday?"

"I think so."

Colin turns back to Barry with a huge smile. "We'll take it."

"Welcome aboard," says Barry. We shake on the deal.

The next day I make a collect call to my parents from my favorite booth at the Port Authority. They're concerned, boring, generous. Do I like New York? Yes. Am I sure I don't miss home? This is my home. Don't I miss California? It's a dim, unpleasant memory, like having been to the dentist's for a filling. I return to The Oven. Colin is lying on his bed, head facing the window, staring up at the ceiling.

"I got the money," I say, lying next to him with my feet to the window. Here and there, through our clothes, our bodies touch. This is as much contact as he will allow. "They'll Western Union it tomorrow."

"So you just call them up, ask for six hundred dollars, and just like that," he snaps his fingers, "they say 'Sure'?"

"They understand that apartments are expensive here."

"And you don't have to pay them back?"

"No."

"You're so lucky! That's so great! You don't have to face life's harsh realities, you've got this wonderful cocoon of money protecting you."

"It's just six hundred dollars," I protest.

"You should be very, very grateful," he says.

"He's right," agrees Nana Leah, suddenly manifesting herself in the corner. "That's a lotta shekels."

"I am grateful," I say, not exactly meaning it.

"My parents don't have any money, just my dad's pension which is, like, nothing." Already Nana Leah is teary-eyed with class solidarity. Colin goes on, "He used to come home from the factory in the morning while I was eating breakfast, he worked night shifts, and he'd have blood on his hands from fixing the machines."

"Gee." I curse myself for not having poor-mouthed a little more.

"Our house was right near the smokestacks. Our backyard was always covered in this ashy stuff. I don't know what it was, but you wouldn't want to play in it."

"Yuck," I say, thinking of the photo I saw showing Colin dressed as a cowboy playing in front of his family's grim little row house. I remember the yard I played in as a child: the magnificent smelling rose bushes and honeysuckles; the little gardening shed I used to climb on top of and play fort; the huge azalea bush that would explode into a mass of hot pink every springtime; the lawn where I played ball; the picnictable where I kept my cactus collection; the tree I used to climb up into and sit eating berries till I was stuffed and stained from head to toe. "Yeah, I'm lucky," I say, for the first time in my life realizing that I really am, but still worrying Colin's going to try and make me feel guilty for it.

"That's great your parents have money but they're not all stuck up and conservative," he says with no hint of sarcasm.

"Petit bourgeois, but reasonably progressive," says Nana Leah.

"And you always had books and art around when you were growing up," he adds.

"Yeah, and I was a big old bookworm right from the start," I say.

"My dad worked for GE. They were totally evil, always screwing their employees. When I was ten there was a strike that went on forever, like six months. The only way we ate was because the union brought us groceries. That's when I swore I'd never cross a picket line. And I never will. My mom's job at the supermarket didn't even cover the mortgage. I delivered papers for a while, but had to stop because bullies would steal them from me. You're so lucky to have parents to pay your rent. Hey, I wonder if the word 'parent' is onomatopoeic. You know, parent, pay rent. These are my pay-rents, mom and dad."

When I get back from work on the day we're planning to move I find Colin in the lobby. "You get Seymour in here," Colin says forcefully to the squat little lady standing at the door of the manager's apartment. "Let me talk to him." She shuffles into a back room.

This doesn't sound good. "Hi Colin, what's going on?"

"They're claiming I owe them money. They locked our room."

"Didn't you pay the rent?" I ask. "I paid you my share."

"I gave them half of it and told them we were leaving three days before the week ended and they're saying we have to pay..."

"For the whole week!" finishes Seymour, a soggy, fat bald man with an unlit cigar dangling from his mouth, as he shuffles into the lobby. I marvel at how New Yorkers are so willing to not only assume the physiognomy of character actors but use the appropriate props. The unlit cigar is perfect.

"But we're not staying the whole week," says Colin. "You can rent that little breadbox out as a room tomorrow if you can find anyone desperate enough to pay for it."

"What does this say?" asks Seymour pointing to a photocopied sheet of paper listing the daily and weekly prices that's taped to the lobby wall. "Does it say half a week anywhere? No, it says 'Daily, Weekly, Monthly.' "

I don't want this to get ugly. "Colin, maybe we should just..."

"Listen, Seymour," says Colin, in a tone I think sounds overly familiar. "Are you feeling all right?"

"I will be when you pay up and get outta my hair."

Oh, that Seymour is a tough customer!

Colin's voice lowers and becomes conspiratorial. "Is it indigestion?"

"Just mind your own business and let me mind mine. Pay your money and take your junk outta here."

Colin's voice lowers even more. "I have a real problem with constipation myself. Wouldn't be that, would it?"

I despair. I'll never get any of my clothes back. All my things will remain locked in that stupid room till Seymour can throw them out.

"Listen, mister," barks Seymour pointing menacingly with the cigar at Colin's heart. "You're getting outta here right now. I'm callin' the cops!" He scowls menacingly.

Colin ignores him, "I know it's rough. It'd make anyone grouchy."

Seymour continues to stab the air in front of Colin with his cigar, but he does not, I note happily, call the cops. "Listen, you owe what you owe..."

"That bad?" asks Colin sympathetically. "Is it sharp pains?"

"You wouldn't believe," says Seymour, all the fire suddenly gone out of his voice.

"Ow!" says Colin, sympathetically mimicking the feeling of pain with his talented face. "And everybody says, "Try prune juice," like you'd never thought of it yourself. And the pain is excruciating."

"People don't know," says Seymour, lowering the cigar. "People are unaware."

"My dad had it bad, too. I used to hear him groan for hours."

"It goes on and on," says Seymour. "And nothing helps."

"My dad," continues Colin, "he had to cut out meat and dairy, eat brown rice and vegetables."

"Ugh," says Seymour. "No flavor."

"I don't envy you," says Colin. "You've got a cross to bear, that's for sure."

"Look," says Seymour, "I got things to do. You get your stuff outta here right now. You got one hour." He hands Colin a key.

"Thanks," says Colin in a perfectly normal voice as he bounds up the stairs. I follow as Seymour retreats into his office.

"I can't believe you!" I say as we pack up our stuff.

"People are only mean for a reason," says Colin.

"But how did you know?" I ask.

Colin ponders a moment. "He didn't look too healthy and... he just had that look."

"It could have just been business. He could have just wanted his money because that's the policy. Renting by the week."

"It's never about the money," says Colin. "Most people in America have so much money they don't know what to do with it. Look at all the stupid jewelry and the big cars and the rooms nobody uses and the skyscrapers full of people thinking up slogans or counting money and everyone having to watch sexy millionaire models on TV every night for hours and hours and the chewing gum and cigarettes..."

"OK, OK, there's a lot of money," I agree. "But Seymour doesn't look so rich."

Colin sighs, weary that he has to explain everything to me. "Seymour does fine for himself. It's just that Americans express themselves by buying stuff instead of asserting their personal style like civilized people. Haven't you ever noticed that the most tastelessly dressed people are the bossiest and greediest? When you have a run-in with someone like that, someone like Seymour, they're not really interested in the money. Every interaction is a little drama for them to act self-important and lord their power over you. You can either submit—which I wasn't in the mood for and anyway I need the money for Barry—or you can challenge their authority, which is hopeless and boring because they're so into winning they just go on and on. Or you can just cut through all the theater, and appeal to them as one animal to another, which is what I did. It doesn't always work, but it did this time."

Colin, I think, is operating on a whole other level.

We taxi our worldly belongings to the new apartment where Cliff and Barry are waiting for us. Cliff has dug a cot out of the basement which Colin lays claim to. He also found a mattress for the loft, though no ladder. Cliff brings beers from his apartment and we all toast our new living situation. After a bit of small talk about the proximity of bars, beauty supply stores and the post office, Barry turns to leave. "You want anything we're just across the hall," he says. As Cliff follows him he winks at Colin, and then at me. I get my own wink! What does that mean?

We open our suitcases. Ta da, we're moved in.

"I'm gonna like living here," says Colin sitting on his cot. "Having Cliff so nearby will be veeeery convenient."

"You better not get caught, that Barry looks like he might just might carry a switchblade."

Colin's eyebrows shoot skyward at my ridiculous lie. "I'll take my chances."

The best thing about our new home is that there's room for a tiny secondhand stereo. Suddenly my life has a soundtrack. Every waking moment I serenade myself with the sounds of Gary Numan, Home Service, Joy Division, the Gang of Four, and Yaz. There's far more variation within New Wave itself than any other pop music genre. Each band is highly stylized and thoroughly distinct: Bow Wow Wow is neo-tribal with a Burundi beat, The Specials are mods who play ska, The Plastics are Japanese art-damaged, Devo are futuristic, and so on. The only common denominator is an alienated ironic sensibility. I like the spare melancholy synthesizer bands best, as does Colin, who naturally also has a theory to explain their innate superiority.

"The reason rock died," he explains "is it uses the guitar as a phallic symbol which makes its sound represent aggression. When punk started out, it turned all that aggression against the rock dinosaur establishment. Now it's just a formula for boys to show off how butch and bad ass they are."

"The good punk bands are all fronted by girls," I note, thinking of X and the Pretenders.

"The synthesizer is gender-neutral, that's why there's so many girls and gays in New Wave," says Colin. "It's the music of a post-macho world."

"And the punks get all haughty and say anything with a synthesizer is too commercial and not authentic," I grouse.

"Technophobia meets homophobia," agrees Colin. "And since New Wave isn't all macho everyone can let go with the fashion and express themselves, even the straight guys."

"Especially the straight guys," I say, thinking of Duran Duran and Adam Ant. "New Wave is much punker than punk. It takes more chutzpah to walk down the street dressed like Boy George than one of The Clash."

"You know who is really punk rock?" asks Colin.

"Who?" I ask.

"Liz Taylor," says Colin. "Have you seen her new black spiked hairdo in those 'I Love New York' ads on the sides of busses? If she were a teenage boy nobody would deny that's punk. And Martha from *Who's Afraid of Virginia Woolf* was at least as punk as Sid Vicious."

This theoretical mingling of gay movie star worship with punk anti-heroism is an intoxicating idea, a soothing balm for our chip-heavy shoulders. It would be perfect for annoying the hyper-butch, fag-hating straight-boys who are increasingly replacing the homo-friendly collection of freaks, art students, and trendy hairdressers that used to make up the punk scene.

"Sometimes, you have to admit, those macho punk boys can be kind of sexy," I think out loud.

"In a tired, predictable, rough trade sort of way," admits Colin.

"Hey, maybe there could be a new Village People character..." I begin.

Colin is way ahead of me. "No, no, no! A whole new band, The East Village People."

"With one punk, one Rastafarian, one no-wave art wreck, and, and..." I've run out of archetypes.

"One neo-mod and one neo-beatnik," finishes Colin.

If we ever followed through with any of our inane ideas, I wonder, would we make any money?

After scrubbing, vacuuming, and laundering at the bathhouse for eight hours (with a vicious hangover) the only thing that keeps me from screaming like an overtired baby as I ride the sweltering, crowded subway home is the thought of a cool shower and sleep. I walk in the door to find Colin standing in front of the mirror wearing only a pair of black slacks.

"Your friend Sheila called," he says, sounding chipper. "The Ventures are playing at the Peppermint Lounge tonight." He holds up a lavender dress shirt to his body, frowns, and tosses it aside.

"Oh, really?" As much as Colin and I despise the dirty, pot stoned, earth toned, hippie '60s, we love the pre-counterculture '60s (what we call the go-go era) when Jackie O. brought true glamour to the White House, TV became so tacky it inadvertently embraced surrealism, doctors handed out speed like candy, adults still had good manners, high fashion embraced day-glo colors and outer space themes, the art world was dominated by swishy Pop artists, and the airwaves were ruled by the brilliant bubblegum of girl groups, the British Invasion, and surf music. That we were too young to experience this fantastical world is a source of never-ending disappointment.

Colin scowls into the mirror. "What're you going to wear? I'm thinking of my blue sports coat and my new op art tie."

"I don't think I can go out tonight. I'm super-tired and it'll be expensive."

"Jeremy! You love The Ventures. The Peppermint Lounge is where they invented The Twist, your favorite dance. What's your problem?"

"I'm just not in the mood."

"I'm just not in the mood," he says à la Norma Desmond as he holds his hand palm out over his forehead and arches his back. "No, I simply can't even consider being seen by my public tonight." I don't respond and Colin turns to face me, arms akimbo. "You're not being fun," he all but growls as his face begins to assume The Look.

"I'm exhausted," I plead, sounding whiny even to myself.

"Fine. You can always catch them later. Seeing The Ventures will be a blast when you're forty-two." He puts on a plain white button-down shirt.

"Why can't I see them when I'm twenty-two?"

"Sure, by all means, start enjoying your life at twenty-two, it's only a few years away. Between now and then you can rest up."

"I'm not moving into a monastery!"

"You can enjoy your next youth. The one you get later." He begins knotting his tie, a process which I know will take him half an hour as he invariably gets it wrong.

"Let me do that for you," I offer.

"No, you lie down. You're tired."

"Good idea." I climb onto Colin's dresser and scramble onto my loft bed. Am I really too tired, I wonder, or am I an old fuddy-duddy? The thought of trying to make myself presentable seems overwhelming, exhausting, and impossible.

Colin puts the Supremes on the stereo. As Diana Ross sings about the love bug the song's beat awakens some primal force within me. I suddenly want to jump up on a table in a crowded restaurant and dance. "Maybe I'm not that tired... no, I think I am."

"Get dressed!" Colin says.

I grudgingly rise and strip off my work clothes. "OK, I'll go, but I'll be so tired I won't enjoy myself."

"Good, come along but have a rotten time. That sounds like a great idea," says Colin in between sips of Wild Turkey.

"It's your fault I'm so tired, taking me out drinking last night."

"Your passive aggression lacks subtlety. I'd work on it."

I catch sight of my mattress. "No, I really am too tired to go." I fall onto my bed and lie corpselike. Colin can only see me on the loft when he's at the far end of the room so he doesn't immediately realize I've stopped dressing. "I'm lying down and it feels pretty good," I say to alert him.

Silence.

"Turn off the overhead light when you leave, please," I request.

Silence.

Suddenly I'm not tired. "Maybe I could go..."

"Will you stop dithering and get dressed!" Colin cries.

"Well, I'm not going if you're going to shout at me!"

Silence. I don't care if I'm not tired, though maybe I really am. I'm going to sleep. I feel something wet fall on my forehead, then my knee. "Colin, what are you doing?" A drop falls on my shoulder. I sniff. I'm being rained on by Wild Turkey. "OK, I suppose I have no choice but to go, but it's your fault if I drop dead from exhaustion." I quickly stuff myself into my thin-lapel gray sharkskin suit.

"You look great," says Colin when I finally hop down to the floor.

I point to his tie, which is knotted all wrong. "Want me to fix that for you?"

"If you must." He looks away as I perform my wifely duty. The tie really is nice; a dizzy-making spiral like something a hypnotist would use. As soon as we're on the street Colin starts hailing cabs.

"It's too expensive!" I complain. "Let's take the subway."

"I'll pay," says Colin. "I have money."

"You should. Since I moved here I've lent you five hundred and thirty-seven dollars." Colin's outstanding debt infuriates me but somehow I never screw up enough courage to demand the money, or even stop lending him more, though I do occasionally make bitter remarks about it. "Five hundred and thirty-seven dollars ought to be enough for door to door helicopter service."

"I'm going to pretend you didn't say that," says Colin, opening the door to a taxi. As Colin gives the driver directions, I smell the Brylcreem in his hair and get hit with a childhood memory of sitting behind high school kids on the bus. Even at eight I'd loved teenage boys with their sweaty animal energy, absurd fashion choices, vaguely hostile jousting, and sexy swaggers. I have a mild epiphany. Colin is a real boy. I'm a... a what? A neuter? A drag parody of young malehood? He's just like the boys I grew up around. Lean. Confident. Sexual. Every molecule of my body wants these boys, demands them. The taxi hurtles towards the Peppermint Lounge and I indulge in a tiny fantasy of myself as a child at a beach where I'd run into two teenage boys, one with golden curly hair, his friend with raven black locks... who'd play Frisbee with me and their dog till sundown when we'd make a bonfire. They'd drink beers and watch the sunset, giving me little sips and laughing as I totter around tipsily... till we're all smashed and lying all three together on a towel staring at the starry sky... It's getting cool out and one of the boys—no, both of them—put their arms around me... The taxi arrives before I can imagine the rest.

As we're standing in front of the club with a crowd of nattily attired young people, Sheila, in a fetching leopard print mini-dress, pops out of a cab. Within moments Colin has unlocked a gigantic geyser of charm. Showbiz gossip and party-patter bubble out of his mouth effortlessly.

"So it's the cast party for *Bye Bye Birdie* and everyone is making toasts to Ann Margaret," Colin pauses to sip some Wild Turkey, his eyes twinkling. How does he do that? I wonder. How does he make his eyes actually twinkle? Could it be an Irish thing?

"And...? And?" begs Sheila.

Colin passes her the bottle. "And they're all saying, 'Here's to Ann Margaret, a lovely young girl who we know will go far,' or 'To a new star in the Hollywood sky,' and stuff like that, really laying it on thick. Finally it's Maureen Stapleton's turn, and she gets up and says, 'And here's to me, 'cause I'm the only one Ann Margaret didn't fuck to get a bigger role in this picture." Sheila cracks up.

By the time we get inside and the band starts I'm so filled with anticipation and Wild Turkey I can't believe I'd not wanted to come. The Ventures look unexceptional, just a bunch of ordinary guys, well into middle age, but when they start to play their super-energized surf tunes, the Spirit of Youth itself reigns in the dance hall. The crowd goes mad and we begin flailing our limbs, twisting, and shimmying crazily. "Do the Photo Shoot," calls out Colin, as he begins miming a fashion photographer clicking a camera at Sheila, who strikes crazy model poses. Getting in the mood I scream out, "The Spy!" and we run around the crowded dance floor pretending to shoot each other and ducking for cover behind other dancers.

When the band's done playing I'm as happy as I ever remember being. My suit is damp with sweat and Sheila looks as if she's just climbed out of a pool. Only Colin has remained strangely dry and debonair. As we stand amidst a mass of people in the lobby waiting to leave Colin emits a gasp verging on a scream, turning heads all around us. Dramatically he raises his finger to point to the wall where a framed photo shows Jackie Kennedy doing the twist on the Peppermint Lounge dancefloor. The dramatic contrast between the wondrous '60s and the awful '80s is too stark. Would Nancy Reagan ever be found pogoing at the Mudd Club? All three of us have no choice but to kneel at Jackie's feet and salaam worshipfully in a fit of retro-induced euphoria.

Morning finds me headachy, cotton-mouthed, and still half-asleep standing over the toilet. As I begin to urinate I feel a searing burn, look down, and see a sickly yellow-green discharge. I pull up my shorts and run back into apartment screaming, "Colin!"

"Nothing to worry about, it's just the clap."

My mouth screams, "What do I do? What do I do?" while my mind thinks, *Unclean! Unclean! Unclean!*

Colin, who's been through this before, gives me directions to the gay men's health clinic on Sheridan Square. I call in sick to work and spend the morning sitting in a miniscule waiting room full of lust-addled homos. Even here their ever-cruising eyes scan and judge, glance away, look again. I take a number and sit on an uncomfortable molded plastic chair. After a long while I stand and stretch, then start reading the bulletin board. A tiny article has been tacked up regarding a surprising outbreak of a rare and deadly cancer, Kaposi's Sarcoma, in seven healthy young gay men (the disease usually only goes after elderly Jews or Italians). The symptom to watch out for is spots on the legs. My shame is now compounded by panic. I've had what I thought was a heat rash on my legs for the last few days. Could it be?

When I was young, one of the more creative grade school sadists used to reduce me to a cowering jelly by bellowing out in a deep voice, "Some day we all will die and face the wrath of God!" I pictured myself at the feet of a Zeuslike figure (growing up atheist, I had a rather hazy concept of the whole god thing) who would skewer me with a trident or impale me on a staff. Something of that feeling returns to me as I sit back down to await my fate.

I'm eventually called to the front desk where a handsome young man asks my name.

"Buddy Freeman," I lie, my head lowered. Unclean, unclean! I answer a few questions about my disgraceful condition then return to my seat to await examination. I know I have no one to blame for this but myself. All those one-night stands and back room encounters. Unclean, unclean!

"I didn't want to bring this up," says Nana Leah, holding one of her little red books, "but homosexuality is a symptom of late capitalist pathology that will gradually fade away under socialism. The decadent bourgeois, who will no longer have the excessive leisure and privilege brought on by owning the means of production, will..."

"Nana, I don't own the means of production, I make four dollars an hour cleaning." Before she can respond I'm called into an examination room where a man in a white coat asks about my symptoms. I tell him about my discharge first. He sticks a cotton-swabbed stick up into my manhood (ouch!) and takes blood. I definitely have something, so I get a nasty shot and some antibiotic pills. Summoning every bit of courage I possess, I then mention my spotted legs. The doctor frowns a little as he examines me. It's only a heat rash. I'm so relieved at this reprieve that his parting instructions, no sex or masturbation for a week, don't even faze me.

The rest of the day I loaf around the house reading, and when night falls I'm actually sort of relieved to have an excuse to stay in and catch up on my sleep. The next day at work I know (intellectually) that many, if not most, people on Earth suffer far worse indignities than I. Still, spending eight solid hours trying not to think about sex while surrounded by such a carnival of carnal frenzy is irritating. That evening I'm jealous when Colin goes out and it's hard to sleep because of my stiffy. The third day my symptoms disappear entirely and all day long I'm consumed with lust. I'd drink myself to sleep but you're not supposed to have liquor with the antibiotics, which are now making me nauseous to boot. The fourth day I give in and relieve my tension before work. The fifth day I give in not only before work, but also again at night so I can sleep. I dream that I've permanently damaged my penis and it falls off. The sixth day, through an amazing feat of willpower, I remain chaste, though nausea makes eating impossible. The seventh day is pure agony all around, and at five o'clock, exactly 168 hours after my first pill, I literally run to a dirty movie theater with quarter booths and find a lascivious teen (algebra text book and looseleaf binder in hand) to help me out.

As I walk home I'm amazed to think that only a few months ago I was a virgin.

Depravity

Working the front desk at the bathhouse can be pretty boring so I doodle, drawing a parade of ghostlike creatures beneath a banner reading "No more bread and circuses!" "Help!" cries one. "My God, why hast thou forsaken me?" asks another. "Positive thinking will bring them back," claims a third. "Were there bread and circuses around here?" queries a small one. "Now I'll have to get some new clothes!" says the last.

"That's really cool," says a coworker looking over my shoulder. I thank him, and for the rest of the day use my spare moments to imagine myself as a celebrated, relentlessly hip, loft-dwelling painter. On my way home I stop at an art supply store where I gleefully fritter away most of my paycheck. The moment I get home I throw E.S.G. on my stereo full blast and stare at the apartment's biggest wall, letting it speak to me. It asks, first, to be covered with two swaths of chartreuse and pink day-glo poster paint. While the wall dries I run out to eat, my mind buzzing so busily with ideas I don't even taste my pizza. I return and the walls beg to be transformed into nebula-like vortexes with the addition of blue and green spirals. After another brief drying period, which I help along with the aid of a blowdryer, I meet the requests that I add lavender swimming spermatozoa, fish, and tiny little ghosts. For good measure I trim the wainscoting with skulls and flowers.

I'm still painting away when Colin comes in the door, stops in his tracks and wrinkles his nose. "God, it smells in here."

"Sorry, I just thought the place needed a little fixin' up." I stand back so he can see my handiwork of which I'm exceedingly proud.

"There's no way I can sleep here tonight. These fumes..." He isn't even looking at the wall.

"Sorry." It doesn't smell too bad to me. "I did open the window."

He takes off his coat and sits on his bed with a miserable expression on his face, which is tilted towards the floor, not seeing the masterpiece directly facing him.

"The paint is supposed to dry in an hour."

"Stinks," says Colin.

"Maybe you could stay at Cliff's," I offer, still hoping he'll say something about my artwork.

Colin glares at me. "I won't be able to sleep and I'll miss work tomorrow and get fired but that won't matter because I'll just call up my rich parents in California and they'll bail me out. They'll make sure I won't go hungry or homeless. Oh, wait... it's *you* who has the rich parents and doesn't have to think about anyone but himself."

"Maybe you could get a hotel room, I'll..." I'm about to suggest that I'll pay but I have no idea how much hotel rooms cost and hardly any money left. Colin still doesn't look angry which could mean he's really, very, extremely angry, or not at all angry.

"You'll what? Pay? Pay your way out of being inconsiderate and never thinking of anyone but yourself?"

"I'm sorry, honest!"

Colin starts changing his clothes. "Lucky for you I have a date tonight."

"With whom?"

"None of your business. You know, you can ask the people you're living with before you start painting."

I can tell this is as bad a chewing-out as I'll get and I'm oh so relieved. Relieved enough to dare and ask, "Well, do you like it?" I switch off the overhead light and turn on a tiny black light. The already colorful wall explodes into a psychedelic riot. I think it's amazing.

Colin looks directly at the wall for the first time. "Don't you think it's a little busy?"

"Most of the time we'll have regular lights on. And I'm not finished yet, it'll be more... coherent later."

"Don't give up your day job." He pulls on a jacket. "Have fun breathing your paint fumes. Try not to die in your sleep."

I'm dreaming of the country. Everything is peaceful and cute, like a scene out of a children's book illustrated by Garth Williams. I frolic with bunnyrabbits amidst toadstools and dandelions, then wander through forests where elves and pixies live inside the trees fashioned into houses with little doors and shuttered windows. Afterwards I sit by a stream, fishing with an old man in a straw hat. The world is safe and sweet, and I'm quietly, completely content and happy. Unexpectedly, I hear a voice emanating from another world. "Get up," it orders.

"No, I'm tired. It's the middle of the night," I respond sensibly, not bothering to open my eyes. I was just dreaming of... what? Something good.

"Get up," Colin repeats, gently shaking my shoulder. My eyes open to see Colin's hand holding a small pill, a black beauty. The clock reads 2 a.m. I shut my eyes. "Get up." I open my eyes again. He's not shouting but his face has assumed The Look I know and dread so well. It's invariably easier to give in than fight so I sit up and swallow the pill. In twenty minutes I'm dressed and doing push-ups, impatiently waiting for Colin to finish in the bathroom so we can go to the Anvil. I wish he'd shower before he wakes me up, I think, taking off my black sleeveless tee shirt. I find some gold latex and paint a few squares and squiggles on the front in a manner I hope resembles Gustav Klimt. It's dry by the time Colin is ready to go.

A surprise Indian summer has warmed the night air and I remove my jacket. The breeze caresses my skin as sensually as any lover. By the time we reach the club I'm in an erotic frenzy. The night of dancing, laughing, drinking, and making love flies by and I'm sad, six hours later, when we have to leave our darkened heaven and walk into a hot bright morning. Everywhere people are propelled by necessity. Mothers push perambulators full of shrieking infants. Delivery trucks, cars, and buses rumble up the street as drivers curse, holler, and honk. Shoppers, already sweating in the heat, lug groceries. "I need a drink," says Colin as he surveys the mayhem of morning Manhattan.

For once I decide to go off by myself rather than follow Colin. He has a sad, tired look in his eyes that just doesn't fit with what I'm feeling. I head toward the subway but can't bear to crush myself into the multitudes of harried, hurried commuters. Everyone looks unhappy and downtrodden, even the well-to-do. Instead I walk forty blocks through streets like canyons up to Central Park and climb around on rocks glittering with flecks of mica making them resemble disco harlots. I roam through leafy glades as benevolent brick castles tower in the distance. The hot thick air, the buzz of insects, the fireworks in my brain... why can't life always be this perfect?

Colin hands me a tiny square of blue paper. "Here," says Colin. "Take this and chew it up real good."

"Huh?"

"Acid," he says, popping an identical square in his mouth.

"Acid's for hippies," I say, though I am curious, having always enjoyed watching the blurry kaleidoscopic simulations of psychedelic trips in '60s movies.

"Oh, live a little," says Colin. I chew my paper. Then, as it's another Indian summer day of lovely heat, we go for a walk around the block. We haven't gotten far when we stumble on a couple of hundred people holding a protest rally. Colin insists we join in. Nana Leah materializes, thrilled that I'm finally showing an interest in politics. "My boy!" she kvells to some geriatric leftists milling about with hand-lettered placards.

A middle-aged man, with muttonchop sideburns and an ill-fitting suit, is speechifying from a makeshift stage. "Reagan says, to hell with the unions. The people say, Fightback! The fossils of monopoly capital on Wall Street say to hell with your jobs, the people say, Fightback!" He mops his sweating brow with a hanky. "And as the imperialist spider spins its web of aggression across the globe, the people say..." The crowd roars, "Fightback!"

"He's good," says Nana Leah enthusiastically.

"You know," I say to Colin. "My grandmother was a communist."

He looks impressed. "Really? That's cool. Not that I believe in communism or anything, but most grandparents are so old-fashioned."

"But she was old-fashioned," I protest. "Just an old-fashioned communist. Communism isn't all groovy and humanistic."

Colin is insistent. "But she wasn't telling you to, like, believe in your country, right or wrong."

"No, not *this* country," I say, as the next speaker, a Black woman with a slight 'fro takes the podium. She cautions us not to be fooled by the 'window dressing of representative democracy'.

"Reaganism and fascism are not aberrations but the truest, most natural form of Capitalist society. And it will get worse! The reactionaries will become ever more desperate as American society crumbles under the weight of bourgeois profiteering while the socialist peoples of the world continue on the path towards peace and prosperity!"

"There is a certain type of sanctimonious bore," says Gramma Bea, alone amongst the crowd shielded from the hot sun by a parasol, "who mistakenly believes that predicting the worst and rooting against the home team are the last words in sophistication and moral superiority."

"I suppose you long for the days when the sun never set on the British Empire," snarls Nana Leah, striding up next to Gramma Bea with her arms akimbo and a pugnacious look on her wizened face.

"Certainly not," says Gramma Bea. "I've always been a Little Englander. As far as I'm concerned, imperialism was a mistake. The less we mix with bloodthirsty, heathen savages the better." This makes Nana Leah so angry all she can do is gasp for air like a fish out of water. Gramma Bea continues in her cool, measured tones, "And I believe Mr. Reagan is an unscrupulous charlatan and demagogue. But surely the United States hasn't always been on the side of wickedness. What about defeating Hitler?"

"That was a long time ago," says Nana Leah, "and America was only looking out for its business interests in Europe."

"Doing the right thing for the wrong reason still gets it done," says Gramma Bea with a condescending smile and a twirl of her parasol. "And if Communism is so wonderful why do they have to shoot people who try to escape to the Free World?"

"And what of the Negro in the south?" asks Nana Leah. "The racism, the lynchings?"

"At least we in the West are moving in the right direction in that regard," says Gramma Bea. "The Communist world isn't moving at all. At any rate, if these speakers really wanted to convert the hoi polloi they oughtn't deliver their sermons in hectoring, vitriolic drones."

As my grandmothers debate, I start to feel a sort of roiling excitement and slip away. "I think I feel the acid," I whisper to Colin. As I speak we both catch sight of a pale, curly haired guy about my age standing with a sign that reads 'The Young Workers Liberation League Demands An End To Imperialism, Racism, Sexism, Poverty and War'. Colin raises his left eyebrow in a way that means he thinks the guy is cute, which he is, in a dorky sort of way. The boy starts chanting with the crowd, "Money for food, not for war, we don't want to die in El Salvador!"

"Money for drugs, not for war, we don't want to trip in El Salvador!" shouts Colin. The boy gives him a worried look. "His ass is incredible," Colin whispers in my ear.

"I don't think he's gay," I whisper back.

"It's the earnest ones who are really good in bed," says Colin, no longer whispering. "All that idealism makes them wild in the sack!" The Young Socialist shoots Colin an alarmed glance and nervously edges off into the crowd, chanting loudly.

"Well," says Colin with a philosophic shrug, "I guess the revolution will not be cruised. Anyway, chanting and slogans are is inherently groupthinkish and propagandistic." Pause. "Oh look!" He's pointing at three Italian-looking, incredibly upscale fashion models in swank Milanese haute couture effetely raising their dainty feminine fists in outrage. Their perfect faces look bored, pouty, and indifferent as if they were staring out at us from an ad in *Interview* magazine. Occasionally they whisper amongst themselves, then frown seriously, pursing their wonderful lips. "Now that is radical chic!" says Colin. "They're like Dominique Sanda from that fabulous movie, *The Garden of the Finzi-Continis*."

Suddenly the acid kicks in for real. I've been vaguely expecting it to be like Peter Fonda's experience in *The Trip*, wild kaleidoscopic hallucinations of foxy chicks with freaky face paint and dwarves garbed in medieval hooded tunics serving soup. What I get are extra bright colors, a few physical anomalies like breathing manhole covers, and the ability to see the patterns of my thought processes as if they were a laser light show. I can't quite navigate simple tasks like walking and talking, so I stand against a lamppost and let everything be.

"You're a lot of use to the revolution like that," says Nana Leah, reappearing with a censorious look in her eyes.

"What exactly should I do? The powers that be have all the military power in the world, all the media, everything on their side. Get in their way and they'll mow you down like red communists, or redwoods, or red Indians, or redheads..." I'm thinking now of how, in Hollywood reality, Lucy Ricardo and Shirley MacLaine and other dizzy redheads are shunted off to the margins by beautiful blondes and power hungry brunettes. I wonder if Nana Leah, being a ghost, can see inside my mind and follow my LSD logic, but I don't get a chance to ask her because she throws up her hands and vanishes.

When the protest is over, Colin and I repair to a bar for draft beers to calm our chemically jangled nerves. Inside, the throbbing High N-R-G (the super-catchy, *Babe We're Gonna Love Tonight* by Lime) makes my spine tingle, then tingle harder, then harder still, till I'm seized with a *Fantasia*-like image of my spinal cord as a set of piano keys being played by the electric hands of the music. Gosh, I think, acid isn't creepy or weird like I thought it would be... This is fun!

Colin is primping in front of the mirror. "I need five dollars," he calls out merrily.

"You already owe me..." I glance at a small sheet of paper near my bed, "seven hundred and eighty-two dollars."

"I just want to get a tuna and Swiss on rye, and a chocolate milk."

"And this is my problem? You make more than I do!"

Colin shrugs helplessly. "But you're better with money than me."

This is undoubtedly true, but Colin's saying so offers me a chance to get morally indignant (always fun) and change the subject at the same time. "Are you implying that because I'm Jewish, I'm good with money? That is such an anti-Semitic stereotype."

"You're only Jewish when it suits your purposes," says Colin. "And the reason you're better with money is that you grew up with it while I didn't."

I'm seized with guilt, once again, over my relative affluence. "Well," I admit, "I do have a few dollars, but I need to get to work and stuff. Really, I've got nothing to spare."

He's shocked, maybe even a little panicked. "This is bad, very bad." He peeks his head over the edge of the loft so he can look me in the face and see if I'm lying. "What about the nine hundred dollars you saved up to bring to New York?"

"Evaporated."

"You're completely devoid of liquid assets?"

"There's some orange juice in the fridge."

He doesn't even crack a smile, just puts his hands on his hips and begins pacing. "This is bad. We'll have to do something about this. You'll have to call your parents."

"They just sent me six hundred dollars a couple of months ago for the apartment!"

He's really upset. "We'll have to do something about this. Right away."

An hour later we're standing at The Haymarket, a hustler bar on 8th Avenue. Though I'm loathe to break my last ten dollar bill, I order beers from the geezer behind the counter. Once we're served Colin leads me back to a small set of steps separating the dark front room from an even darker room with a pool table. A dozen johns, all looking incredibly johnish (balding, portly, gray, desperate... just what you'd expect), sit at the bar drinking highballs. Around them, strutting like chickens in a cage or posing like *West Side Story* delinquents, are about two dozen skinny, street-tough hustlers. One elfin boy sits on his enormous john's enormous lap, the disparity in their sizes making them look like a ventriloquist and his dummy. The jukebox plays a song, "This time, I'm holdin' out for love. Made up my mind, I'm holdin' out for love," which, given the circumstances, makes me giggle. Colin glares and I hush up.

"What now?" I ask.

"Just wait," Colin says. "Some guy will ask you home, but work out the price first and get the money *before* you have sex."

"OK." As we stand against the wall I compare myself with the other boys. They're all about my age or maybe a little younger. No, they're definitely younger. "Colin, I'm too old. Nobody will want me."

He looks at me appraisingly, giving my fears full consideration. "No, you're all right."

The boys all look so at ease with themselves as they shoot pool, smoke, flirt, do all the bad kid things I never do. "Colin, do I look uptight?"

"You *are* uptight, that's your charm. Everyone wants to deflower the classy virgin. The girl who runs around showing her breasts, well, yeah, the guys will fuck her, but they won't respect her. And why pay for what you can get free?" This has the sound of homespun wisdom, or at least something gleaned from old movies, so I have no choice but to believe him.

After a long while, a huge be-suited man with pock-marked skin comes up and offers me a drink. I ask for a beer. He goes off to order and Colin smiles at me.

"Good job. I'll see you later," he stagewhispers.

"Where are you going?"

"Home. This place is slow tonight."

As Colin takes off, the man returns with my beer.

"I'd like to take you home with me, but I don't think I'm in a position to afford you."

"How much of a position are ya in?" I ask, feeling ever so bawdy.

We haggle out a price, then ride in a taxi to his small, neat Soho apartment. The guy, Francis, hands me a joint and holds out a lighter. Will it be laced with angeldust? There was a girl in high school who took a hit off an angeldust-laced joint at a party and jumped out a fourth story window. No, wait, that was a movie.

"You first," I say, trying not to betray any nervousness. He puts the joint to his lips and inhales deeply. Normally I loathe pot on principle (too mellow and hippie), but here in New York, it seems streetwise and sexy to want to get high. I reluctantly take a few tokes. Francis removes his suit. Naked, he looks like a beached sea mammal. Ick. Suddenly the pot hits me and everything turns into a math puzzle. As I shimmy out of my clothes, my body is a collection of circumferences and planes.

Lying on his enormous body I'm obsessed by the ratio of my mass to his. Integers and functions fill my mind as I fulfill my contractual duty.

"Here you go," he says, handing me the money that I now remember I was supposed to ask for up front. "You'll be able to buy yourself all the hot dogs you want with that, won't ya?" We both laugh, probably for different reasons.

Now that I'm a whore maybe Colin will like me, I think as I fondle the crisp fifty-dollar bill on my way home. He won't think I'm a spoiled rich kid anymore. I imagine him throwing his arms around me as I show him the money, pulling me onto the bed, rewarding me. We could be like a glamorously doomed hustler and pimp team out of Genet. I walk into the apartment and find Colin reading *ZG* magazine and give him a blow-by-blow account of my adventure.

"See, hustling's not hard. I knew you'd be good at it," he says with a proud parental smile.

I saucily tuck the fifty into Colin's shirt pocket and bring my face as close to his as I dare. In his eyes is a twinkle that makes my spine tingle. "Thanks," he says pulling away and standing up. "I'll bring you the change after I get my snack from the deli." He leaves and I have no choice but to scream.

"We just have time to make the next showing," says Colin, looking up from his *Village Voice.*

"Of what?" I ask.

"*The Cabinet of Dr. Caligari.* It's a silent with incredible German Expressionist sets. Get dressed. And hurry." When we reach the theater we discover, oops, it's Wednesday not Tuesday. Today's movie is Charlie Chaplin's *City Lights.*

"How could you get the day wrong?" teases Colin.

"You did, too!"

"But you're supposed to be more on top of things," he says. "I'm a genius, I can't be bothered with petty details like what day it is."

"Well, this is supposed to be a classic," I say, reading a blurb in the window of the theater.

"Chaplin was a progressive," whispers Nana Leah in my brain. "He went to the Soviet Union and championed the common man."

"And you know he was English," adds the disembodied voice of Gramma Bea.

"Well, we're here," Colin sighs. "Let's go in."

Despite Mr. Chaplin's popularity with my inner grandmothers, the movie is too slapstick for my taste. Chaplin plays (surprise!) a lovable tramp. In between clownish escapades with a drunken millionaire he courts a beautiful blind girl who sells flowers on a street corner. She mistakenly thinks he's a wealthy young man (he doesn't set her straight) and is charmed enough by his kindness to hold his hand. After many a trial and tribulation, Chaplin gets money from the millionaire for the flower girl to have an operation restoring her sight, but in the process gets sent to prison without ever having a chance to reveal his true identity to her. The girl, once she can see, lands a job at a posh florist. She ogles a handsome young man in tails and top hat and wonders if he might be her mysterious benefactor.

In the final scene Chaplin, much the worse for wear, is released from prison and goes looking for the flower girl. She sees him first and, not recognizing him by sight, laughs when some rascally newsboys persecute him with a peashooter. When he finally sees her he stares adoringly and she laughs even more. "I've made a conquest," she says to a co-worker. The tramp's face falls, and ashamed at having hurt his feelings, she gives him a coin. As he takes it, she realizes from the touch of his hand that he's her mysterious benefactor. Up to this point, as in most silent films, facial expressions have been exaggerated to mean only one thing. On recognizing her benefactor, however, the flower girl's face simultaneously registers shock, pity, self-pity, confusion, gratitude, love, loathing, fear, and sorrow. The film fades out on a close-up of Chaplin sadly and nervously biting on the stem of a rose, aware that he's not what she expected and can never, ever be what she wants or needs him to be, but still, ever-so-slightly hopeful.

It's the saddest thing I've ever seen and as I stare at the credits, it's only my deep-rooted aversion to public displays of emotion that keeps me from crying. The lights come on and I manage to croak out, "Do they get together or not?" asking not only Colin, but myself, my Grammas, and whatever deities may be listening.

Gramma Bea, the first to speak, is unexpectedly, frighteningly hard. "She can't go with him, of course. A girl has to think of her own happiness, her children's futures."

"Who cares?" says Nana Leah. "He'd be better off without that little social climber."

"Gosh," says Colin. "Gee whiz." He says these things ironically, but I can tell from his face he's flamboozled. "What a strange ending. Quite unconventional for that era."

As we walk home I can still see the look on the flower girl's face, the look on the tramp's face. "What would you do if you were her?" I ask Colin.

"I don't know," he says, possibly for the first time in his know-it-all life.

Fall is really here now and our apartment is always chilly. I don't mind. I'm snuggling under the covers watching the wind bluster through the patchwork yellow-orange-red-brown leaves of the tree outside our window. Only when my thoughts turn to the perpetual gray fog of San Francisco do I shiver. Colin, entirely impervious to cold, is lying on his bed in his underwear reading magazines. Without warning, his booming theatrical voice interrupts the quiet.

"A social secretary at the White House named Muffie Brandon says, and I'm quoting here, 'The White House is experiencing a terrible tablecloth crisis. One set of tablecloths, to my complete and utter horror, went out to the drycleaners and shrunk.'" Colin looks up from the paper. "Where did all these preppies come from? All the Muffies and Skips? They just popped up overnight like mushrooms."

"I had a pair of pennyloafers a couple years back," I admit guiltily. "Before they were preppiewear."

"It's time to give up '50s retro," says Colin. "The whole parody of hyper-formality and mid-century modernism has been appropriated by Reagan and the preppies."

"I wasn't parodying anything. I really do believe in good manners and boomerang-shaped coffeetables. The pennyloafers, they were a mistake, but I still like dressing up in suits."

Colin is unswayed. "Mark my words. By the time Muffie and her cronies get through with their dirty work, you won't want anything to do with that stuff. You'll be running around with your hair in an Isro."

"What's an Isro?"

"Like an Afro but for Jews."

"My hair isn't quite that kinky."

"The point is, all that '50s stuff is getting tired. You're going to want really modern clothes like they're coming up with in London. Like Vivienne Westwood designs. Fashion is the new frontier of cultural activism. We really need to go shopping."

"Us and what money?"

"Well, as soon as we get some money."

"He certainly has a head on his shoulders," says Nana Leah, sitting on the edge of my loft and dangling her feet, "but I'm not sure about what it is he keeps in it."

"He's brilliant, Gramma."

"If you ask me, he makes simple things very complicated. The rich have declared war on the workers and you've got to choose sides. Do you think the peasants of Central America care what the teenagers in London are wearing?"

"Fashion is an important means of self-expression," I say. "It allows you to define yourself instead of being defined by some uniform."

"*Men babrist noch di klieder, men begleit nochen saicyhel*," intones Nana Leah. "One is greeted according to one's clothes, bid farewell according one one's wisdom."

"It's not just fads and fashion," I reply. "Colin is interested in avant-garde art and literature..."

Nana interrupts. "What good does any of that do for assembly-line workers without health insurance, or political prisoners in Chile?"

"Well, the workers can read and go to museums," I begin, wondering what on Earth I'm saying. "Art and books are for everyone, and they can change people's opinions, and everyone should be able to make their contribution to... to express themselves."

"Ach! You try earning a living while raising a family and see how much you feel like expressing yourself at the end of the day. You just try it, mister!"

Actually, I think, I'd rather not try that.

Colin wants to go to Alex In Wonderland, a gay club he describes as being full of suburban wannabes.

"Why do we want to hang out with suburban wannabes?" I ask. "What's wrong with urban ares?"

"I get tired of people who know all about contemporary art and culture but don't know anything about their own bodies and desires."

This sounds like something he's read, and I don't feel like arguing. "OK, lead and I will follow."

"You need a little loosening up yourself. Here." He hands me a pill.

I swallow it, then think to ask, "What was that?"

"A Quaalude," says Colin. We walk in silence for a bit, then, once we're right outside the club, Colin turns to me sheepishly. "I spent all my money on the Quaaludes, you gotta lend me some to get in. I don't have enough money to cover him so, feeling noble, I run across the street to the parking lot by the piers where I'm instantly solicited by a john in a VW bug. I get in and sit on the passenger's seat and negotiate. Ick! Still, I don't want to bother finding another customer so I lower my head, close my eyes and... double ick! Surely, I think, Colin understands how distasteful this is for me. Surely, he'll realize how much of a sacrifice I'm making on his behalf. Surely, he'll see this as an act of love, and love me back. The whole thing is over in a few minutes and I run back to find Colin leaning against the wall outside the club. He takes the money with a quick "Thanks," and we go in. At least he thanked me this time.

After we've gotten our beers Colin ambles off towards the back room with a muttered "See ya later." I start to follow him but he turns around with an exasperated look and says, "Go have fun somewhere on your own." Stung, I slink back to the bar.

"Hey," says Eddie, Colin's co-worker, emerging from a dark corner. He's wearing his usual clone look only now he's grown a light beard and mustache combo. Totally uncool, totally *not* New Wave, but I have to admit to myself that he's handsome in spite of it.

"Hi," I say.

"Wanna dance?"

I do. Eddie, like the rest of the crowd, is smoothly funky. I, New Wave to the end, hop around spastically trying to make my body angular and emphatic. The music is on his side (High N-R-G) and I can't quite get with the rhythm. It doesn't help that the 'lude is hitting me now so I'm perpetually losing my balance. It's slightly embarrassing, but deep down I really don't care what all these disco bunnies think of me. Nobody here's ever heard of Pete Shelley, let alone the Silicon Teens.

"Here, you look like you could use some help." Eddie hands me an upper, which I swallow without water.

Is he coming on to me? I wonder. I kind of hope he is, though the facial hair would make things difficult. Soon the pill sends me to another world where time passes both very quickly and practically not at all. I catch the groove of the music and just dance,

dance, dance. After an hour, maybe two, maybe three, I start to wonder what happened to Colin. I wave good-bye to Eddie, whose glazed eyes show no sign of having noticed me, and push through the crowd towards the darkened sex maze. After my eyes adjust to the dimness I begin poking around. It doesn't take long to discover a crowd of men watching something that turns out to be Colin lying on his stomach being sodomized by an ill-favored lumberjack type.

This is weird. Colin likes pretty boys. Even worse, four other trolls of varying shapes and deformities are waiting in line, *an actual line*, for their turn at my beautiful Colin, who I realize with a shock, is utterly passed out. His eyes are closed, his mouth slightly open and emitting faint moans. Paul Bunyan finishes, zips up, and walks away with a hideous smirk on his face. I want to kill him. Colin moans a little more. A small voice in the back of my mind whispers, you could have him right now and he'd never know. A round little man with skin white as a marshmallow moves towards Colin's inert body. I rush in front of him and shake Colin's shoulders. How many vile creatures have already had their way with him?

"Colin! Colin! Are you OK?"

"Hey, I was next," says the marshmallow man. I glare at him and he slinks off into the darkness grumbling, "Stuck up pretty boys."

Colin sits up. "Wha's goin' on? Where am I?" His face is puffy, his eyes bleary. "Ohhh, I shouldn't have taken all those Quaaludes." How many did he take? He only gave me one.

"We have to go," I say. Nodding meekly, Colin stands and pulls his pants up from around his ankles.

He prefers this to me?

The image of Colin in the back room is depressing me, so I'm dying my hair cranberry red. Nothing cheers me so much as my image in the mirror with a strikingly novel and unnatural hair color, proof positive that I'm not locked into my identity or fate.

As I comb the noxious smelling chemicals through my locks, Gramma Bea and Nana Leah materialize. They're agitated and keep shooting each other little looks. I assume they've been discussing me in the Other World or wherever it is they go when they're not pestering me.

"Jeremy, it's time to face facts. Colin will never be yours," says Gramma Bea, pacing nervously. "I wish I could say he's leading you on, but he hasn't given you the slightest encouragement. Quite the contrary."

"But I have a Plan," I protest.

"A five-year plan?" asks Nana Leah in one of her rare attempts at humor.

"I'm thinking more like five months," I say. "Maximum."

"Dear, you're obsessed and not thinking clearly," says Gramma Bea coming to a standstill and addressing me with a grave look. "You are perhaps the last person on Earth Colin will form a romantic relationship with."

"That's how I know he'll finally go for me!" I say. "It's always the one you least expect who gets the guy in the end."

"In escapist Hollywood fantasies," says Nana Leah, shuddering with righteous indignation at the very thought of Hollywood and all it represents.

"In this instance I'm afraid she's right," says Gramma Bea. "It's all very fine to emulate Cary Grant, but he never had to rescue Katherine Hepburn from voluntarily drugging herself so she could pass out in a room full of sex fiends."

"It's probably a phase," I suggest. "When he's ready to move on, I'll be there to give him a helping hand."

"*Meshuggeh*," mutters Nana Leah. She shoots a subtle glare toward Gramma Bea. "He's been confused by bourgeois, romantic claptrap."

Gramma Bea sighs, "Watching these boys carry on is almost enough to make one want to go back to arranged marriages."

"Or at least heterosexuality," says Nana Leah.

"I'm going to rinse my hair out now," I say acidly. "Thanks ever so for dropping by." I tap my foot impatiently, waiting for them to go which, mercifully, they do.

I come home from work and find Colin lying on the floor, eyes closed, with one stereo speaker pushed right up to each ear listening to Bill Nelson's "Flaming Desire" at top volume. "Hello," I scream. No response. I go down the hall to wash off the day. The music is so loud I can hear it in the shower, now it's Heaven 17's "Penthouse and Pavement." Back in the apartment I turn down the volume.

Colin sits up. "Hey, I was listening to that!"

"It was hurting my ears," I protest. Colin turns off the stereo and sits on his bed, stretching his long body attractively.

"Oh, poor Granny can't abide that fearsome rock music," he says in a kooky voice. Then seriously, "You have to lend me twenty."

I'm about to hand the money over when I see Nana Leah floating in the kitchen. "*Borgen macht zorgen*," she says, shaking her head from side to side like a metronome. "Loans make groans." Her warning given, she vanishes.

This stiffens my resolve. "No way! You already owe me close to a thousand dollars. That's more money than I brought to New York. And anyway, I lent you five dollars yesterday."

"I'm aware of that," he replies neutrally while sticking out his hand.

"What do you need it for?" I ask, feeling like the parent of a teenager.

"I have my purposes," he says, arching an eyebrow.

"Well, I need it," I say, instantly making the fatal error of admitting I have the money in the first place.

"OK," he responds. "I suppose you don't trust me."

"Augh!" As I jump onto the dresser, then onto my loft bed, the towel around my waist falls off revealing my damp, naked body.

"And put some clothes on!" says Colin turning his head away in a parody of an outraged Victorian.

I pull on some pants as Colin emits a petulant whine. "Now, can I please just borrow a few measly dollars so I can go out for dinner and drinks."

"Can I go with you?" I ask.

"Well, since you're paying," agrees Colin.

Outside, the first snow of the year is coming down in huge confetti-like flakes, imbuing the city with a festive air. As a Californian, this strikes me as unbelievably magical, but even the New Yorkers look unusually happy as their urban squalor is covered with a pristine white blanket. After our leisurely pancake dinner, Colin and I are slightly disappointed that the snow has turned black with soot.

We decide to check out a new bar, The International Stud. The place is small but for some reason it has six bathrooms all in a row which guys go into to have sex, despite there being a perfectly nice back room for that purpose. Colin and I perch ourselves at the bar and order warming brandies, then observe. The chic thing here turns out to be dressing in the un-coolest clothing imaginable. We're not talking nerdy '50s gas station attendant uniforms; we're talking high-water designer jeans. There are still people wearing designer jeans un-ironically just down the block, albeit not "floods." This is true perversion, I think. Having Colin around to share my amusement makes the evening just that much more delightful. If only I didn't have to pay his way.

It's Tuesday night at the Haymarket. The place is half-empty and nobody has spoken to either Colin or me in an hour, but we're broke, so we wait. After a dozen forevers a gray little man with the gait and bearings of a "Lady Executive" from an old Perry Mason episode swishes up to Colin and begins furtive negotiations. After a couple of minutes, Colin, with an ugly expression on his handsome face, comes over to where I'm poised against the wall trying to look nonchalant and perhaps slightly dangerous.

"That guy over there, Lyle, is a voyeur. He wants to watch us fuck."

"Oh?" I play it cool, but inside I feel like Julie Andrews spinning around on top of that mountain at the beginning of *The Sound of Music.*

Colin scowls. "I said yes because it's getting late, but don't think I'm going to enjoy this."

Drunk with joy I follow Colin, who follows Lyle out of the bar and down dark streets crowded with ne'er-do-wells and unsavory characters. Soon we arrive at a ancient fleabag hotel of the sort that might easily be haunted by the ghosts of murdered dipsomaniac flappers, handsome immigrant stable boys, or muckraking newsmen who crossed Tammany Hall one time too many.

"Oh, Gawd," murmurs Colin disapprovingly.

"This is the place," says Lyle with a crooked, dirty grin as he leads us into the minuscule lobby. Behind an iron grill sits a white-haired man wearing wire rim spectacles and a green visor.

"Yes?" asks the man. He has the craggy face of an old Yankee as painted by Norman Rockwell.

Lyle rents the room and the man gives directions to our love nest in his creaky, cranky voice. "Ya take these here stairs two floors up, that's two." He sounds angry, like he's used to dealing with people who can't count. "Ya go left, then left. There's yer room, right there. Two twenty-three." He pushes some keys under the grill.

Colin and I follow Lyle up the narrow stairway littered with flakes of paint that have peeled off walls in jagged, and to my eyes, rather pretty shapes. Our ascent is suddenly and dramatically halted by a spindly boy, who dashes up the stairs and stands in front of us and blocks our way with his arms. "Man, I been lookin' for you everywhere!" he says to Lyle with a desperate look in his bloodshot eyes. "You gotta give me da money now,

OK?" His English is Ricky Ricardo but his body language is jittery junkie.

"Pedro, shush!" commands Lyle, making a lowering motion with his hands.

"You said you give me da money las' Tuesday!" Pedro insists loudly. Though extremely handsome, he looks malnourished. I have the urge to buy him a bowl of soup. "Then you disappeared!"

The hotel manager (who I now think of as "Pops") looks up from behind his grill and frowns menacingly. "What seems to be all the commotion?"

"Pedro, I gave you everything you have coming to you," says Lyle pertly.

"No, man, no, you gotta give me a hun'red dollars." Pedro is vibrating with excitement and, though he's not wearing a coat, sweating.

"You hear me?" asks Pops loudly.

"Oh dear, oh dear, I thought we'd settled this," says Lyle, looking around him as if for help.

"I don't have all night. I want to get this over with," says Colin.

"C'mon, maaan!" Pedro grabs Lyle's arm.

Jerking his arm away Lyle huffs, "I don't have to put up with this."

The boy slams his hand against the wall. Whap! "You gonna fuck with me?!" Colin and I flinch.

"Take your arguments outside. I don't want no trouble!" screams Pops. "This is a respectable establishment!" Colin twinkles his eyes at me and I raise my eyebrows at him, our method of sharing a private giggle at this absurdity.

Pedro's whole body seems to burst into tears. "Man, this is so fucked up!"

Lyle pulls out his wallet and starts fumbling, "Very well, here's... five, ten, fifteen..."

"A hundred!" shouts Pedro.

"No monkey business on my stairs or I call the police," barks Pops.

"I'm so sorry," says Lyle to Colin and me, his face suddenly looking worn out, like he's been playing this scene on Broadway for a year and can't bear another performance. Pedro starts babbling in Spanish and shaking Lyle who whines piteously, "Please, Pedro, stop shaking me so I can count!" Pedro doesn't stop.

Pops picks up the phone. "Should I call the police? That what you want? Don't think I won't! I'll call them, yes I will. Be here in two shakes of a lamb's tail." Pedro lets go of Lyle who resumes the count with trembling hands.

Colin sighs. "I'm bored."

Pedro notices Colin and me for the first time and squints at Lyle. "Who's these guys you're with?"

"Er, friends," sputters Lyle. This time Colin and I laugh out loud.

"You laughin' at me?" asks Pedro with unfriendly urgency.

"No, no," says Colin quickly.

"Oh, Pedro, won't you please calm down?" begs Lyle.

Before Pedro can resume his harangue Colin turns haughty. "Look, this has simply wrecked my nerves! We have to go." He grabs a twenty from Lyle's hand. "For our trouble," he explains as he marches down the stairs with regal aplomb.

"Wait!" screams Lyle. "Come back!"

"You've had your chance," sings out Colin.

"Cops'll be here in a heartbeat, they will! Won't tolerate no shenanigans in my hotel." Pops now looks grim enough to have been painted by Edward Hopper.

I follow Colin onto the street. "Don't you want to wait? Lyle'll be done in a second. We could get a hundred dollars." Even as I speak I know it's useless.

"We've got enough for dinner and then some," says Colin, pocketing the twenty. We walk in silence for a minute. "Whew! That was close," he says, as if he'd narrowly escaped decapitation instead of sex with me.

I'm on my way to an East Village watering hole where I plan on meeting Colin later. A few blocks from my destination a granite-faced woman in her fifties wearing a starchy white nurse's uniform and dark blue cape stops me.

"Sir, please excuse me. I am Mrs. Kalishnova," she says in a thick Eastern European accent. "I am sorry to take your time, but I am most worried about my nephew Peter. I am his guardian and mostly he is a very good boy, but it is also the case that sometimes he is headstrong. I have had an argument with him earlier this morning that we do not finish because I must go to work at the hospital. When I come home this evening he is not in, and I wait and I wait and he is not coming home. Then I find a note in which he tells me he has gone out to play the pinballs. He is only thirteen years old and it is not safe for him to be out so late." She's wringing her hands nervously, pulling invisible rings off her fingers. "I must find him, but I am afraid to go alone to these pinball parlors as there are the criminals and robbers. You have a kind face. I beg of you, will you help me?"

Is my face really kind? I wonder. Is that sexy, having a kind face? I agree to help since she reminds me of Nana Leah, who lived in this very neighborhood half a century ago, and we start walking towards the pinball parlors located in the depths of Alphabet City. As we make our way through streets where Caucasians are a distinct minority she holds onto my arm stiffly, afraid but brave. She probably wouldn't be so friendly with me if she knew what sort of person I am, I think. Gay, Jewish: which would she think is worse?

The first arcade we find is a cavelike arcade fully open to the street, but it's so full of teenagers that you can't see the back. The bing, bing, bing, of the machines and the roar of the crowd would make calling out his name useless. "You will have to go inside to look for him," says Mrs. Kalishnova sorrowfully, as if she were asking me to swim with piranhas. "He is a large boy. Chubby, you say in America. He is fair and has the blonde hair. You will recognize him."

If he's in there, he'll be the white one, I think as I go inside and begin prowling. An attendant is making change for teens who can't get the quarters from him fast enough, so rabid is their lust for Pong and Pac-Man. He gives me an odd look so I ask for some quarters hoping he'll think I'm a pinball enthusiast and not a sex pervert. I'm relieved that the kids look right through me.

I hear Nana Leah's voice. "The masses try and forget their lives by gambling."

"It's not gambling," I explain. "You can't win anything except more games."

"So much the worse," she says.

There are no chubby teenage Slavs to be found so I go back outside where Mrs. Kalishnova stands, nervously peering around the streets.

"No luck."

She sighs. "Let us try the next one." We walk in silence for a moment. Then she speaks, her voice betraying a weariness that would drive any self-respecting thirteen-year-old out to a pinball parlor. "When I was a girl in Odessa, we obeyed our parents. We tried to make them happy. I love America with all my heart, but the children here are so spoiled. Why does he need to play with these pinball machines?"

"Unwholesome," agrees Nana Leah. "Youth should be sent to the country where they can work in the fresh air, build socialism with their own two hands and see the results; eggs and chickens, factories, railroads. People need to be useful."

"My mother used to say that fun and games are only the icing on the cake of duty," says Gramma Bea. "At the time I found her outlook terribly old-fashioned, but I suppose it is true that living solely for one's own amusement ultimately leads to unhappiness."

"Why?" repeats Mrs. Kalishnova, and I realize that I haven't responded.

"Well, it's fun," I say. "I like Pac Man. It takes your mind off things. It's an escape."

Mrs. Kalishnova sighs. "What is so terrible about being a schoolboy that he should need to escape?"

I want to scream. How can people grow to maturity in this or any country and not realize that being even slightly unpopular, let alone a raging nelly, nancyboy or a fat Ukrainian kid, can be hell on Earth? I want to ask her if children where she came from were actually good-natured, if you could be different and not get pounded black and blue, spit on, and generally humiliated. Instead I say, "Let's try in here," and pop into another arcade. No luck.

We visit three more places with no success. "Where is he? Where is he?" Mrs. Kalishnova asks under her breath as we walk up the street. Her panic is starting to freak me out.

"Hey, maybe he's gone home already," I suggest, imagining their minuscule apartment: lace doilies, faux Faberge eggs, overstuffed armchairs, pictures of the old country, the smell of boiled cabbage. "Why don't you call and see?"

"Yes, you are right. I will telephone." Mrs. Kalishnova disengages from my arm and goes to a nearby phone booth that miraculously works. I'm truly relieved when I see her hand fly to her heart and a huge smile break her face in two. As we walk back to the relative safety of Second Avenue she thanks me again and again and again, then disappears into the night. I walk to the bar feeling terribly noble.

Golddiggers of 1981

Colin and I are sitting at the bar of the International Stud. I'm trying to look cute and hoping someone will speak to me. It takes a good long while (oh, what I wouldn't give for the courage to initiate conversation), but finally a short, balding man in his late twenties wearing a beautifully fitted charcoal gray suit, worn without irony thank you very much, introduces himself. Davis Douglas Hiram III. He's not my type but there is a certain sort of dapper cuteness about him. "Rather like Fred Astaire," observes Gramma Bea. He tells me he's a lawyer, and in fact comes from an eccentric wealthy Los Angelino family in which everyone (mom, dad, uncles, aunts, everyone) is a lawyer. In no time he's inviting me over to his apartment on West Tenth for caviar and vodka. Flattered that someone with such fancy snacks would fancy me, I accept.

"Hey Colin, I'm going home with the guy in the corner over there..." I pause for effect, "for vodka and caviar."

"Oh really?" he says, one eyebrow arched, as he examines Davis. "Have fun." The way he says "fun" makes it sound he's dubious such a thing is possible with such a person.

After a short sobering stroll through the brisk night air, Davis and I arrive at his swank apartment building. Even the lobby is deliciously toasty. I am, I think, wrapped in the arms of luxury. When Davis opens the door to 8C, I'm not disappointed. The largish living room is furnished with sleek modern furniture, and there's even an ugly expensive-looking steel sculpture on a white pedestal in the corner. Davis pops a tape into his high-tech sound system and disappears into the kitchenette to fix drinks and snacks. I loll about on the thick clean white shag carpet listening to the crazy, jazzy music feeling ever so sophisticated. Davis comes back in with a pleased look on his little face and a tray of goodies.

"Who's this playing?" I ask.

"It's Nino Rota's score from *Juliette of the Spirits*."

I sample caviar adhered to crackers with a little smear of cream cheese. "I love it. You've got great taste in music."

Davis sits in a little chair and sips expertly from his frosted martini glass. "Thanks. You've got a great body."

"Thanks." I stretch myself out ostentatiously at his feet, imagining that we look something like a couple in a magazine advertisement for Scotch.

"Who's that?" I ask, pointing to a large framed black and white photo of Davis with a mini-skirted, go-go-booted drag queen about twice his height.

"Jordanelle. She's Australian."

I sample the vodka. Yum. "Jordanelle looks like Nancy Sinatra would if she'd been stretched on a rack," I observe.

"Ha ha," laughs Davis obligingly. "I met her in Sydney when I was on vacation, but she lives here now. She makes jewelry."

"I'm going to get my ear pierced," I declare, having just decided.

"Really?" He's obviously not in favor of this.

"Yup."

"Your ear," he says in an oppressively tolerant voice. Then he oh-so-casually runs his hand down my back as if petting a cat. "With a body like yours I guess you can do what you want."

I can feel myself blush. If only Colin were here! Never in my nineteen years have I felt more like a sex kitten. I'd purr if I knew how.

"So even your mom is a lawyer?"

"Even my one of my grandmothers was a lawyer! I hate it though. I'd like to quit and let someone who wants to be a lawyer have my job. I want to run a gallery."

"So why not do it?"

"Money," he says without elaborating.

"Maybe some day," I say encouragingly. Davis sighs, then gives me a look that leaves no doubt what's on his mind. I stand up and he takes my hand (his own little hand is softer than my mother's) and leads me to his bedroom.

I've just finished dying my hair black again and am about to walk out the door on the way to the Laundromat when Colin looks up from his bed where he's sprawled out reading yet another magazine. "Wait, wait! Could you wash this for me, pretty please with sugar on top?" He smiles angelically as he tosses a pair of pants at me.

I sigh a long sigh like my mother. "Huuuuuuh."

Colin mimics me, "Huuuuuh." I hate it when he does that. If only he used his powers of mimicry for good instead of evil.

"I've already got two of your shirts in here, and some of your socks too if I'm not mistaken. I am not your maid."

"No, of course not. You're the boy who grew up with a maid to do your wash for you."

"I did not! All we had was a cleaning lady come in once a week and I never let her in my room because she put everything away in the wrong place." I pick the pants off the floor where they've fallen and toss them back to Colin.

He catches them. "Of course she still had to clean your house, even though she had a home and children of her own to take care of."

"Don't try and make me feel guilty. I didn't hire her. And anyway, all she ever did was push the vacuum around over the same little patch of rug in the living room while she watched soap operas." This is a rather lame thing for me to mention since I hate housework so much that even pretending to clean for a day would affect me like bamboo shoots under the fingernails.

"She was Black, right?" asks Colin. This is a lucky guess. I'd never volunteer such embarrassing information.

"She was Jamaican. Don't blame me for my parents though. I... am... not... your... maid."

"No, you're just the boy I took in and found a place to live and who repaid my kindness by sexually molesting me." He tosses the pants back at me. They land on my head.

"I will do your pants this one time," I say, shoving them into my bag. "But don't expect me to ever do them again."

"Thanks," he says, already back to reading his magazine.

Davis and I start to see a lot of each other. Our dates always begin with me joining him at his apartment for drinks (Davis won't come over to my place because he thinks it'll be "depressing"), after which we eat out, attend an opening, or go clubhopping. No matter where we are, Davis runs into affluent-looking, attractive people who greet him with hugs and air kisses. Often they have drugs and funny stories to share. They're mostly older, his age, late twenties, so I seldom connect with them. I just stand around wondering what to say till someone asks me if I'm in school or gives me a line of cocaine. Davis treats me when we go out, but at unpredictable intervals he'll expect me to pay my own way. Since I make four dollars an hour and everything in New York is incredibly overpriced, this is a problem. To make matters worse, Colin continues to extract "loans" from me on a weekly basis. Where to get cash?

"Perhaps your father would give you some money," suggests Gramma Bea. "You really mustn't lose this Davis. He's quite a catch, a real gentleman, not like those bedraggled nancyboys you usually run about with. It's really such a shame your parents couldn't provide you with an income." She sighs, looking at me in a way that makes me feel like Oliver Twist or The Little Match Girl, just the feeling I need to overcome my pride and call home.

This time I only net three hundred dollars that I squirrel away under my mattress without telling Colin.

Of course, I relate every detail of my affair with Davis to Colin, exaggerating the swankiness of the parties, clubs, and openings we attend, ("I'm pretty sure Jackie had been there earlier"), lingering over the description of each hors d'oeuvre and decoration. Though he's never met him in person and only seen him once, Colin thinks Davis is a creepy troll. "You're such a whore!" he says. This is an ambiguous comment since usually Colin loves whores. He regularly sees one West Street hustler whose mom, a hooker, sits smoking and putting on makeup as Colin and her son sodomize each other on the bed of their one-room apartment. Could Colin be jealous? Involuntarily I envision Colin and Davis together. It's like seeing a statue of a Greek god next to a lawn gnome. If Colin is jealous it could only because he wants me all to himself. The Plan is working!

In Davis's milieu, pet boys are taken for granted. I accompany him to social events in Midtown or Soho where I mix with the rich and successful. They usually appall me. For every occasional fun person like Jordanelle there are two boring lawyers and, worse, three precious artistes. The latter invariably claim to be fascinated with some seemingly obscure but actually mundane facet of urban life. "I thought it would be interesting to focus on islands," one says, stretching out the word 'island' to make it sound exotic. "Because, you know, we live on an island, and cross traffic islands every day, and when we want to get away from it all, we think of tropical islands, yet... no man is an island." Mr. Artiste explains this while standing on one of a series of islands floating on a small artificial sea in a vulgarly gargantuan Soho art gallery. Davis finds this intriguing. I don't even need Nana Leah to tell me this is pretentious bourgeois nonsense, or Gramma Bea to tell me it lacks the charm of a pretty picture.

Davis takes me out to meet his pal Brad at a Mexican restaurant. Unlike California where Mexican food is fast and cheap, here it's an upscale novelty cuisine produced by soignée young chefs for trendy gourmets. Brad turns out to be a blandly handsome photographer who proudly shows us a clothing ad from *Interview* magazine that uses his work. The photo features a gaggle of blonde boys dressed all in white lounging in front of a palatial white Georgian country home. One of them has his polo shirt falling off his body so that his every-muscle-perfectly-toned torso can gleam attractively in the sun and make us want to buy the overpriced preppy duds all the more desperately. I don't know whether I'm more offended by the ad or the cover, from which smiles Nancy Reagan, the Eva Braun of the 1980s.

"Wow, you got to work with him?" drools Davis, his stubby finger rubbing against the semi-nudist as if he could feel the taut, depilated flesh through the photo.

"He's a sweetheart," says Brad in a voice that implies an intimate familiarity.

My egalitarian fervor fueled by two margaritas, I switch to attack mode. "And I'm sure he comes from fine Mayflower stock," I say with my jaw clenched in a parody of upper-crust speech patterns I've learned from watching old movies. "A real Aryan from Darien. My gawd but those boys look pure. Ron and Nancy would be proud."

"Let's not talk about politics," says Brad with a worried look in his eye.

"Well, what do you think of the Reagans?" I ask.

Brad looks at his taco. "Politics divides. I want people to come together."

"But you're gay, right? The Republicans hate gays."

"If you think those Mafioso union thugs who run the Democratic Party are gay people's friends, you're sadly mistaken," says Brad. "Affluent people are much more tolerant of homosexuality than the poor."

"Then why are the only politicians who favor gay rights liberal Democrats?" I ask.

Brad doesn't deign to answer this but launches a diversionary attack. "You want to talk about oppressed minorities? What about rich people? Rich people are taxed more heavily than anyone else, more than other minorities. If anyone tried that with blacks you can just hear the outcry."

I'm incredulous. "But rich people are taxed at higher rates because they derive more benefits from government services." I can hear an unattractive shrillness creeping into my voice, but I can't stop it.

Brad gets a tiny bit shrill himself. "So do Blacks. Just look at how many are on welfare. Not that I think that's wrong, I understand it's hard to be poor and that they suffer from racism or whatever. But that doesn't justify persecuting wealthy people. I mean, who creates all the jobs? Who gives the most money to charities? Rich people, that's who."

Davis intervenes. "Did I mention my friends Randy and Sarah asked me to go in with them on Imij?" He turns to me, "It's a photo gallery they're opening in Soho. I'm really doing it."

I'd like to switch the subject back to Brad's obnoxious reactionary comments, but unfortunately the margaritas have done their work too well and my mind is filled with sand. I let it slide. When Davis and I get back to his place, however, he lashes out. "Look, I know Brad is a snob and somewhat politically naive, but you need to learn to get along with people different than yourself. You really embarrassed me."

Was I really disagreeable? I wonder as Nana Leah shakes her head no and Gramma Bea shrugs like, maybe. I guess I did put him in on the spot. "OK, sorry," I say, more because I'm too tired to fight than out of any real regret. "It's just that if nobody says anything to people like that they'll never learn when they're being stupid. Those boys in that picture! Brad is just trying to make everyone insecure about their status so they'll buy expensive clothing."

"Brad is just trying to make a living as a photographer. The people who design the ads are the ones you should be mad at," says Davis.

I'm not ready to get down from my high horse. "And the blonde thing, it's so Nazi. I mean, would it have killed them to have one brunette? And the clothing was so ugly."

"Not everybody can wear day-glo, black, and zebra print all the time," hisses Davis. "We can't all be New Wave."

"Why not?" I ask, truly and honestly not knowing. "Give me one reason!"

"Because we're not all teenagers," says Davis.

"I saw a little old lady in a hot pink winter coat with a leopardette pill box hat on just the other day. I thought she looked great. In fact, my friend Lizzie and I always used to say we couldn't wait to become elderly eccentrics. Of course, little old men can't dress any way they want, but by the time I'm old I'll just switch and become a lady."

Davis is only half-listening to me. "I can't take you anywhere nice. That's what I get for dating rough trade."

"Rough trade? I went to two semesters of state university!" I protest, though I'm secretly flattered. What could be sexier?

"It's all relative," says Davis. "And nobody says you have to read those upscale magazines. Let Brad and all the stupid people from Connecticut read them and spend all their money on those stupid clothes. There's nobody saying you have to buy them. We still have freedom of choice in this country. You go on being you." This sounds sort of conciliatory and I think we've reached the end of our row. "But just remember," Davis adds with a scowl, "nobody likes a bitter New Wave chicken."

It's December 25th so Colin and I are avoiding Christianity by eating dinner in a Chinese restaurant with a shrine in the corner; a little dollhouse-like pagoda with a Buddha statue, electric candles, incense, and oranges left as offerings to the gods. I tell Colin about the episode with Brad and Davis's rough trade comment, but he doesn't respond the way I expect.

"You, rough trade? That's a laugh. I don't know why you put up with Davis and his idiot friends. I suppose you must find it comforting to be with people of your own class."

"They're not of my own class!" I shriek. "I just told you, Davis even called me rough trade! He's rich! I haven't seen bank books or tax returns, but maybe even filthy rich."

"His money comes both from working and owning capital, so he has what's called a contradictory class position," elucidates a suddenly apparent Nana Leah, who's obviously been eavesdropping. She puts on a huge scowl, "But a man of the people he's not!"

"Well, I just thought you hated all that preppy crap. Jeez, I mean, those old money WASP conservatives are getting their revenge for the '60s, turning the country into a boring, repressed plutocracy."

I strike back with the first available weapon. "So what's with Andy Warhol interviewing Nancy Reagan anyway? You're always saying he's such a genius and here he is fawning over this woman whose husband..." I'm momentarily stymied because there are so many atrocities to choose from when discussing the President, "wants to count ketchup as a vegetable in school lunches, appoints a Secretary of the Interior who doesn't want to save the environment because he thinks Christ is about to return..."

Colin turns defensive. "Warhol didn't interview *Ronald* Reagan, he interviewed *Nancy*. She's not responsible for everything he does."

"She's bad enough! What about the two hundred thousand dollars' worth of china she just had to have for the White House while people are starving?"

"Warhol is just showing America its own face in the mirror. He's not endorsing Reaganism any more than he was endorsing Campbell's soup or Brillo pads. That's Pop Art. Now, you can argue that Pop, as an artistic project, is played out and that it's time to politicize art, but you can't deny that it has its place in art history, that it was an important reaction against the desperate groping for authenticity of Pollock and the Abstract Expressionists."

"So where is it written that you can't deny that?" asks Nana Leah. "You most certainly can deny that!"

Colin isn't finished. "And you're the one hanging out with Davis and his creepy preppy friends. How different is it for you to hang out with Davis and Brad, and Andy to hang out with Nancy?"

"He's right," says Nana Leah. "Absolutely right."

"Hmm," I say. "I guess I'll have to think about that one."

As we leave we're delighted that the waitress doesn't wish us a merry you-know-what.

Getting my ear pierced is a little scary, but even scarier is that I decide to have Cliff do it. Without telling Colin of my decision, I show up at Cliff's table.

"Hi." I glance over the snowdomes, cheap scarves, and New York themed tchotchkes.

"Hey, Jeremy."

I flash what I hope is a winning smile. "I wanna get my ear pierced."

Cliff gives me a huge grin, made all the more adorable by the way his hair flops boyishly over his forehead. I would gladly trek to the North Pole on hands and knees if I could come back looking half as adorable as he is to me right now.

"OK, lemme show you some studs. Pick one you like 'cause you gotta wear it for a month while your ear heals."

I choose a plain silver one. "This."

"OK, c'mon and sit down here." He points to a plastic chair. "I just shoot it into your earlobe with this gun and we're done. It's like getting a shot at the doctor's. Stings for a second, doesn't really hurt." He swabs my ear with alcohol. "Brrr, kinda chilly today. You seen Colin?"

A pang of jealousy shoots through me. "Not since this morning."

"How come you're getting your ear pierced?" Cliff doesn't have a pierced ear. Does he think I'm a dork?

"Just 'cause."

"Well, you've got the look to carry it off." He's just making small talk but I'm flattered beyond words. I can feel his warm breath on my neck as he centers the tip of the gun on my earlobe. *Zap.*

"Ow!"

"That's it. All done. Look in this mirror... nah, it's too small. Come back in here. Hey Louie," he calls to his co-worker (a stocky boy with a Flock of Seagulls coif), "cover me for a while." Cliff leads me into a small room behind the table. There's a safe, a tiny chair, a sink, a mirror, and an odd New Yorky smell I can never place. I look in the reflection at my strange new self, then, before I know what's happening, Cliff and I are kissing. Hands find their way under winter layers and enthusiastically run up and down bodies.

Cliff's hands unzip my fly. "Ooh!" he says. "Colin said you have a really big dick." I think gay guys talking about cock or dick is just as tacky as straight men talking about pussy or boobs or gazongas (not to mention potentially offensive to my grandmothers, who after all might pop in at any moment). Fortunately he doesn't say anything more till we're done.

"Thanks," I say.

"I better get back to work," say Cliff, already heading back outside. "See ya!"

It's so frosty out that by the time I get home my whole body is numb. I turn on the stove full blast and stand in front of it, my thoughts still twirling like snowflakes in a blizzard: if I'm cute enough for Cliff, and Cliff is cute enough for Colin, then I should be cute enough for Colin...

I'm startled by the sound of the door opening. "Hey stud, I just saw Cliff. He told me you two played around. I told him you were hung so I figured he'd want a sample." He joins me in front of the stove, taking off his mittens and sticking his hands in.

"Sample?" I ask.

"He's a big size queen. He said he didn't think you were really all that big. But he said it was nice anyway. I'm glad you two are getting to be friends."

"Friends?"

"I was worried you were jealous of him or something stupid."

"Stupid?" I seem to have echolalia.

Colin turns to me with an unusually serious look on his face. "Y'know, I think I love Cliff, but he'll never leave Barry. Did you know they've been together eight years? Hey, lemme see your ear!"

I turn my head.

"Very you," says Colin.

My composure returns. "What's that supposed to mean?"

"Just what I said, very you."

"Cliff was the one who started it."

"I know."

"You're not jealous?" I ask.

"Don't be so suburban," says Colin.

I stare into Colin's eyes. "Cliff will never be all yours, but I would."

"You're not my type," says Colin, his face calm, reasonable, and blankly unreadable.

"How come?" I sound desperate even to myself. Why was I cursed with such a whiny voice?

"Everyone has a type, and you're not mine."

"But I love you."

"Well, you want to fuck me, I know that much."

"It's more than that," I say. "I mean it's not that at all! I love you."

"Look, we already do *everything* else together. What more could we *do* together?"

For that I have no answer.

Colin and I are chomping away in a pizzeria on St. Mark's when Lisa and Benny walk in and order slices.

"What?" asks Colin, no doubt seeing my frown.

"Those kids are from my high school. Drama worms."

"They look like mods, or half-mods, anyway."

"That's their thing: they're always a little this, a little that, a little snotty. We always hated each other. I was sort of punky back then and they used to laugh at my dog collar and thought the Ramones were stupid. They were only into punk and New Wave from a connoisseur angle. Like they thought having one Talking Heads album and a skinny black tie meant they had brilliant taste. Total jerks." I'm slightly embarrassed by my own vehemence, but with Colin I never hold back. Half the time I don't even know what I'm feeling or thinking till I hear myself blabbing to him. Without spotting me, Lisa and Benny sit down and begin to eat their slices—using forks and knives.

"So you're saying they're poseurs?" asks Colin.

"Sort of. Yeah."

"And what were most of the kids at your school listening to?" he asks.

"Peter Frampton. Kiss. Icky stuff."

"Well, then Benny and Lisa did have superior taste."

"Not superior enough to appreciate the Ramones, or the Sex Pistols, or any band that wasn't sort of..." My mind runs out of words, but Colin has only asked as a formality. He already knows what I think and has found the holes in my logic.

"They don't like bands that are loud and angry. But why should they be angry? They're cute, rich, white, heterosexual Americans. Being angry would be pretentious for them. You were angry because you were gay and getting beaten up and made fun of."

"But still, they just have this way of seeming like it's all an act for them. Everything they say is in quotation marks. They project an invisible stage around them wherever they go. Even when they dress up, their clothes seem like costumes. They're not really fun or wild or anything, they're just performing."

"They lack authenticity? As if you were a real punk? As if you were really a Cockney nihilist? People like Lisa and Benny put on shows all the time, but shows are fun. Costumes are fun. Being on stage is fun." His eyes narrow into accusing slits. "Being a little snot who disapproves of theater like some seventeenth century puritan is not fun."

"Not that I care now, I guess, but I used to think... still think, it watered everything down the way they went punk all half-hearted and 'Look at me, aren't I cool' and copying every last little detail from magazines."

"And you got your ideas from...?"

"Well, magazines," I admit. "But I didn't follow them slavishly."

Colin looks at me with pity.

"OK, maybe I was a little harsh on them."

"Interjecting theatricality into everyday life is a great way to express yourself, provided you do it well. If Benny and Lisa seem half-assed, it's just because they're bad actors and you think their lack of talent will rub off on you, make you look like a poseur. See, you like to think you're a wild boy while they're marionettes, tied with invisible strings of privilege to the controlling hand of respectability."

"You have got to have read that marionette thing somewhere," I protest. "You did not just come up with that on the spot."

"But you're both just kids out for a good time. It's just that you happen to like slumming."

"Slumming?" An image from a forgotten movie flashes through my brain—a gaggle of 1930s socialites, men in tuxedos, women in floor-length satin evening gowns, all with martinis in hand and laughing uproariously ("Cecil, can you believe we're on a *subway*?") as they ride off to Coney Island on a lark. "Colin, I am not slumming!"

"And when the time comes, and it might not be for five or ten years, you'll use your very precise diction and family connections..."

I interrupt, "I don't have any family connections!"

He ignores me, "...to get a decent job and all the little goodies you grew up with. And that's natural, who wants to suffer? C'mon, Benny and Lisa are just having fun. You rich kids are so mean to each other."

Being read to filth by Colin is like a walk in warm rain; I want to get out of the way, but the experience isn't entirely unpleasant.

At least he's paying attention to me, treating my ideas and opinions as if they matter. As Benny and Lisa start towards the door Lisa catches my eye. She quickly turns her head and pretends not to see me. On the street Benny does a little twirl and soft-shoe step as he waits for her. Boy, oh boy, oh boy, do I hate them!

Colin feels that New Year's Eve is for beginners, so the night of December 31ˢᵗ finds us blasting my new Altered Images album and cleaning the apartment. As he mops the floor, Colin holds forth on the importance of hedonism:

"What you have to try and do is meld with nightlife the way a Sufi becomes one with his dance."

"How's that again?" I ask as I squash a gigantic roach I discover under the kitchen cabinet I'm wiping down.

Colin explains. "The sexuality of the West Village and the artiness of the East Village are like the yin and yang of a vast ever-expanding party; a party that's slowly undermining the foundations of bourgeois civilization by seducing people away from drudgery, blandness, and respectability."

"Are you saying partying will replace The Revolution?" I ask, already anticipating Nana Leah's objections to this heresy.

"Revolutions are wars, and wars don't work," says Colin. "Partying does, though. America pulled out of Vietnam, basically, because kids were having too much fun surfing and going to discothèques to want to become cannon fodder. And now people are running away from the whole boring, suburban consumer lifestyle to move to cities where they can be creative and go out at night. That's why Manhattan is so expensive: everyone wants to live here and be part of the fabulous party."

"So what about the people outside lower Manhattan?" I ask.

"Someday the party will swallow everything," says Colin.

"And in the meantime?" I ask.

Colin rests his head on the mop handle. "Too bad for them."

We hear the sound of horns honking and people screaming from outside. It's 1982.

"Hooray," I cheer weakly.

"Go get dressed," says Colin, dropping the mop.

"Why?" I ask.

"We're going out," he says, as if the answer should have been obvious.

"I thought you said New Year's was for beginners!"

Colin can't believe how dense I'm being. "Yeah, but New Year's is over now."

Davis, my wealthy sort-of-boyfriend, invites me to his twenty-ninth birthday party at his new photo gallery, Imij. I want to look my best (it's sure to be a super-swanky event) so when I pass a shoe store with some cool boots in the window I have to go in and try them on. They're thin-soled black suede with a useless flap in front—totally Adam Ant meets Robin Hood new romantic—and they look stunning. They're also way too expensive, but I don't even try to resist. Leaving the store I'm only sorry I never learned to walk on my hands because so few people get to see my boots way down there on the sidewalk.

I bring Colin and Sheila with me to the party, tempting them with descriptions of lavish hors d'oeuvres and rich eligible bachelors. We arrive fashionably late at the gallery which consists of one medium-sized room so full of people you can hardly see the luridly tinted photos of cheese in various states of moldering decay that hang on the walls. There's a DJ blasting music over a portable sound system so everyone's screaming instead of talking. I don't see Davis anywhere.

Colin examines a huge photo of some chartreuse-tinted rotting Camembert. "Art is a mistake," he says, shaking his head sadly.

Sheila scans the hors d'oeuvre table's disturbingly small quantities of exceedingly pretty food, most of which has already been eaten. "Maybe the photos are supposed to make us lose our appetites so we won't be disappointed at the spread."

"Look there's a bar," I say, embarrassed that Davis isn't as lavish as I've claimed. We get cocktails then return to scavenge the last of the comestibles.

"Hi," says Davis, popping out of nowhere and pulling me by the arm away from Sheila and Colin. "I'm glad you're here." Instead of hugging or kissing he continues to hold my arm, hostlike.

"Happy birthday. Here." I hand him a tiny package.

"Oooh!" he says, ripping off the wrapping paper to reveal a tiny blue plastic cat with a head that bobs up and down on a spring, the sort of thing a teenage girl might have gotten for her birthday in 1964. "Thanks. So you haven't seen the gallery before, have you? What do you think?"

"It's a nice, er, space," I begin, as someone's elbow accidentally jabs me and I drop my drink. I look down expecting the worst, but miraculously my boots are dry. Davis's light gray suit-pants, however, are splattered with dark wet splash marks. He doesn't notice so I keep mum. No point in making him self-conscious, especially not on his birthday.

"I think we can do a lot with it," says Davis as a preppily dressed guy about my age walks up to us. He's a head taller than Davis and me and has an expensive camera slung around his neck. "Oh, Jeremy, this is my little, and I use that word loosely, brother, Lawrence. Lawrence, this is my friend Jeremy." We shake. "Lawrence just got back from Italy. Dad sent him there because Lawrence just came out and Dad somehow got it into his head that Italy would turn him straight. Instead he just had this whirlwind affair with an incredibly rich handsome Italian count!" Davis laughs and Matthew's wildly handsome face smiles over-politely, leading me to believe that Davis delivers this potentially embarrassing tidbit of information with every introduction.

"That's crazy," I observe.

"I told you my family was crazy," says Davis proudly. "Hey, take our picture."

"OK," says Lawrence. Davis and I put our arms around each other's shoulders. Click.

"Well, I must mingle," says Davis, traipsing off into the crowd. Lawrence stares at me for a second, smiles coldly and excuses himself. He looks nothing like Davis, I think. And boy, is he ever cute.

"Who was that you were talking to?" asks Colin coming up from behind and startling me.

"Davis's little brother. I kinda get the feeling he doesn't like me."

"Young fags never like each other, they're competition," explains Colin.

"Oh."

"C'mon, let's get another round."

We do get another round, and another, and are just starting on our fourth when Davis again pops out of nowhere and grabs my arm. This time the crowd is too thick and he can't lead me away. I seize the opportunity to perform the social pleasantries. "Colin, this is my friend Davis. Davis, my... roommate Colin."

"Oh, gee, yeah, hi," says Colin doing a tolerably good impersonation of Andy Warhol at his most blasé.

"It's my birthday!" says Davis, who is now quite gloriously smashed.

"Yeah," says Colin.

"What?" asks Davis, unable to hear over the hubbub. "Huh?"

"Uh, happy birthday," says Colin as if the words pain him.

Sheila comes over, glaring at a tiny canapé she holds in her hand as if she was trying to decide if it was worth digesting. "An actor/model/waiter-type over there just told me I was a fine, cheeky lass."

"Which one?" demands Davis. "It's my birthday."

"Happy, happy," says Sheila. She points to a handsome and rather gigantic man in a suit. "Him."

Suddenly I recognize the face. "I think that's Jordanelle!"

"Called himself Jordan," says Sheila.

"His girl name is Jordanelle," explains Davis. "He's only dressed like that 'cause he just came from the theater. He said he'd change into his girl duds here."

"What kind of drag does he do?" asks Sheila.

"Nancy Sinatra-esque," I explain.

"But he likes girls," adds Davis. "Straight as an arrow."

Sheila scrutinizes Jordan, an act possible only because he stands a head taller than the rest of the crowd. "Hmmmmm."

Davis is seized with a mission. "You two should make it!"

"Really!" says Colin, turning into an outraged Queen Victoria.

"And you see how tall he his. Well, have you considered, uh, you know." Davis looks down towards his crotch.

"Vulgar, vulgar, vulgar," says Colin, shaking his head slowly.

Davis glares at Colin. Colin rolls his eyes. I start to worry. My dating Davis won't make Colin jealous if they just plain hate each other.

"Maybe I'll go talk to this Jordan," says Sheila, raising one eyebrow in a coquettish manner.

"Do," suggests Davis. "And fuck him!"

"Indeed!" says Colin.

"Wish me luck," says Sheila, throwing back her shoulders and sauntering off towards her prey. Davis turns to me.

"Everybody should go home with someone tonight. I say so... and it's my birthday!"

Colin ostentatiously picks up the last cracker, spreads some Brie on it, then winces. "Hey Davis? Want some cheese?" He holds out the cracker. I down my drink hoping to douse the panic rising in my gut.

Davis glares. "No. You eat it."

"I've lost my appetite for cheese." Colin's eyes are brimming with contempt. "And it smells funny. At least I think it's the cheese that smells funny."

"Get up there, child," commands Gramma Bea, pointing to the hors d'oeuvre table. "Get up there and dance. Hurry!"

"Not in the mood for cheeeese," says Colin, elongating the word bratishly.

"Uh, Colin..." I don't know how to ask him to stop being obnoxious without being obnoxious myself.

"Can't think what's put me off cheeeese, but I'm not in the mood."

Gramma Bea is stern. "Jeremy, do as I say!"

"You prefer dick cheese, I suppose?" taunts Davis. "Port Authority fresh."

"I will not have such vulgarities mentioned in my presence," says Colin.

I jump on the table and begin to shimmy. "Hey Sheila!" She turns from where she's talking to Jordan, sees me, and scampers up onto our new go-go platform. We begin twisting.

"Whooooo! Go, go, go!" screams Davis, completely ignoring Colin, who's left holding the Brie-smeared cracker in the vicinity of Davis's ear. Deprived of his quarry, Colin wanders away with a sour look on his face.

"It would seem the crisis has been averted," says Gramma Bea. A few couples around the room begin dancing. "Though if you continue seeing Davis I think you should speak with him about his drinking. It doesn't bring out his best."

"It's my birthday!" shouts Davis, holding his drink aloft like a frat boy.

"Take it off!" shouts a chubby man standing next to Davis, his voice thick with irony. This is not actually a command to take it off, but a bitter mockery of all taking it off, and by extension, the sort of activity that might lead to such an idea.

Davis laughs. "Yeah, take it off! It's my birthday!" Less irony. Undetectable levels of irony.

Sheila and I try to do the bump, except my booty keeps missing her booty. "Whoo!" says Davis. "Take it off!"

Gramma Bea is apologetic. "By now you really ought to know that men are...," she searches for the right word, perhaps inhibited by the fact that I'm a man, "...creatures. Perhaps you'd better take it off."

I stuff my shirt into my back pocket.

"Whooo!" screams Davis happily.

"Get down from there!" shrieks Nana Leah, materializing next to Gramma Bea. "Don't sell yourself cheap."

"I talked to Jordan," says Sheila.

"And?" I ask.

"He's changing in the bathroom."

"Changing his clothes, not the world," says Nana Leah.

"Oh, be quiet, woman!" screams Gramma Bea, squinting at Nana Leah in a manner that I think makes her look like an owl. "Go away and let Jeremy have some fun. The boy needs to kick up his heels."

I'm starting to sweat from the bright lights and exertion, I feel self-conscious, and worst of all, I've accidentally stepped in the remains of some dip with my new boots.

"Reactionary!" says Nana Leah, clenching her fists with anger.

"Killjoy!" Gramma Bea sniffs disdainfully.

"Never worked a day in your life!" hisses Nana Leah. "Except on your back."

"Get funky!" yells out someone in the crowd with about seventy-two percent irony.

Gramma Bea reddens with anger. "He's got to find someone now while he's young. In five years he'll resemble a burly falafel salesman thanks to your swarthy genes!"

Nana Leah gives Gramma Bea a little shove. Gramma Bea slaps Nana Leah across the face with the palm of her hand. They're not hurting each other, but it's still pretty shocking. I just about want to cry.

"Wooo!" screams Davis. Next to him, Lawrence glares at me as if I were an especially large cockroach.

Jordanelle, resplendently attired in a blazing orange wig, translucent orange sleeveless mini-dress, and white patent leather go-go boots, leaps up on the table next to Sheila and screams, "Yeehah! Dance, you motherfuckers, dance!" Our combined weight is making the folding table shake alarmingly. As a woman dressed like a drag queen beckons me to lean down so she can ironically shove a dollar tip into my jeans, I spot Colin at the back of the room chatting up what appears to be a winsome French schoolboy. I jump down from the table, accidentally twisting my ankle a bit in the process. Lawrence, who was standing nearby though facing away from our dancing, walks off in what may very well be disgust. Davis smiles luridly. "Your friend what's-her-name and Jordanelle make a cute couple."

"Yup," I agree, standing stork-like on one leg. "Will you excuse me?" I hobble off towards Colin, gratefully noticing that Gramma Bea and Nana Leah have vanished into the crowd. Before I can reach him he starts kissing the French schoolboy who I decide can't really be a French schoolboy because he has a tiny pigtail protruding from the back of his mussy black hair. This aesthetic gaffe reassures me; Colin could never get serious about anyone with a tiny pigtail. I turn around and hobble back.

"Let's go home and fuck," Davis says, putting his clammy hand on the sweaty small of my back. I really don't want to, but between Colin and my Grammas I'm so upset I'd leave with Attila the Hun to get away from the party. I pull on my shirt and let Davis lead me onto the sidewalk where a chill wind slaps me in the face. Ouch! I want to slap it back, but can't because it's the wind. Davis ushers me into a rented limousine (my first time in such a politically problematic vehicle) and as we ride to West Tenth he blathers on about the stunning success of his soiree. What a geek, I think, first about him, and then about myself.

When I go over to Davis's now I often run into Lawrence. He's never more than coldly civil to me and is forever sipping cocktails (only after watching him did I realize that I gulp mine) with other well-dressed young adults. His photographs of minor celebrities now appear in several local papers and galleries and he's on the verge of becoming a celebrated photographer. Though his success is due entirely to connections (Davis introduced him to everyone he needed to meet), he thinks of himself as a hardworking Horatio Alger type. When I tell Colin about Lawrence, he just says, "That's how New York works. There's no justice in this town, it's who you know."

The next time I drop by Davis's, he suggests we go out to dinner at an Alsatian restaurant that's just opened up around the block. As we're about to enter I glance at the menu. The prices are obscene. "Um, Davis, I can't really afford this."

"My treat," he says with less warmth than you'd really want to hear in those words. The restaurant gives you crayons so you can color on the paper tablecloths. I draw sperms, ghosts, televisions, all spinning in a vortex. Davis draws cubist faces. The food is horrible. By the time we're done with dinner it's raining out and we have to run back to Davis's apartment. "How about a hot toddy?" I ask, not knowing exactly what a hot toddy is, but knowing that's what you drink when you get wet.

"OK," says Davis. "I'll whip up some hot buttered rums, you get some towels from the bathroom." While I'm drying off and trying to imagine what hot buttered rum will taste like, Davis rather over-casually lets fly with a little remark. "Lawrence thinks you ought to bring your own liquor over here instead of drinking mine all the time."

"Oh?"

"Here," says Davis handing me my drink.

"What do you think?" I ask.

Davis thinks a little. "Well..."

Before my brain can finish processing this information my mouth takes matters into its own hands, if a mouth can be said to have hands, which it probably can't.

"I don't think we should see each other anymore," it says. Then Gramma Bea whispers into my ear the right words to finish the deal. "It isn't fair to you. There's no way I can ever repay you for all your kindnesses."

"I understand," says Davis. I kiss him on the cheek (an act I immediately regret), down my cocktail, and leave. The rich really are different from you and me. They're cheaper.

Will Yourself To Be Gorgeous

Colin looks up from his *Village Voice*, his face a supernova of excitement. "We're going to the movies. Get dressed!"

"What are we seeing?" I ask.

"You'll see," he says. "Be ready to go in five minutes. I'll go see if Cliff wants to go."

As I dress, I fret. Colin hasn't asked Cliff to do stuff with us so far. Is this a new trend? Moments later Cliff, Colin, and Barry are all in the apartment. I'm glad Barry's coming along.

"Hi," says Cliff with a little nod that makes his bangs flop adorably. I want to scream out, "Stop being so perfect!" but I just say, "Hi."

"Howdy, Jeremy," purrs Barry, soft and friendly. "I always see you rushin' in and rushin' out of the apartment. I never get a chance to visit with you. How you been doin'?"

Everyone else in New York is terse to the point of rudeness, why does Barry have to hold onto his weird Southern charm?

"I'm fine," I say in the flat tone usually reserved for relatives.

As we walk out the door Barry turns to Colin. "What's this movie again?"

"*Fox and Friends*. It's by this brilliant gay German filmmaker, Rainer Werner Fassebinder."

"Does it have Hannah Schuygulla in it?" asks Cliff.

"Who's Hannah Schuygulla?" asks Barry.

Cliff explains. "She's his big female lead. She's German, but she's got old Hollywood glamour."

"There was this review in the *Voice*," says Colin, "that was talking about how she's not naturally beautiful like Marilyn Monroe, but she's actually more attractive because she wills herself to be gorgeous."

Cliff pats Barry on the back. "Kinda like you, honey." Does Cliff really think Barry is gorgeous?

"Natural beauty is boring unless you do something fun with it," declares Colin.

"I want to will myself into being gorgeous," I think aloud.

"You're fine the way you are," says Cliff, giving my hair a playful muss. The physical contact shocks me a little.

"But this movie doesn't have Hannah Sch... whatever-her-name is?" asks Barry.

"No, it's about a poverty queen who's used and exploited by evil rich fags," says Colin, giving me a little look.

"The poor are the salt of the earth," says Barry.

"You better believe it, mister," agrees Nana Leah.

"Romantic claptrap," says Gramma Bea.

"Too much salt isn't good for you," says Colin.

"Without salt you'd die," says Cliff.

"So just how do you go about willing yourself into being gorgeous?" I ask.

Colin and I are standing in The Slot, a thoroughly disreputable leather bar, eating free peanuts roasted in the shell (yum!), and washing them down with draft beer. Around us are legions of manly leathermen, nearly all of them sporting hankies in their back pockets advertising various perverted sexual proclivities. While I have no clue about the meaning of the colors (I can't even remember if right is top and left is bottom or vice versa) Colin claims to be able to read the codes perfectly.

"Green is for sex al fresco. Navy blue is for cornholing. White is for virgins. Black is for Satanism. Baby blue is for diapers. Gold is for Eurotrash. Pink is for nellies. Mauve is for foot binding. Chartreuse is for water torture. Brown is for..."

"Don't tell me, don't tell me, don't tell me!" I interrupt.

"Princess prude!" he reprimands.

I suspect Colin only likes this scene because it's as dirty and un-Catholic as you can get, a way of thumbing his nose at whatever little part of his brain still believes in the whole God-and-sin bit. He even pretends to get in the spirit of things by shoving a ladies kerchief (cream-colored with cartoon ladybugs all over it) into his left rear pocket. Now and again I see men staring at his ass with confused looks on their faces. After a half-hour I get bored and start nagging. "OK, we're all full of peanuts, we've had our beers, let's go dancing."

"Settle down, these places don't get really fun till right before they close when everyone realizes they have to pick someone up or sleep alone. Hey, look at him!" Colin is pointing towards a short, youthful, and entirely adorable bar back running around shirtless, picking up empties. "You always like guys smaller than you."

"Sure, so I can be the big butch one," I say in a joking tone, though it's the absolute truth. "But so what? He's gorgeous. He'd never go for me."

"The thing about you," explains Colin, "is that you're a trophy hunter; you want the boys everyone else wants. But not all trophy boys only want other trophy boys. It's not impossible that that bar back has a fetish for your type."

"And what type would that be?" I ask. "Nervous Jews?"

Colin sighs, looks at me as if he wants to say something, then thinks better of it. Instead he walks over to the bar back and starts whispering in his ear. This is absolutely unnerving and I consider bolting out of the room except that the bar back is now smiling and looking straight at me. I compulsively munch peanuts I'm not the least hungry for.

Colin saunters back across the room. "It's all set. His name is Rex and he thinks you're cute. He gets off work in half an hour. I told him you'd take him home. Don't worry, Barry's out of town. I can stay with Cliff tonight."

A peanut skin goes down my throat the wrong way, inducing a huge fit of coughing. When I can look up I see Rex leering at me from behind the bar. "Colin! What did you say to him?"

"Just that you thought he was cute and that you had a huge, fat dick and would fuck him really hard and really fast all night long."

"Colin!" The raunchy language is bad enough, but it's also irksome to be reminded that Colin's not really a prude like me. He just sometimes pretends he is to be funny.

Colin sniggers sadistically. "You can take a boy out of the suburbs, but..." He doesn't finish because Rex comes over.

"Bartender said I could go early," he says with a big smile. Even Rex's teeth are cute.

"Time's a-wastin', get on out of here!" says Colin.

As we leave Rex, displaying unselfconscious exhibitionism of a natural trophy boy, doesn't even put on a shirt. Back at the apartment I grab some vodka from the freezer and skibble up onto my loft from the dresser and invite Rex up. Being a superhumanly built Greek God-type, he leaps up with the grace of a cheetah. We sit for a second on the edge of my bed. Before I know what's happening, my body is on top of his and, for the first time ever, acts of its own accord. I don't need to issue commands like, thrust or grind, it all just happens. Now I know what sex is like for monkeys and insects.

Eventually we fall asleep, sweaty and exhausted, in each other's arms. It's almost too much. In the morning, after having slept for all of an hour or two, I wake up to find Rex gone. My bleary eyes search the apartment, but I only see Colin standing in front of the mirror playing with his hair.

"Hey Colin..."

"Hello, love machine. Gawd, were you two noisy last night. I heard you right through the walls. That Rex must have been something. The way he howled!" He stops teasing his hair up for a second and hands me a small slip of paper from off the dresser. "Here, this is for you."

"Jeremy," I read aloud. "Last night was really special. I feel like we reached a place where hardly anyone goes, like we just had one body, if that makes any sense. I really want to see you again." Underneath Rex's name is a telephone number.

"Yippee!" I say.

Even scrubbing and laundering all day at the bathhouse doesn't dampen my spirits. That night I wonder if I should call, or is it too soon? Will I come off as desperate?

"Wait," say Nana Leah and Gramma Bea.

"Call," says Colin. "Barry is still away, so if you want the apartment again tonight, it's yours."

I call and we arrange another date for when Rex gets off work, fourish. This gives me time to sleep and primp. What should I wear? I decide to greet him at the door in a pair of gym shorts with my hair a little messy so it looks like I just woke up. When he rings my bell wearing nothing more than a pair of boots and some cutoff shorts I all but swoon. We don't even wait to get up on my loft, but make furious love on the kitchen floor. When he leaves in the morning, Rex gives me a kiss on the lips that has me wanting to start all over again. I could do this every night, no problem.

"You mustn't let yourself get carried away by this Rex person," says Gramma Bea. "You don't know the first thing about him, who his people are, where he comes from, or what he wants to do with himself."

"Gramma!" I just don't feel like being nagged.

"Living entirely on the physical plane is extremely dangerous. Have you ever wondered what would happen to you if you got in an accident and lost your looks?"

"I don't have any looks," I say, half-believing it.

"Stuff and nonsense," she says. "The point is, were you to find yourself with a giant scar across your face or missing a leg, would this person still like you? One ought to cultivate intellectual and spiritual bonds with the people one..." she searches for the appropriate word, "sees."

"Oh, I know," I say guiltily.

"I'm not being prudish," she continues, "Commit all the sins against nature you like, but try for something a little bit more."

"If Colin would be my boyfriend..."

Gramma Bea doesn't have to say anything, she just gives me a pitying look and I shut up.

"OK," I agree. "I'll try and be less shallow."

"All one can do is try," she says as she vanishes.

"How'd it go with Rex?" asks Colin when he gets in.

"Um. It's the hottest sex ever," I begin. "And I'm going to try to get to know him better so we can be like boyfriends or whatever."

"Uh oh," says Colin.

"What's that supposed to mean?"

"Boys like Rex," he says knowingly, "are pure sex. There isn't a lot else going on. Just go with it. Get rid of all those middle-class theatrics you use to mask your sexual desire. All that repression is just so you can look down your noses at the working poor who haven't got time for it."

"Well, I'm going to try anyway," I say.

During the next few dates I try to establish some rapport with Rex, asking a question here, venturing a tidbit about myself there, but he never takes the bait. Then, after we've been seeing each other for a couple of weeks, Rex puts me off. That's fine. I have sleep to catch up on. Rex does come over the next night, but something is different in his kisses. It's like he's not there and the sex somehow just feels like friction, like using three-dimensional pornography. I wake up the next morning to find him gone and a note by my bedside reading, "Jeremy, that was really great. Thanks for something real special. Love, Rex."

All my apprehension flies out the window. He used the word "love." It's too good to be true. I dance through the whole day, imagining futures that involve four hours a night of erotic passion. Only once or twice do I let myself hear the soft voice in the back of my mind whispering, "If you get serious with Rex, Colin will really get jealous."

That night when I call Rex he's busy again. Not to worry, I think, this has happened before—he just needs a break. When it happens again the next day I panic.

"If you get clingy," says Colin, "you can kiss him good-bye."

"He said he loved me!" I say, waving the note around like evidence in a courtroom drama.

"Oh, Jeremy," sighs Colin.

I wait two days to try again, and again get the brush off. Rex, I now realize, is through with me.

Colin and I are wandering around as he tells me, lectures really, about the movie, *Funny Face*, that I simply must see. It contains a scene in which a magazine editrix (based on Diana Vreeland) with a whim of iron suddenly declares the whole issue about to go to press must be scrapped as she's been seized with the inspiration that pink is about to be the in color. The ensuing Think Pink fantasy sequence is apparently an unsurpassed marvel. Colin is waxing rapturous in his description when he stops in mid-sentence, his eyes fixating on a sweaty bunch of guys in a basketball court. "Hey, I think those guys are trying to get a game going. I'm gonna play." He darts through the door in the chainlink fence into the world of real men. All the musical tones vanish from his voice as he confers with his soon-to-be teammates and his body becomes fluid and pantherlike as he starts messing around with the ball, bouncing it up and down real fast (is that "dribbling"?) and tossing it to other players.

I've always known Colin loves basketball (when he was a teen, it was his only form of socializing. The other boys didn't mind his fagginess since he was a good player), but I've never seen him play before so I stand and watch for a minute. Though his transformation from high falutin' queen to regular guy was momentarily fascinating, the game itself, like all sports, strikes me as deadly dull. Why on Earth do gay men find athletes so attractive? Sure, jocks have nice bodies, but so what? So do most drug-addled nightclubbers, and they can also think pink.

I wake up for the third day in a row with a huge, mind-crushing headache and a fever that makes me feel as if I'm immersed in a lake of fire. I call work and tell them I won't be in again. "If you don't show up today, I suggest you don't show up tomorrow as you won't have a job here," hisses Allen. I hang up on him.

The next day I'm feeling if not better, at least well enough to sit up. "Maybe I should beg for my job back," I wonder aloud.

"No way," advises Colin. "You were out for less than a week and you were even really sick!"

"It is unfair," I agree.

"Even if you weren't, it should have been all right. I mean, aren't they queens, too?"

"Absolutely."

"Then they should show a little solidarity. It's not like flamboyant gays are allowed to work in the real world."

"Am I flamboyant?" I ask.

Colin gives me an appraising look. "Musical voice, theatrical mannerisms, silly clothes; yeah, you're flamboyant. So basically you can forget about working blue collar jobs, corporate jobs, or going into politics, the military, the Church..."

"Or synagogue, as the case may be," I interject.

"Or the police," continues Colin, "or the fire department, or teaching school, or pro sports."

Enumerating the areas of gay professional exclusion should be depressing, but since all I really want to do is go dancing at nightclubs, it doesn't bother me. I am, however, reminded about the perilous state of my finances. "Oh Colin, about that eleven hundred forty-six dollars you owe me..."

Colin frowns. "I'm a little short this week."

The next day I'm fully recovered and begin what turns out to be a two-week frenzy of want ads, interviews, applications, and desperation. I'm nearly out of money and my dreams are haunted by ancestral misfortunes, pogroms, and potato famines. "One winter during the First World War, all we ate was turnips," commiserates Nana Leah. "Your great-grandfather spoke German and Polish so he could work as a translator for the army or we might not have even had those." Though she's trying to cheer me up I find this unspeakably depressing.

I'm also embarrassed. Jews are renowned the world over for their conspicuous overachievement, having invented Christianity, stand-up comedy, psychology, sociology, gay lib, Israel, international finance, communism, Las Vegas, 2nd wave feminism, and Hollywood, all the while winning a mind-boggling number of Nobel prizes. Yet here I am scanning the papers for minimum wage jobs.

Still and all I must eat, so I call the number of a bicycle messenger service near Grand Central Station. The address the man on the phone gives me turns out to be accessible only through a freight elevator that lets me off in a maze of corridors in which the rooms aren't numbered consecutively. I have to roam and roam before I locate #436. Inside I discover a room covered in scraps of mismatched industrial carpeting with walls of splintery, unvarnished wood. The only furniture consists of a few cast-off school chairs and one huge gray metal desk, behind which sits a sweaty pink man with serious ring-around-the-collar. He's busy writing something in a log and doesn't see me. After a few seconds I clear my throat.

"Uhm. I'm here about the job?"

The man looks up and hands me an application, which I quickly fill out and return. He glances at the form for a millisecond then turns to me. "OK, I'm Greg," he says a gruff, permanently aggrieved voice. "You wanna be here tomorrow at 8:30." I guess this means I'm hired; apparently the only real qualification is having two legs. I go home feeling relieved and terrified at the same time.

The next morning I arrive for work ten minutes early but there are already twenty or so other messengers, all but a couple of whom are Black or Puerto Rican, hanging around the office smoking, cursing, and grumbling resignedly. One lanky fellow with terrible acne asks me a question, but his Spanish accent is so thick I can't understand him, so I smile and say, "I'm Jeremy." He looks confused and wanders off.

Greg glowers at me like I'm gum at the bottom of his shoe, then turns to a guy with a big gold tooth and a bandana around his neck. "Hey Roscoe, this here's Jeremy. Will you get him started?"

"C'mon, white boy," says Roscoe, "I show you 'round." I follow him into the hall. "Water cooler," he says, slamming his hand down on the plastic drum producing a loud THWUMP. "Bathroom." He opens and slams a door marked Bathroom. "Wheels is in here." He beckons me into a room with a rack of rickety old bicycles. "Take one a these." As I try to find one that's my size, Roscoe leans against a wall and looks me up and down. "You won't be here long. I been here six months. Can't stand it. Got two kids though, gotta bring home some money." I'm amazed that someone around my age has not one but two children. I still feel like a little kid.

After pawing through the bent, rusty bikes I settle on an ancient green three-speed and wheel it back into the dispatcher's office. "You get your assignment based on seniority," says Roscoe. "Once you get you some seniority you can make some money. Right now you last in line so you gonna wait in here awhile 'fore you get sent out."

"How much can you make, I mean once you get some seniority?" I ask.

"Oh, you know, depends on how fast you are, how busy it gets. Hey, good luck." Roscoe wanders off to join his friends in the far corner of the room. As I stand around waiting for my first mission I read a small metal plaque devoted to one of the boys who "gave his all" in service of his job, which is to say, he was mowed down by traffic while trying to deliver a package.

Finally I'm given my orders and I set out. The spring sky is blazing blue, the air is fresh from recent rain, and whizzing around is fun, fun, fun, even though the traffic is absolutely insane. After my first delivery I call in for my next job. There isn't one, so they tell me to call back every half-hour till they have something for me. I end up spending half the day by a phone booth at an Orange Julius, frittering away too much money on papaya smoothies and hot dogs. At three I get another delivery, then another at four, after which I'm called back to the office to turn my bike in. I wonder if I'm really going to be able to make a living at this.

The tiny paychecks from my messenger job barely cover rent. "You need to turn some more tricks," Colin says, "but try a classier bar than the Haymarket. Go to Reflections. If you're going to sell your body you might as well make some real money." I agree and he fusses around like a nervous stage mother, telling me what to wear, showering me with advice and attention. "You want to dress a little fancier," he suggests, "but the clothing still has to be tight enough for them to see your body. And try parting your hair instead of spraying it up all *Eraserhead*. Here, let me do it." My own mom wasn't this attentive on my first day of school.

Reflections is near 53rd and 3rd, an intersection I know is a pick-up spot for hustlers because of a Ramones song which naturally gets caught in my head as I make my way into the unobtrusive bar/restaurant. Before my eyes can adjust to the darkness a huge, meaty-faced Mafioso bouncer in a black suit greets me. "Hey fella, how's it going?"

"OK. Yourself?" I say, trying to sound casual.

"Can't complain." He's openly staring at me, his bushy, Neanderthal brow furrowing in scrutiny. Am I a drugged out piece of street trash who'll steal some john's wallet or puke in the bathroom? No. I saunter over to the bar (this skill has taken some practice, I used to just walk over to a bar) where some drab businessmen are hunched over their highballs. While I'm waiting to be served I survey the back of the room where there's a dining area with white tablecloths and candles, a place where a few trophy chickens are being wined and dined by their sugardaddies. Across from the bar is a sort of bleacher covered in gray carpet on which sit the hustlers, about a dozen guys, all of whom are either thinner and prettier or butcher and more muscular than I am.

Once served, I take a seat on the bleacher, feeling like a transfer student on the first day of school. The boys are all busily chatting with each other and don't even trouble me with so much as a sidelong glance. The bouncer bets one of them five dollars he can't do fifty push-ups and the kid is instantly on the floor proving him wrong. The scene reminds me of high school jocks clowning around with their favorite coach. I could strike up a conversation with one of my fellow harlots, but without Colin around I revert to my true self, a pitiful wretch as terrified of strangers as a 19th century New England spinster abroad for the first time amongst heathens and cannibals.

After sitting alone for a while I'm reminded of the novel *The Persian Boy*, wherein the eunuch protagonist comes across a foreign land where the women, on reaching the age of marriage, have to sit all day every day in the local amphitheater till a man picks them for a wife. There's one ugly girl who's way too old to be there and out of pity the eunuch picks her so she won't have to spend her life waiting for a man who'll never come. She's incredibly grateful until she discovers she's been chosen by a eunuch and bursts into tears.

I slide into a harem fantasy. Perseus, send for my catamites, I am feeling amorous!... A youthful shepherd with a garland of laurel leaves, soulful black eyes, and skin the color of pancake syrup is sent in... He is shy at first, cowering before me, so I beckon him forward. "Come, forget your sheep for awhile," I command.

"Am I to be yours tonight, my sire?" asks the boy.

"Evening," interrupts reality in the form of a runtish businessman with monklike male pattern baldness. "Name's Leopold. Care for something to drink?" It doesn't take long before Leopold solicits my services. Unfortunately, he says, he's a little short of cash and will have to give me half in cash and half in the form of a check. I've read enough about street life to know that no check from this man will clear. Still, the other boys are so much cuter than me and there aren't enough johns to go around, and I've been here for close to two hours nursing the same beer, so I agree. In no time I'm back at his miniscule apartment, the floor and every available surface of which is covered with papers, manila envelopes, and notebooks. Leopold and I strip and fall onto his single bed. Mercifully, the act only takes a few minutes. After we're done he gets up and miraculously finds a checkbook in the midst of the chaos on his desk.

"Gee, that was good. Here you go," he smiles, handing me the check.

"What about the cash?" I ask.

"What are you talking about?" asks Leopold. "I told you I was short of cash."

Could I have misunderstood? That strikes me as unlikely since I'm a native English speaker. If only I'd remembered to ask for the cash up front! Maintaining what I hope is an ominous, even threatening, silence, I pull on my clothes while glaring at him and wondering what to do. Trying to locate cash in the rat's nest of an apartment would be hopeless. He might not even have any. I ought to rough him up, but I don't know how. Strange really. I was beaten up constantly all through school, how could I not have learned how to work someone over?

"The check's good," insists Leopold. "And I'm really out of cash." He pulls his wallet from his pants and opens it up to show me it's empty. I'm sure he's done this before.

"Look, you told me half in cash," I say, picking up the worthless check from the nightstand and shoving it in my jeans. "You said *cash*." I stalk out of the apartment feeling like the world's lowest loser. Just for kicks I go to the bank the next day. I'm told that Leopold's account has insufficient funds.

After the Leopold debacle I feel utterly doomed for days. I'd cheer myself up by painting but I don't want to poison Colin with fumes, so I decide to write. As if from nowhere, an idea pops into my head. Hours stream by as I lie on my bed scribbling and revising. Sometime in the middle of the night I decide I'm finished.

I peek over the edge of my loft. "Colin!"

He looks up from his bed. "You don't have to yell, I'm five feet away from you."

"I wrote something."

"I thought you were reading up there. You don't read enough."

"Listen."

"All right already, I'm listening," says Colin.

"I call it *In Defense of Chiang Ch'ing, or I was a Gay Teenage Frankenstein*." I note Colin's lips curling in a way that doesn't quite reveal if he thinks the title is funny or stupid. I continue:

"Chiang Ch'ing is one of the most hated women in the world today. Starting out as a deservedly unknown actress, she rose to a position of power in communist China by marrying Chairman Mao. Once at the top she proceeded to terrify the nation with her petty revenge and diabolical whimsy, which she cleverly disguised as routine political persecution. While I normally disapprove of such untoward behavior, there is still a soft spot in my heart for Ms. Ch'ing. It has to do with a particular "atrocity" she committed: It seems that she had the three most beautiful actresses in China tortured to death before her very eyes out of sheer jealousy.

"Bravo! I say. If that's not politically correct, what is? Chiang Ch'ing can be my comrade any time! She's done what I frequently dream of. In fact, a favorite fantasy of mine is surgically grafting Halloween masks onto the perfect faces of film idol Robby Benson, musical pretty boy Shawn Cassidy, and porno god Kip Knoll. Better yet, I'd like to send my private army into Studio 54 or some other enclave of the physically perfect, have them drag out all the beauties and force feed them something to make their skin break out (Sarah Lee chocolate layer cake, perhaps). You see, I want to be one of the beautiful people, and the only way accomplish that (even with extensive plastic surgery) would be by knocking off a lot of the competition.

"The competition for young guys in New York is tough. The streets are filled with really, truly, fabulously gorgeous young men around my age (nineteen) with peaches-and-cream complexions, smugly WASPish noses, long lanky legs, and, of course, high, high cheekbones. Oh, those cheekbones! I cry with envy and desire, and it's exactly that combination of envy and desire that I find so torturous. Do I want to sleep with little Sean, Chip or Corey or do I want to hate him for being so much competition?

Before you get the idea that I'm some junior league elephant man, let me state that all my limbs and facial features are more or less intact and that I have no diseases more exotic than acne. My family tells me as a compliment that I am the spitting image of my grandfather Herschel as a young shoe repairman back in the Ukraine. Were this some mundane decade, like the 1950s, I'm sure that I would be considered an average-looking guy.

"Alas, this is the 1980s, and even average looks will get you about as far as the nearest Chock Full O' Nuts. The surplus of beautiful boys is so acute that for the less-than-fantastically gorgeous, getting a date for Friday night is like finding an apartment. Why should someone date Mr. Average while there are eleven or twelve eager young fashion models within spitting distance? On the more amusing side, one can now see boys who in another era would have been actors, models, or porn stars working as busboys, ice cream scoopers, and file clerks. But this is little solace to the ugly come five o'clock when the world is again sharply divided into the gorgeous and not-so-gorgeous.

"It is not my intention to offer solutions to this abominable state of affairs, only to cash in on it. Robert Patrick, Joan Rivers, and Rodney Dangerfield, among others, have made nice careers for themselves by complaining about their unattractiveness. What I propose is a similar arrangement for myself. Remember, it's best to appease me: you wouldn't want another Chiang Ch'ing on your hands. And by the way, if you have any little brothers around my age who are 'unattached' and looking for a date, I just might be free the next few evenings."

I glance up from the page to see Colin's reaction. There's a semi-Satanic look in his eyes and I know he's got me on something.

"Better not step in any puddles."

"Why?"

"You're so shallow you'd drown in anything deeper than an inch. Why can't you less-than-gorgeous boys, you not-so-perfect types, why can't you date each other?"

"Uh..." I've never considered it.

"You could, but no, you run around slavering over pretty boys. Listen, looks aren't everything. People have minds too, you know. You don't have to be a face chaser."

I realize Colin's completely right and hang my head in shame as he elaborates.

"Ralph, for instance. Remember Ralph from work? He told me he thinks you're hot. He thinks you're a God. But just because he's overweight and has a face like an Easter ham you'd never consider even having sex with him."

"But you wouldn't either! You only have sex with cute guys. That's natural. Isn't it?"

"Nature has nothing to do with anything. Sure I like pretty boys, but if some handsome lad rejects me I don't make a whole federal case out of it. I don't complain." The way he says "complain" makes it sounds like smearing the walls with your own feces.

Suddenly I'm overcome with weariness. "But everywhere you go all anyone is looking for is cute guys, nobody's looking for..."

"Character?" Colin interrupts. "No, nobody's looking for character in the gutters you hang out in, but there's a whole world out there. You could volunteer to help old people in nursing homes or join the Episcopalians or something."

The thought of leaving the world of instant gratification makes me slightly hysterical. "Even before I knew what sex was, when I was a kid, I got crushes on cute boys! When I'm walking down the street and I see a cute young guy it's like he's in color and everything else is black and white. Like he's from Oz and everyone else is from Kansas. And forests or cars or paintings or sunsets are nothing compared to cute guys. You just don't understand because you're cute."

"I'm not that special," says Colin. "You just think I am because you're in love with me. Fall in love with someone else and he'll look plenty cute. You'll see."

Now I have him on something. "Hey, if I think anyone I'm in love with is cute, then that means I'm not just a face chaser!"

"I guess that's true," says Colin. "And it means it'll be that much easier for you to find someone to fall in love with who isn't me!"

That doesn't sound easy, I think, collapsing on my bed and tossing my essay to the floor.

I'm lying around the apartment thinking about Rex. Rex, I imagine, is not his real name. He's probably really named Stanley, but changed his name to Rex because it sounds like sex. "I don't think it's very clever of you to always be mooning over these boys," says Gramma Bea. "It isn't any fun, and what's the point of being a playboy if you're not going to have fun?"

Of course, she's right. It's my day off and without really formulating a plan I go for a walk. After drifting aimlessly for a while I find myself at a vintage clothing store where I absentmindedly buy an extra-girly '50s ballgown of pink chiffon. On the way home I stop at a beauty supply store for eye shadow, mascara, and a shade of blue-based pink lipstick that makes me think of Swinging London. I remember Lance Loud from *An American Family* saying he thought he was more interesting than his friends because he wore silver nail polish and so I pick up some of that too. The woman behind the register doesn't even blink when she sees my purchases so I don't bother with my cover story that the make-up is for my bedridden sister.

Back at the apartment I spend the balance of the afternoon painting a pair of old Converse sneakers day-glo green accented with meaningless yellow hieroglyphics, then dress up in my new duds. I look like a butch Cyndi Lauper. I love the way the tulle swirls around me as if I was standing waist deep in a pink cloud. I decide against falsies since I'm not trying to look female, just fabulous. Then I paint my face, loving the way my eyelashes get all Tony Curtisy with the mascara. I'm doing my nails when Colin comes in.

"Work was gruesome today," he says. "Really ghastly."

"How long does it take nail polish to dry?" I ask.

"Oh, fifteen minutes, half an hour. We had to throw out this drunk who peed his pants. It was so disgusting I had to take an extra twenty from the till to compensate for my emotional distress."

"Half an hour! If they can send a man to the moon why can't they develop nail polish that dries right away?"

"Because men control all the research money and men don't wear nail polish."

"I'm a man," I say, eager to puncture Colin's know-it-allness.

"The sort of men who control the research money," he sighs.

I examine myself in the mirror. "Hmmm," I say aloud, broadcasting my indecision. Colin mutely lies on his bed and starts reading a basketball magazine. While being careful not to smudge my nails I put on my newly painted sneakers, some studded leather accoutrements, belts and wristbands, then some day-glo love beads that I always keep around just in case. "Getting there," I say. Colin goes to the fridge and takes out an apple.

"What should I do with my hair?" I ask.

Colin is exasperated. "Since you're obviously dying for me to notice that you're in drag so you can talk about yourself, I suppose I'll offer the obvious advice." He takes a bit of apple and chews it very, very slowly.

"What? What? What?" I beg.

"Put on a wig," he says.

"But I don't have a wig."

"Then a hat."

"Don't have a lady's hat."

"Here," says Colin, handing me a silver metallic scarf from a pile of clothes near his bed. "Wear this around your head." I try to wrap it like a turban, but the result looks ludicrous. "Oh, let me do it," he commands, staring at my head like a sculptor staring at a block of marble. Then, in an instant, he's wrapped the scarf just right—once around and tied in back so that it falls *just so*. Best of all, a tuft of my hair poufs out on top like Ari Up from the Slits.

"Thanks," I say. "So you think I make a good transvestite?"

"Please, you're a drag queen, not a transvestite."

"What's the difference?" I ask.

"If you put on make-up with your fingers, you're a drag queen."

"OK, do I make a good drag queen?"

"Fair."

"I'm going to the Slot. Wanna come?"

Colin looks at his magazine, looks at me, back at the magazine. "Oh, I suppose," he says, though I notice him stuff the magazine in the pocket of his coat before we leave.

To avoid death at the hands of the militantly intolerant and unfashionable we take a taxi to the bar. The place is practically empty, but I still manage to slip into a dark corner unseen by either the bartender or Rex, who's running around half-naked and perfect as usual, his fat-free body glistening slightly under the dim lights as he hauls around a box of Millers. As Colin orders us drinks the bartender catches sight of me. Fortunately, instead of throwing me out for violating the dress code he rolls his eyes like, kids will be kids. This is all the encouragement I need. I run up to the jukebox and put on the Thompson Twins' "In the Name of Love" and run back to the shadows. Colin has started in on the peanuts. "Here, Sugar. They didn't have any strawberry daiquiris so I got you a beer."

"Sugar?"

"You need a girl name. All gay men used to have girl names, not just drag queens. You know, before liberation." The way he says "liberation" makes it sound like a Veg-o-matic or an electric toothbrush, something you're supposed to want but can't quite work up the desire for. "You look like a Sugar."

"You should be Judy," I say. "Like Judy Jetson, Judy Garland, or Judy Holiday."

"I can live with that," says Judy.

A few minutes later my song comes on. Going to the middle of the bar where a light illuminates me like a spot, I dance and lip synch to the anguished, lovelorn lyrics. Rex manages to continue with his duties in every part of the bar without glancing my way. Fun, fun, fun! Finally, as the song ends, I leap in front of him.

"Haven't seen you around, baby," I purr, wishing I had a better line prepared.

"Been busy," Rex mumbles.

Now I'm starting to feel the Hollywood sex-kitten magic, to really get into my role. "You never even said good-bye. What kind of way is that to treat a boy?" Even in the dress and make-up I'm pretty androgynous so I keep the masculine pronoun. "I've missed you, baby." I decide I like calling guys "Baby."

"You know..." He looks around the bar. The half-dozen customers are ignoring us but his bartender buddy is enjoying my little scene.

"No, baby, I don't know. Why didn'tcha ever call? Don'cha like me?

"I... I met someone else." He clearly just wants this to end. Suddenly I catch sight of myself in the mirror behind the bar. I look really, really good, not in a passing or a sexy way, but definitely like someone who could be hanging out in a fashion forward club in London. *ID* magazine-worthy.

"Well, I just wanted to kiss you good-bye. Would you let me do just that one little thing, baby? Just one little kiss as a favor to me?" The look on his face is easily worth the money I spent on getting dressed up and taking the taxi. "One itsy, bitsy little kiss?"

Rex leans back, away from what he clearly considers a fate worse than death, but says nothing. As I plant a big, juicy, Technicolor kiss right on his lips I pull him against me so that he can feel my hard boy body against his and maybe, just a little bit, remember me and miss me. He stays rigid for a moment, then I feel him soften, get into it. It becomes a real kiss. That's all I wanted. I let him go. "Bye, Rex," I say in my normal voice as I turn on my heel and march away.

Colin is pretending to read his basketball magazine. "I'd like to go now," I say.

"Sure," he says, stuffing the magazine in his pocket as we march out the door.

"I wanna go dancing. Since I'm all gussied up."

"Let's," says Colin.

Later, on the dance floor, the music is great: the preternaturally perky "Beat The Clock" by Sparks, the madly Teutonic arias of Klaus Nomi, the anthemic "Don't You Want Me" by The Human League, the cold metallic mockery of "Money" by the Flying Lizards. When "In The Name of Love" comes on, Colin picks me up swirls me around with a big smile on his face. Score one for The Plan!

A Rural Escapade

I'm wedged into a seat next to Colin on a bus whizzing down the highway. I look up from my magazine to gaze out the window. I behold cows spotted like Dalmatians grazing on the lush green carpet of grass that extends as far as the eye can see, a few majestic old trees rustling in the cool spring breeze, a red barn is perched jauntily on a hilltop; all the usual disturbingly alien and slightly sinister sights of the countryside. These people probably all voted for Reagan, I think as we pass through a small Connecticut town. They probably all hate homosexuals and blame their problems on Jewish bankers and Negroes. I don't like leaving the city, but duty calls. I'm to provide moral support for Colin while he attends his Uncle Mike's funeral.

"We should be there in twenty minutes," says Colin grimly. He takes a morose bite out of a candybar and chews it slowly, like a condemned man savoring his last dessert, then looks over at me. "God, why did you have to bleach your hair? You look so fruity."

"Are your parents going to, I don't know, say anything?" I ask.

Colin gets testy. "Of course not. Just because they're not rich like your parents doesn't mean they're ignorant and bigoted."

"I never said they were," I say. "And my parents aren't rich." I suspect the fact that I'm out to my parents while Colin isn't bothers him. In his mind, he's the brave iconoclast while I'm the whimpering play-it-safe type.

"You're such an elitist," snarls Colin. "My parents voted for McGovern. They read books."

"OK, OK," I say, wishing I didn't sound so defensive.

"My dad even met Tallulah Bankhead," he adds, slyly proud.

I try to be agreeable. "She was an actress, right?"

"Are you sure you're gay?" he asks.

"I'm only nineteen," I protest. "I haven't had time to memorize the name of every single Hollywood actress who was ever fabulous."

"Well, you'd better hurry up, you're not getting any younger. Anyway, Tallulah Bankhead was a witty alcoholic bisexual actress who loved gay men, a real fag hag. My dad met her during the war when he was in the army and hung out with her at some club."

"Wow."

"I used to wonder if they ever slept together, 'cause my dad is really handsome, but now I wonder if he wasn't, you know, a little bit..." Colin wiggles his hand in the universally known sign for gay. He sighs and goes back to his magazine.

Soon I'm staring out the window at the outskirts of Colin's hometown. A thin film of grime and hopelessness covers the buildings, none of which display much of New England's highly touted quaintness. As we pull into the downtown area I notice that all the people on the streets are fat. How did skinny Colin emerge from such a porky town?

"Hey, Colin, look how fat everybody is."

"Yeah." He thinks a moment. "Maybe that's why there are so many pederasts here. Everyone over twenty's lost their sex appeal by blimping out."

"Pederasts?"

"The place is crawling with them."

I look to see if anyone on the bus has heard us. I don't want them to think *we're* pederasts and put us in stockades or stone us in the town square. Nobody is looking our way so I assume we're safe. "How do you know there are so many pederasts?" I whisper.

"You can't be a cute kid here without all the solid citizens trying to fiddle with you," announces Colin in a voice that's entirely too loud. The bus pulls into the station's parking lot. "Welcome to Peyton Place."

Colin's dad, a tall but collapsed looking man, is waiting inside. I can't imagine Mr. O'Malley drinking with Tallulah Bankhead, though he is wearing a fedora as if it was 1949 or something.

"Heya Colin!" he calls out. They shake hands and then I'm introduced. We trade pleasantries as a beat-up stationwagon carries us through streets of shabby homes, vacant lots, boarded-up stores, and squalid warehouses. Small gaggles of children play ball in the streets or loaf insolently. I try to imagine Colin amongst them, a flamingo in a dog kennel. Soon enough we're at the door of the O'Malley's house. I feel a surge of excitement. This is where he comes from.

"Hello?" A timid voice comes from the kitchen followed by its owner: a small, wrinkly woman drying her ruddy hands on a grayish apron. She lights up with a crinkly smile and hugs Colin. I say hello and express my condolences on her brother's death.

"He's gone to a better place," she says with unfeigned Roman Catholic conviction. I get the creepy feeling I used to get as a child when I ate dinner at the houses of friends who prayed before their meal. My own family was decidedly atheistic, and I always secretly worried that their deity would turn out to really exist and decide to cripple or blind me for my insolent irreligiosity. "Now you boys go and wash up, supper's about ready." She turns to me. "Colin's brothers arrive tomorrow but they'll be staying at my sister's, so you'll have the boys' bedroom all to yourselves."

I follow Colin up the stairs, down the hall and into a room with three beds and dressers. It's small, I think, as I set my overnight bag on the floor. How did three tall boys ever fit in here?

"You take that bed, this one's mine." Colin flops down on his old bed. His old bed! I feel the same tingly pins-and-needles on my scalp as when encountering ancient artifacts in museums. But none of them—not the eerie and majestic Indian totem poles, not the spooky, giant Olmec stone head that gave me nightmares for a week, not even the mysterious and probably-still-living-but-in-a-state-of-suspended-animation Egyptian mummies—affected me as much as Colin's childhood bed. I know I could die happily right now and here if I could just lie on it with Colin and have him hold me in that most sacred of all human spaces.

"So, this is your room..."

"Was."

"Was," I echo as I look out the window at the leaves of a maple tree. I recall my own childhood, how I'd stare out the window and see shapes in the leaves the way other people always do with clouds.

"I'll be back," says Colin springing up and taking a towel from a pile on top of his dresser. I hear the shower through the thin walls as I snoop around the room. Archetypically boyish pictures adorn the walls: basketball players, a rocket ship. The closet is crammed with boxes which I don't dare open for closer examination, though I'd love to. An odd, musty smell in the room reminds me of summer camp. Is it mothballs? Rotting wood? I imagine myself as a child coming over to play. That would be the best, just to be Colin's friend as a kid. His only and bestest friend. "Wanna play at my house?" he'd ask after school, all TV child sweetness and enthusiasm. "Sure!" I'd say, exuding the same adorable innocence. We'd come here, sit on the bed and play Monopoly, or else it'd be a sleepover. His brothers would be away, but they'd have insisted that Colin's friends not mess up their beds, so I'd have to stay in his bed. Wearing fresh pajamas we lie together under the woolen blankets, not touching each other, not yet... then Colin would roll over and... my fantasy ends as a damp

Colin tromps into the room. "The bathroom's all yours. First door on your left."

At dinner the conversation is as flavorless as the food. Lots of "and whatever happened to cousin so-and-so" talk. Everyone has married and produced children, moved from one town to another, or been laid-off from the plant. Now and again Mrs. O'Malley sighs and says something meant to be comforting about the death of her brother. "Not three weeks ago he turned to me and he said he'd had a full life and wouldn't mind meeting his maker for a one-on-one, that being the way he was apt to describe a little chat." Or, "No, he wasn't one to want to go on and on just for the sake of it. When he retired he said his work was done and all he wanted was to see a grandchild or two, which thankfully he did."

After the meal Colin's parents go off to his aunt's house and we're left alone with instructions not to touch a single dish in the sink as Mrs. O'Malley will take care of all that when she gets home. "Maybe we should do them," I say, looking at the stacks of plates and pans. "I mean, she is in mourning."

"It's better for people in mourning to have something to do," says Colin walking into the living room and throwing himself down on the sofa. "Oh, I ate too much," he confides, patting his stomach. "Still, there's something comforting about stuffing yourself with bland food."

I look around at the small but tasteful living room full of old dark wooden furniture. One wall is covered with a bookshelf, one has a hi-fi and a ton of records, one has a reproduction of Van Gogh's *Starry Night,* and one has a window looking out onto the barren backyard. "This is nice. The room, I mean."

Colin flares. "Were you expecting plastic knickknacks and pictures of big-eyed children on the wall? Just because my dad worked in a factory doesn't mean we're stupid."

"I didn't say that," I bleat defensively.

"I used to come home after school," says Colin, calming down as quickly as he heated up, "and sit here doing my homework and listening to my brother's show albums."

I twist my face a little in disapproval. "Show albums?" As much as I share the general gay male obsession with old movies and musical theater, I feel that actually listening to show albums is going a bit far.

Colin reads my expression. "Sure, they can be corny, but they're fun. Inspiring even. There's nothing like a musical to make you feel good when the whole world's against you. Let's put something on." He gets up and flips through records. "Here's one, *Applause*. There's this one song, "Alive", that's like the best song ever. Lauren Bacall is Margo Channing; I think I told you the story, didn't I? She's depressed so she goes out with her gay hairdresser and this song..." he stops talking as the music comes on. The throaty voice warbles about being up and down at the same time, feeling partly Jane Fonda and partly Jane Austen, then halfway through, the number turns into a bombastic go-go freak out. Colin starts doing the Monkey so I leap up and Frug, both of us achieving a soul-refreshing level of frenzy in no time. At the song's conclusion we collapse on the couch.

"That was fab!" I say.

"Ow! I shouldn't have done that on a full stomach," says Colin as he wraps his arms around his midsection.

After a moment's pause, Colin starts lecturing. "There's not much on Broadway these days to get excited about, but in its day that was the music that cut through the everyday and gave you a glimpse of something beyond. Like New Wave is today. It was social commentary and fantasy and transcendent vision all rolled into one." I wonder for the thousandth time where Colin learned to talk like this as he continues. "And all the stars of musical theater had totally over-the-top personalities. Like, there was Ethel Merman..." He gets up to find another album. "Think of it being, like, 1943 and Hitler's conquered half the world, and you're some Rosie the Riveter girl in a factory with your man overseas

in a trench. You need someone to give you the courage to go on..."
He drops the needle on the record and a noise comes out of the
speakers that's more a force of nature than a voice. "There's
nooooo business like shooow business!"

"That's the sound of human courage," says Colin. I listen for
a minute to Ethel. "You can see why they call that sort of singing
belting," says Colin. "It hits you with the force of a belt."

"Wow," I say.

Colin hands me the album cover with a picture of big, ballsy
Ethel. "She's about the only singer, male or female, who you could
put in a boxing ring with Mussolini and be fairly certain that she'd
come out the champ."

"She'd rip his head off," I agree, imagining the fight in my
mind's eye and especially relishing the triumphant yodel coming
from Ethel as she holds aloft Il Duce's neatly severed noggin.

Colin leads me on a brief tour through two more musicals,
Annie Get Your Gun and *Gypsy*. I can't believe I've survived for
nearly two decades without these uplifting masterpieces. I'm
ready for more. "What about these?" I ask, holding aloft *The King
and I* and *Finnian's Rainbow*.

"They're good too," says Colin, "but I need a drink." He gets
up and starts searching through the kitchen cabinets. "Nada. We'll
have to go out. There's this one bar in the hotel the next town
over, and when I was at the Community Theater they used to say
the actors who were "that way" hung out there and met older
gentlemen. Theater aficionados." The way he says "aficionados"
makes it sound just like sex perverts.

"How do we get there?" I ask.

"We'll hitch."

Though I'd love to be the sort of tough adventurous boy who
thinks nothing of hitchhiking, I've never done such a thing for
fear of being murdered, raped, tortured, dismembered, or worse.
"Are you sure this is safe?" I ask.

"There are no busses at night and we don't have a car. How do you propose we get there? Hire a taxi? Hire a limo?" Colin gives me The Look.

"No," I say in a small voice. Colin gets up and puts on his jacket.

"C'mon, then," he says, opening the door. I haul myself up, grab my jacket and follow him outside. I note that the air smells like rain just as a small drop of water lands on my face.

"Colin?"

He gives me The Look.

"Shouldn't we at least take an umbrella?"

Silence. The Look. More silence.

As I trot alongside Colin I feel another drop, then another. Five minutes later we're in a light drizzle. Still, the magic that is Colin has bled all over his hometown, making everything of interest to me.

"What's that big building?" I ask.

"My high school."

"Wow. It's so... industrial looking. What's that over there?"

"Used to be the rec center. Now it's closed. The town has been dying ever since the layoffs."

"That's too bad."

"No, it's not. Who cares if they close all the factories? I'd rather die than work in one of those places. Literally. They should just close this whole stupid town down and let the Mohicans come back and take over."

"What's that over there?"

"Community Theater building. Oh, my god! See that guy going in there? That's Hank Westfield, king of the drama queens. I can't believe he's still here. Probably working in his dad's clothing store, doing Community Theater on the weekends, and blowing the interns. What a loser." I crane my neck to see this specimen of small town loserdom and am rewarded with the sight of a nondescript guy in his mid-twenties wearing icky beige slacks and a pink sweater.

"How can he be in the closet if he's wearing a pink sweater?"

"Small town closet queens never fool anyone. They just keep up the act so people won't have to talk about it and get uncomfortable. I mean, even if he didn't have a pink sweater on everyone would know."

"How?" I ask. "Telepathy?"

Colin raises his eyebrows to indicate his annoyance with having to explain this perfectly obvious point. "Anyone can tell if someone wants to have sex with them just by looking in their eyes, even straight guys. The first thing the human animal asks when it sees another human animal is, does it want to hurt me? The next question is, do I want to fuck it?

"I don't think all that!" I protest.

"Sure you do," says Colin. "Unconsciously. And there's no hiding your sex drive. Oh look! There's the church my family went to. What a dump."

After another five minutes, kept lively by Colin's descriptions of his miserable hometown, we reach a freeway on which there are no cars. According to a luminescent clock in the window of a nearby dry-cleaning establishment I see that it's nine o'clock. "Hey, don't you think it's a little late to..." I'm stopped by The Look. Colin sticks out his thumb. As if on cue, a burst of thunder announces the arrival of a truly awesome storm and we're pelted with cold rain. Lesser people, I think, would suggest that Colin turn back at this point. I, however, am ahead of this game. If he wanted to turn back he would, so if I suggest it he'll snap at me. I'll keep my mouth shut.

Three minutes later I begin to whine. "Can't we go back? I'm soaked. You're soaked. There's nobody out here. It's cold." Colin doesn't even bother with The Look, just pretends he doesn't hear me. I repeat my whine at five-minute intervals, timed by the clock in the dry cleaners, until 9:30. Colin, I think, is incontrovertibly insane. I should call a policeman and beg him to take me back to the house so I can pick up my bus ticket and return to civilization. Rather than act on this common sense inclination, I decide to give it ten more minutes, then ten more. Then, miraculously, a huge truck pulls to the side of the road a few yards in front of us and we rush towards the opened door. Colin jumps up onto the step and sticks his head inside to confer with the man behind the wheel: a lean, older man with eyes that have seen woe. After a moment Colin stands aside and gestures for me to get in.

"Hi," I say, feeling as I always do in the presence of blue-collar types, as if I was dressed like a fairy princess from a Victorian production of *Midsummer Night's Dream*. Surely this person, this man, can tell I'm a homosexual and will say something unkind, snub me, push me away, push me out of the truck and onto the road, perhaps while the truck is speeding down the highway at sixty miles an hour.

"Don't you look like you just crawled out of the pond," the man laughs good-naturedly as Colin slides in next to me. "Name's Allen. Good thing I came along here when I did. You sure picked a fine night to go traveling."

"Yeah, you sure did," says Colin turning to me with apologetic, ironic eyebrows. "Whatever could have possessed you to insist we go gallivanting about on a night like this?" Though I'm charmed and amused by Colin's implicit apology, I'm unnerved that he's being such a camp in front of Allen.

"Yeah, what could you have been thinking?" asks Allen, joining right in the game. "'Tis a night not fit for man or beast."

"And try not to drip so much water on the nice man's truck," says Colin.

"On my deluxe interior," says Allen in a mock haughty tone.

"These street urchins have no manners," sighs Colin.

"Nonesuch whatsoever," agrees Allen, still putting on airs.

"Here we are in this gentleman's fine coach..." begins Colin.

"...Delivering highly refined and important vegetables to highly refined and important supermarkets," continues Allen.

"...And you have to go and drip," concludes Colin.

Pause.

"You from 'round here?" asks Allen.

"Me yes, him no," says Colin. "But I got out."

"Good for you!" says Allen with real feeling. "Getting pretty bad around here since the layoffs. Not for me, but I got cousins..." He and Colin proceed to discuss the ailing local economy for the next ten minutes as I, seated between them with just centimeters to spare on either side, try and fail to think of something to say. Finally we pull into a parking lot next to a white-shingled two-story Colonial style house with green shutters and a lawn jockey next to the door. "Nice meetin' you boys," says Allen with a wave as we jump down from his truck.

Moments later we're basking in the warmth of an overly charm-laden dining room. Though the place is three-quarters full of affluent middle-aged diners, it's unnervingly quiet.Against the wall to our right is a long bar at which sits one tweedy man staring into space. Colin and I slosh our way over and, at my suggestion, order hot buttered rums. Colin goes off to the boys' room and I surreptitiously take stock of our fellow patron, trying to determine if this extraordinarily ordinary man could be a closeted small town homosexual. He sighs (frustrated and forlorn: probably gay), eats a salted peanut (not watching his figure: probably straight), looks at his watch (no limp wrist: straight), stands (nothing to go on here), throws a few dollars on the counter without hardly looking at them (spends money ostentatiously: probably gay), and walks off (no wiggling hips: straight). The entertainment is over.

"Gee, and we came all this way," says Colin, returning to his seat.

"And how are we going to get home?" I wonder aloud.

Colin starts to give me The Look but stops as he catches sight of a small stone fireplace in the middle of the wall facing us containing a cheerful little blaze. "Ooh, that looks cozy," he declares, marching through the center of the room, ignoring the tiny stares and glares from the eerily silent diners. I want to follow, but can't. Surely if we make a spectacle of ourselves by standing (and dripping) in the center of the room we'll be shown the door by an officious hotelier.

"C'mon!" calls out Colin.

I join him by the fire. "You can't yell across the dining room," I whisper.

"What?" asks Colin in a voice that I'm sure is deliberately just a tad too loud.

"Shush," I whisper.

Colin leans over mock-arthritically so that his ear is inches away from my mouth. "Aye? You'll have to speak up, sonny, I can't hear so good these days!"

"Colin!" I whisper/scream.

"Hey," says Colin pointing towards the bar where two men, both about thirty, WASPily good-looking and wearing expensive suits, are taking seats. "One for you and one for me."

"They're not my type," I sniff.

"Beggars can't be choosers."

"Who says I'm begging?" I ask.

"Well, you want to get laid..."

"So what? Nineteen-year-olds always want to get laid. It's biological."

"I bet you never made it with a real preppy," says Colin.

"I'm sure I have," I say, "somewhere, sometime."

"I don't mean some backroom tryst. I mean going to their little white clapboard house and meeting the golden retrievers. The whole experience. Preppies are wild in bed. It's all that money."

Unsure if I'm being teased, I remain silent.

"You take the one on the left," says Colin.

"They're not exactly cruising," I point out.

"This is not Greenwich Village. You don't 'cruise' here. You actually have to speak to people and have conversations. You're just like some randy old dog." I fervently wish Colin would lean to lower his voice. "C'mon." He walks over to the bar. I have no choice but to follow.

Colin is about to take a seat next to our quarry when the pair of them look up and the one on the right says, "Hey girls!" I can feel myself blush crimson. Even the unflappable Colin is clearly taken aback.

"My word, it's pouring out there," says a female voice coming from behind us. Colin and I turn and see a pair of expensively dressed women slide up against the men, who are clearly their dates or husbands. "Time to build the ark and start rounding up the animals," jokes the other woman as the four of them all laugh politely.

"All right," says Colin. "It's getting late. Let's get one more drink then go."

"Do we really need another drink?" I ask.

The Look. Colin settles in at the bar and suddenly unleashes a torrent of charming blarney, weaving a fantastic tale of what my life would have been like had I grown up here instead of crazy California (I'd have graduated high school early and be at Harvard studying economics, but still be a closeted virgin). Then Colin tells me about the neighbors he had while growing up: the woman who wore muumuus and started drinking at brunch; the grade school teacher arrested for shoplifting tomatoes; the man who went insane and ate his dog (or so the older kids said).

Two drinks later a quaint grandfather clock chimes 11:30 and we head outside where the wind roars dully and the rain has gotten cold enough to feel like little slivers of glass or tiny frozen bullets. We walk to the edge of the parking lot and cower under the one street lamp that illuminates a small patch of slick highway and wait silently. All around us are forests. I've always been terrified of forests at night, believing them to be the preferred hiding place of psychopathic murderers and malevolent supernatural beings, so I keep a sharp lookout for any pairs of eyes that may gleam or glow out at us from the dense flora. Mercifully the were-ghouls and deranged veterans of my nightmares are otherwise occupied and leave us unmolested. After half an hour, during which time several clumps of people from the restaurant leave, giving us tiny concerned looks as they pass Colin's outstretched thumb, the establishment closes.

"Owwww," I whine. Just then one of the waiters emerges from the Inn and unlocks his car. Colin runs up to him and says something, then waves me over. The waiter, cute but unquestionably straight, barely says a word as he gives us a ride all the way back to the doorstep of Colin's parents' house. While we're walking from the curb to the door the rain lets up and a tiny patch of sky peeks through the clouds, allowing a brilliant moon to shine down prettily.

Colin waxes philosophical. "Nobody can say we don't try to have fun, that we don't put any effort into our partying. I think we made a heroic attempt tonight. Truly heroic."

I give him The Look.

The next morning I wake up to find myself alone. A note on Colin's bed explains that the family is off at the funeral, they didn't want to wake me, and won't I help myself to breakfast? Quickly I shower, dress, chomp my cereal, and begin an exhaustive snoop of the premises. The closet in Colin's room: boxes of old toys, board games. Hall closet: towels and linens. Girl's bedroom: horse pictures, more toys. Master bedroom: dull as dishrags. Downstairs mystery room: sewing machine and cot (presumably for when someone was too drunk to make it up the stairs). Downstairs closet: ashtrays, candles, tablecloths, and finally, gold: a family album.

Decades' worth of photos show worn people with pale, resigned faces and thin, angry lips imprisoned in claustrophobic black and white snapshots. Colin's birth (or is it Postwar Prosperity?), however, works a miracle. Smiles creep onto people's faces. Drab clothes give way to colors and prints. Space opens up around the slightly less defeated looking relatives as they smile at me from their backyard barbecues and baby showers. Photos taken in the '60s show Colin as a mischievous redheaded imp, but I'm most transfixed by the shots taken in the '70s. They show the angelic teenage Colin, a boy whose mind is clearly in the heavens.

Was Colin really such an angel or was that just the power of his beauty? Could anyone be as wonderfully pure as he looks in these pictures? He doesn't seem angelic now. Even when he's in a good mood, he's sort of bitter. And when he gets angry, which he does a lot, he's devilishly cutting and cruel. Unfortunately, the last few years are missing from the photographic record, so I can't see the transformation from angel Colin to the Colin I know. Where did all that anger come from? What happened? I only have a minute to run over the clues in my mind before I hear a car drive into the garage. I stash the album back in the closet and dash to the kitchen. Colin and his parents troop in gloomily to find me at the sink washing my bowl. An hour later we leave.

I hate to talk about it while we're sitting on the bus, but I can't help myself. "When you said that about the pederasts," I say in a voice somewhere between a whisper and a murmur, "that they won't leave a kid alone, did you mean that somebody, anybody, did anything like that to you?"

Colin looks at me searchingly for just a second. Is he wondering if I can be trusted? Then he twists his face into a familiar expression of cynical exasperation. "I had to fend off my share of advances."

"Did anyone ever get away with anything?" I ask.

"Not really," says Colin, his face looking less composed. "Nothing much."

"Then what exactly?" I ask.

"None of your business," says Colin acidly. He turns away from me to stare at some fascinating cow pastures.

I want to ask who it was, if it hurt, if he told anyone, how it felt, if there's anything I can do, but I know he won't answer.

From Chicken to Beef

We're back in the city, lying on our respective beds reading when the alarm rings, an odd thing for it to do given that it's 10 p.m., but then Colin is prone to nothing if not oddity.

"What's that for?" I ask.

"We're doing acid," announces Colin, reaching into his shirt pocket, removing a few small squares of paper that he divides evenly, "and we're going to The Saint. It's a membership-only club for older disco guys, but Varlena's dating some guy who got us passes. You could get lucky and meet a sugardaddy, so wear something young looking."

Alert to the tragic fleetingness of my youth, I dress in my extra-New Wave best. As we walk through the cool spring night the acid hits, transforming the familiar streets of the Village into an unearthly landscape. By the time we make it through the front door of the club I'm light years away. Physical space becomes fluid or irrelevant and mixes into the velvety folds of time. It's like living inside a choppy movie montage. Inside, surrounded by a sea of clones, I discover a spaceship. I stare at it for years (it's the first space ship I've ever seen) till Colin becomes concerned. "Snap out of it. Stop staring at the light machine."

I'm surprised that light comes not from the sun but from a machine in a lower Manhattan discotheque. Later (before, suddenly, then, now, who knows?) I'm on the dance floor. Though I've forgotten how to use my limbs, I manage to sway to the music a bit, careful not to fall into any black holes or time warps.

"You're sooo out of it," observes Colin, staring into my eyes with concern. "Do you feel all right?"

I look around me. I'm in a frosty white tank. A word insinuates itself where my mind used to be. Bathroom.

"Are you all right?" Colin repeats. Though speech is beyond me, I manage to nod yes. I note that Colin, even though his face is a mask, is incredibly handsome. I feel a magnetic attraction emanating from my sternum, pulling me towards him. Doesn't he feel it? He must!

The bathroom door swings open and Varlena slinks in. "Hey boys!" she sings out gaily. A tired muscle-preppy at the sink rinsing the sweat off his gleaming tanned torso glares and hisses snake-like. Varlena doesn't notice. "Like my new outfit?" She has on a purple spandex unitard that leaves one shoulder bare, and a short black cape. "I just finished it." She twirls around like a movie star.

"Incredible," says Colin.

"Uh, great out looking... look out... fit look..." I give up.

"I think I gave him too much acid," confides Colin.

"I been there, honey," says Varlena, putting a hand on my arm. I notice she has silver nail polish on as she squeezes my bicep a little. "That's a fabulous bracelet!" She's eyeing my three-tiered, studded leather wristband.

"It's yours," says Colin, unfastening it from my arm.

"I couldn't!" Varlena laughs.

"Take it," says Colin, holding the wristband out to Varlena.

"Are you sure?" asks Varlena, delightedly looking from Colin to me and back again.

"Sure!" announces Colin. I stare at my naked wrist, speechless.

Varlena puts my fabulous accessory on her own skinny wrist and holds it up for us to admire. "It works perfectly with this outfit!" she squeals as yet another muscle-preppy comes into the bathroom and glares.

That cost fourteen dollars! objects some subterranean part of my brain that can still articulate. That man is staring at us as if we were street trash. Colin doesn't love you. The toilets can breathe. Your arm looks under-accessorized. If you don't watch it, the grid pattern from the floor tiles will consume the universe.

"You better take him out of here," suggests Varlena to Colin, looking at me with what might be pity. "He looks a little panicked."

"Back to the dance floor," commands Colin, his hand on my shoulder guiding me out of the bathroom.

By the time we get home the next morning, sequential time and contiguous space have returned. I'm relieved at the orderliness of existence, but truly devastated by my loss.

"How, how, how could you just give Varlena my studded leather wristband? And by the way, I'm sick of you telling me what to wear and what drugs to take and who to have sex with."

"You're just mad because you want to have sex with me. Your petty little ego can't take rejection. And anyway, who gave you the acid last night? Who got you into the club?"

"There's this little thing called private property, a quaint custom we follow here in America..."

"No wonder you don't have any friends. You're so selfish."

"What do you mean, I don't have any friends?"

"You have one dopey girl you listen to records with. And me. And I don't know that I even want to be friends with someone who's so attached to things." The way he says "things" makes it sound like I'm suffering from an obsessive need to collect used napkins or hassocks. I know that Colin isn't attached to things. He'll give away whatever he has without a second thought. When it comes to shopping he'll spend his last penny without thinking, but if he can't afford something it doesn't pain him. He only works jobs that entertain him; the pay is irrelevant. There are no profit and loss statements in his world. I love him for this, for being the opposite of the dull, greedy, lifeless suburban world I grew up in and which rejected me like a bad loan. But on the other hand, MY STUDDED LEATHER WRISTBAND!

"You have to buy me another one and say you're sorry."

Colin smirks. "The only things I *have* to do are stay queer and die."

"Fine. I will never do your laundry for you again. I will never lend you money again. I will never speak to you again."

"You're such a little drama queen. You owe me for all the effort I put into making you into a human being instead of a cringing, whimpering virgin." The way he says "virgin" makes it sound absurd, like flagpole sitter or Popsicle stick collector. "You should pay me to put up with you," he concludes.

"Leave the apartment this instant!" orders Gramma Bea. "And don't forget to hold your head up high." I look at the door but can't walk through it.

"Socialism means collective ownership of the means of production, not studded leather wristbands," observes Nana Leah. "Though why you would want such a thing, I have no idea."

As if by instinct, I pick up a shoe throw it at our full-length mirror, which shatters loudly. I turn to Colin, suddenly aware, and strangely proud of, the tears in my eyes. "I hate you!"

"Bravo! Bravo! Fabulous performance." Colin claps his hands slowly then puts on a deep, awards ceremony announcer voice. "I think we can safely predict a new addition to the Rabinowitz household, and his name is... Oscar!"

It's late at night and I'm bouncing along the sidewalk, wondering as I often do at the miracle of Colin. My mind has me lying naked in his embrace, our tongues engaged in a wrestling match, when back in the real world a large hand (not my own) tries to shove into my front pocket.

"Eek!" I squeal, immediately dismayed that I've expressed my panic in the manner of a cartoon lady confronted with a mouse. "Help!" I cry out in a lower register as my body, thankfully acting of its own accord and oblivious to its public image, hurls itself away from my attacker and against the brick wall of a building. The hand, I now see in the sickly yellow streetlight, belongs to an extremely tall man dressed in filthy rags.

"Ha, ha," chuckles my assailant, who is red-eyed and clearly stoned and/or drunk, as he stands in front of me and ineffectually tries again to fit his huge hands into the pockets of my skin-tight Levis. He can't. They're so tight even I have trouble getting my wallet out. Painted on, as they say. I scream bloody murder and the mugger takes a step back. I scream again. He makes a disapproving face and ostentatiously puts his hands on his ears like a bad actor miming out, "Too loud."

Before I know it, I'm pushing past him to get away. He grabs my shoulders and I can smell his rank sixteen-days-without-washing odor. I pull away and run, run, run, endangering my life on several occasions as I ignore red lights in order to put more distance between myself and the grim specter of death. Six blocks later I stop for breath, turn back, and can't see my assailant.

As I pant, Nana Leah appears. "Poor man. He may be a social parasite, but only because he's been crushed by capitalism. I feel sorry for him." For a moment I try to imagine the fleabag single room occupancy hotel the man would live in. Yellowing walls. A single bare mattress, a broken sink, a dresser. Would he have a dresser, or only a paper bag on the floor with more filthy rags in it?

Gramma Bea turns up as well. "Jeremy dear, if you must prowl about at night at least keep yourself to the better-traveled streets."

"You could carry a gun for protection," suggests Nana Leah. "Then when the revolution comes you could use it to..."

"Oh, tommyrot," harrumphs Gramma Bea.

"In the Soviet Union there is no crime," says Nana Leah.

"In the Soviet Union there's nothing to steal," says Gramma Bea.

The two of them glare at each other as I, suddenly famished, dash into a deli for a cheese stollen (like a Danish but much better). When I emerge I find that they're both mercifully gone. Do other people have to live with ancestral specters like this? If they do, why don't they ever mention it? Sometimes, I'm not exactly sure what I think because I'm so busy sorting out what they think. That can't be good, but on the other hand, if they disappeared, I know I'd feel lonely.

There's never enough work at the messenger service and I fill the time between deliveries by reading. Colin has no end of literary suggestions (issued like commands): Christopher Isherwood's *Goodbye to Berlin*; the short stories of Tennessee Williams and Flannery O'Connor; *Maiden Voyage* by Denton Welch; *Midnight Cowboy* by James Leo Herlihey; James Kirkwood's *Good Times/Bad Times*; Mary McCarthy's *The Group*; the list goes on and on. After I've finished each of these, he grills me to make sure I've understood the work correctly, which is to say, I agree with him about its merits and message.

Money is tight, and my addiction to novels becomes a slightly obsessive means of avoiding worry as well as a time killer. The moment I arrive at the dispatcher's office I bury my nose in a book. This perplexes my colleagues who use their own down time to smoke or discuss sports and girls. "You reading for school or something?" asks Roscoe.

"Nope, just for fun," I say tersely, not wanting to explain that when I stop reading I start panicking.

One day I'm asked to pick up a delivery from a clothing manufacturer. The office is just off a vast, noisy, over-bright room full of women hunched over sewing machines. After I grab the manila envelope I run out with the same reflex that would pull my hand off a hot stove. Nana Leah, I know, worked in hellholes like this for fifty years. I wouldn't last a single week in such a place. Physical exhaustion and boredom would combine to kill me.

And how much better is this messenger job that doesn't pay enough to live on? And what happens when my parents retire and can't help me out? And what if I got sick or was in an accident and couldn't work? And what if there were a depression and I couldn't get a job? My mind fills with images of breadlines, riots, people sleeping in cardboard boxes, doctors sadly shaking their heads as they draw starched white sheets over the faces of the recently expired. For the first time ever, I wish I was back in California. That would be safe, I think, except for the earthquakes.

While my mind is busy spinning out worst-case scenarios, a bus smooshes my bike against a parked car. I'm not hurt, but the handlebar is pretzelized and the front wheel locks. I walk the bike back to the office where Greg barks that repairs will be paid for out of my wages. "Robber barons!" declares Nana Leah. "You should organize the workers. Get the company to cover the repair cost."

"This is just how they do things," I explain.

"When I started out working in the garment trade, not only did they pay us by the piece, they made us pay for our own needles. We worked twelve hours a day and half-day Saturdays and only earned enough to live six to a room and eat soup and bread. Then you know what happened?"

"What?"

"We organized!"

"You mean a union?"

"Exactly, The International Ladies Garment Workers Union. When I was fifteen years old, there was a huge strike. It wasn't easy, we didn't always have food even, but eventually we got some of the progressive press and politicians on our side. Louis Brandeis was called in to arbitrate. Later he was a Supreme Court justice. It was Brandeis who negotiated the protocols of peace. You probably learned all about this in school, right?"

"No," I admit.

"Bourgeois school systems!" snorts Nana Leah. "Well, we were still underpaid and overworked. But the Protocols laid the groundwork for all our future gains by giving us the right to collective bargaining. By the time I retired we had the eight-hour day, an end to piecework, and even a few benefits. Individually, workers are at the mercy of the boss. Together with your coworkers, you have some power."

"So what would I do?"

"Discuss the situation with the other messengers. Ask them if they've ever thought about a union. Talk it up."

"Half the guys barely speak English."

"I worked with women who spoke Rumanian, Russian, Yiddish, Turkish, you name it. When your life depends on it, you find a way to communicate. See if any existing unions are interested in helping out. Sometimes they'll give you pamphlets and legal advice. But find a progressive union, not one full of class collaborators. A lot of union leaders get paid off or go soft, start siding with capital. They tell you to be patient. No wildcat strikes. No militancy. No revolution. You'd make your grandmother very proud if you organized a union. Think about it." She evaporates.

The next day I call in to work and give notice. Maybe I could find a way to communicate with my coworkers if my life depended on it, but it doesn't.

The phone rings.

"You've got to get the new James White and the Blacks album. He does a cover of "Heat Wave" that's unbelievable!" says a wound-up Sheila. "Promise me you will get this album."

"Sure, sure," I say. I'm depressed and not in the mood for too much enthusiasm. "What's up?"

Her musical edict imparted, Sheila's voice relaxes. "Jordanelle just took me on a carriage ride in Central Park, of all the hokey things, but it was so fun!"

"How nice for you."

"I honestly think he's the man for me. It's like having a best girlfriend and boyfriend all rolled up in one. We can trade clothes *and* have great sex."

This is more interesting. "Do tell."

"He's into all sorts of role-playing: mommy/daughter, lady acrobat and bearded lady (for when he doesn't shave), and my personal favorite, lesbian golfers."

"You're very, very lucky," I say, jealously. "Doesn't it bother you that he's so old?"

She ignores my dig. "And I really respect his jewelry. It's not hippie dippy craftsy stuff. It's elegant, though mostly nothing I'd wear. Plus he makes a lot of money from it."

"How much money?" I ask, wondering why don't I know how to do anything.

"I don't know exactly, but he take me out to eat all the time at nice restaurants. I think he misses Australia. He's always talking about it. He says maybe he'll take me there. I don't know though, the bands from down there are so lame."

"You sound like you're getting married."

"He hasn't mentioned marriage, but he did say he'd like me to have his baby."

"That's disgusting!" I say. "I hope you told him where to get off."

"I think it'd be cute," says Sheila. "Having a baby to dress up."

"Sheila, a baby is not a fashion accessory."

"Yes, it is. Can't you see my little Sheila Jr. in her leopard-print diapers?"

"How do you feel about changing messy diapers?" I ask.

"I hadn't thought of that. You're right, that is totally gross. Maybe I'll skip the kid, or we could adopt one who's already potty trained or something."

"Fine," I say. "You lead a life of domestic bliss and I'll just molder away in damp basements sodomizing strangers and getting V.D."

"What's with you, Jeremy? You lonesome? You need a boyfriend, that's what you need."

"Gee, a boyfriend. Why didn't I think of that? Thanks, Sheila."

"Well, I gotta run. We're going to lunch. Call me later, OK?"

"Auuuugh!" Bubbling with jealousy and self-pity, I head for the International Stud. After an hour of swilling beer and fending off the advances of a man old enough to be my grandfather (why do sixty-year-olds think a bonafide teenager would go home with them just because they buy him a beer?) I head into the back room. It smells like sex and in no time I'm adding to the odor.

A jaw-droppingly perfect fellow approaches me and pulls down his pants revealing his underwear-clad buttocks. How does he keep them so white? Maybe he just bought them today, or maybe he's an underwear model (he's that handsome) and gets dozens and dozens of free pairs. As the man pulls down the exceptionally clean jockeys revealing his flawless posterior, he mutters, "I want you to fuck me."

Maybe he never wears the same pair twice, I conjecture. I recall reading an article that claimed Jerry Lewis never wears a pair of socks twice. I wonder, does he throw them away or give them to the poor? Are there people so poor they'd wear used socks? Well, even I would if they'd been worn by Jerry Lewis.

"Are you gonna fuck this worthless fuckin' whore ass?" asks the underwear model.

"Sure," I say as I wonder if his use of the term "whore ass" means he's a prostitute, or if he really is an underwear model but regards modeling as an inherently prostitute-like activity. The same article revealed that Jerry Lewis is addicted to corn nuts and keeps a fifty-pound bag of them in his car, lest he be caught without them. Suddenly Gramma Bea materializes.

"You know," she says with a dreamy look on her face, "in my day if we loved someone, and they didn't love us, we'd wait for them. Not just weeks, months, or even years, but sometimes a lifetime."

Nana Leah is right behind her. "Enough with your pining and waiting. Marxist-Leninist analysis teaches us that sex isn't that important. It should be like drinking a glass of water, something you do so you can get back to living, back to work, back to revolution."

Gramma Bea sniffs haughtily. "Do you call this," she gestures at the orgy around me, "drinking a glass of water?"

Nana Leah shakes her head. "This, I don't understand."

Gramma Bea fans her face with her frumpy Queen Mum hat as she peers around uncomfortably. "The people here are just as crude and coarse as can be. And the dirt! The walls are..." she runs a white-gloved finger over one and examines it, "...quite disgusting."

"I've worked in factories that make this place look like The Winter Palace," brags Nana Leah. "But still, you'd think Jeremy could find nicer places to socialize."

"Did you try sending Colin flowers?" asks Gramma Bea. "Perhaps a bit of romancing would help him come 'round."

"He's not that kind of a boy," I explain. "He'd think that was corny."

Nana Leah brightens up with a memory. "I didn't fall in love with your grandfather until he showed me what he was made of. It was the strike of '26. The first one after the Party won control of the local chapter of the union. There was a meeting where all the reactionary elements were trying to convince us to settle for arbitration instead of going on strike. Your grandfather got up and started to sing the *Internationale*. Everyone joined in and drowned out the class collaborators. I knew right then I wanted him to be the father of my child."

"So what are you suggesting?" I ask.

"Work for social justice. Then, if he's a real progressive, Colin will respect you."

"Do you think he's a real progressive?" I ask.

"No," says Nana Leah, glancing around the room with a look of pure mortification. "And the sooner you get away from him, and this, the better." She vanishes.

I pull away from the underwear model. He immediately solicits a gargoyle lurking in the corner and I get the sickening suspicion he thought he was degrading himself by having sex with me. I slump up to the bar and order a beer.

Gramma Bea sits down next to me. "You know, I was something of a flapper when I was your age. Oh, you take after me a bit, I'm afraid!" She lets out a little laugh. "Not that I was wanton," she adds, with a quick glance at the back room, "but I was always looking for a bit of fun. I worked as an usherette at a review." Her eyes get all dreamy and she stares off into space as if looking into the past. "I didn't want to marry just yet, though my mother was always warning me about becoming an old maid. I hadn't been there long when your grandfather started courting me at the theater, and though I discouraged him, he wouldn't take no for an answer. This made me nervous. You see, men in those days would assume things about a girl in the theater, even if she were just ushering. Anyway, he was amazingly persistent. He would wait for me to get off work, often as not with flowers, and talk with me as I waited for the trolley. Well, you know how much I love flowers, so finally, after about a month of Sundays, I agreed to meet him for tea.

"What a surprise! Not only did he bring the loveliest violets, he'd remembered my saying I liked poetry and also gave me a book of verse. It turned out that he remembered everything I said, even off-hand comments. I was flattered enough to agree to a dinner date. Before I knew what was happening, there I was holding a bridal bouquet. And do you know, he brought me flowers once a week till the day he died? So, though he wasn't the wealthiest or the wittiest man alive, I grew to love him for his small kindnesses." As she finishes her reminiscence her eyes refocus on me, and she smiles brightly.

"You don't know Colin. He'd never go for any of that old-fashioned stuff."

"How do you know it won't work unless you try?" asks Gramma Bea as she disappears with a wink.

How do I know?

"What's this?" asks Colin, staring at a bouquet of blue daisies sitting in a thrift store vase next to his bed.

"They're for you," I say. "From me."

Colin picks up the card and reads. "My love for you, it springs eternal, so I humbly offer you this present vernal, of my esteem 'tis but a kernel, write 'Jeremy loves me' in your journal." He looks up at me, his face both laughing and scowling with disapproval. "Oh brother! Nice try but I'm allergic to flowers. I'll have to get rid of these right away. Maybe Cliff will want them." He stalks off, carrying the vase as far away from his body as his arms will allow.

"I'm sorry! I didn't know you were allergic!" I call out after him just as I recall that I did know. Moments later I hear the faint sound of laughter coming from Cliff's apartment.

"Surprise!" call out Colin, Barry, Cliff, Jordanelle, Sheila, Eddie, Varlena, and two cute boys I've never seen before as I walk into my apartment.

"What's all this?" I ask.

"Happy birthday!" some of them add by way of explanation.

Being the center of attention has frozen me, but I manage a small "Wow, thanks" as I accept a drink from Barry.

"This here's Tuscaloosa Punch, an old family recipe. Better sip it slow, it knocks Yankees on their asses." Barry stares at me, waiting for a reaction, so I try the punch. It tastes like rubbing alcohol, sugar, Hawaiian Punch, more rubbing alcohol and more sugar.

I manage a "Mmmm."

"So you've hit the big two-oh. It's all downhill from here on in, baby," Barry teases.

"First your vision goes," says Cliff, who's wearing campy, big thick black glasses himself.

"Then you lose your sex drive," says Colin.

"Then you start wearing beige," says Sheila.

"Then your drag makes you look like Milton Berle," says Jordanelle.

"I like older men," says Eddie, lewdly grabbing my privates and giving me a friendly kiss (the first one I've ever received from someone with facial hair... it scratches).

Varlena and the two boys I don't know talk amongst themselves.

"I told everyone to bring booze instead of presents," says Colin. "So there," he points to the top of the fridge on which sits a six-pack of beer, a bottle of cheap champagne, and a half-empty bottle of gin.

"Thanks everybody," I say taking a big swig of Tuscaloosa Punch which I suspect contains the better part of my birthday gin.

"We brought you a present anyway." Sheila hands me the new B-52s album, *Mesopotamia*.

I thank her and put the album on. One of the two mystery boys says, "Turn it up!" so I do and we all have to start dancing except Barry and Jordanelle, who're old.

"Now I like how you've done this place up," says Jordanelle, examining my artwork on the wall. His fingers trace the route of the ghosts, TVs, and spermatozoa swimming in the vortex. His eyes squint appraisingly. "You should be a painter."

"You already live in a filthy garret," says Cliff.

Colin turns to Barry. "Isn't he talented? Look at that, it's as good as anything in a gallery." Does he mean that? He's never said anything nice about my painting before.

"Yeah, it's really great. And to think it was painted by someone so young!" says Barry, fanning himself as if the thought of youth heats him up so much he needs cooling down.

"I'm not so young. Not a teenager anymore," I say sadly, the awful truth of it finally sinking in.

"From chicken to beef," says Eddie.

"So you're like, twenty?" says one of the mystery boys. "I'm twenty."

"So'm I," says the other mystery boy.

"Three twenties," I say, trying to think of how to work this angle into a three-way.

"I'm nineteen," announces Eddie smugly.

"I have an appointment," says Varlena, smoothing her hair in front of the mirror. "Boys?" The mystery boys line up behind her. "Bye-bye, happy birthday, and all that jazz," she shouts over her shoulder in a parody of off-handedness as she marches out into the hallway.

"Yeah, bye," says one of the boys as he shuts the door.

"In the South, somebody would have introduced them," sniffs Barry.

"I fancied the one with the giant mole," says Cliff.

"I thought the one with the puppy eyes was cuter," says Colin.

"They were both cute," I say.

"Dey're stuck-up bitches," says Eddie. "La-dee-dah Fifth Avenue whooores."

"I love the way you Americans pronounce 'whores'," says Jordanelle. "Whooores."

"I don't pronounce it that way," says Sheila. "But then I generally just say 'demimondaine'."

"Dese two ain't no demimondaines, dey're whooores," says Eddie.

"This is sooo colorful!" says Colin, with an ironic eyebrow arch.

Cliff nods his head. "Absolutely. Is somebody taking notes? Will our lives be immortalized?"

"Speaking of immortalizing, you could paint a portrait of us... or me anyway?" says Jordanelle. I could pay you with a bracelet or a necklace."

"Miss Butch Thing doesn't wear jewelry," says Colin.

"Except earrings," Cliff adds.

"And studded leather wristbands." I glare at Colin.

"Do you love this album or what?" Sheila interrupts.

"I wish I had a boyfriend," I say without meaning to.

"What de fuck is dis music?" asks Eddie.

"Honey, if you can't get a boyfriend at twenty it's only 'cause you're being too picky. No offense," says Barry. "And if what I hear about your dick is true, that goes double." I cringe inwardly.

"We're out of gin," says Colin waiving the empty bottle in front of our faces. Clearly someone has been re-spiking the punch.

"Time to take this party to a bar," says Jordanelle.

"We've gotta be gettin' home," says Barry, taking Cliff by the hand.

"What bar?" asks Eddie.

"Boots and Saddles," says Colin.

"Danceteria," I say.

"Yay, dancing!" says Sheila.

"Bye," say Cliff and Barry, each of them kissing one of my cheeks.

"Actually, I got business to attend to," says Eddie. "Plus a proctologist appointment in de morning."

"Ouch," Colin sympathizes.

"Ciao," says Eddie.

"Nobody says 'ciao' anymore," says Sheila after he's left. "It's so seventies."

"The young can be so intolerant," says Colin to Jordanelle.

"Belligerent babies," he replies.

"Don't talk about me in the third person on my birthday!" I command.

"C'mon," says Sheila, pulling on her red leather jacket. Jordanelle heaves his bulky frame up from Colin's bed where he's been sitting and I can see that he's wearing a rather daring micro-mini.

"So how's Davis?" I ask as we all tromp out of the apartment.

"He's got himself a new trophy boyfriend," says Jordanelle as we walk out the door.

"A new one? Was I a trophy boyfriend?" I ask.

"Will you stop talking about yourself!" says Colin. "It's not charming in the least."

I feel my face flush crimson. "Well, so long as he's happy."

Colin is having none of it. "Like you care if that little troll's happy."

"His new boyfriend is pretty dense," says Sheila falling back to walk beside me. "He wants to be a DJ but he only plays disco."

"Heavens, he doesn't play the fashionable music of the moment," says Colin in mock horror. "How could anyone who isn't an up-to-the-second trendoid dare to put a needle on a record. The nerve."

"You sing a different tune when you're out and somebody puts on *I Will Survive* for the six-thousandth time," I note.

"Liking disco instead of New Wave is evidence of a flawed moral system," says Sheila.

"Yeah," agrees Colin, "but not everyone has all the moral education you two do."

"What are you riding them about?" asks Jordanelle.

"I think they should be a little more tolerant of the ignorant masses," explains Colin.

"I don't want to be tolerant," I say, giving myself a birthday indulgence to be bratty.

"Have a drink," says Jordanelle, handing me a beer from the pocket of his white vinyl raincoat.

"Thanks, I'll wait," I say, imagining the long night of dancing before me. "Gee, you guys, this is the best twentieth birthday party ever!"

Walking past the stores selling cheap and irregular clothing on 14th Street, I'm seized with an inspiration. Pushing through the crowds of little ladies I manage to purchase a pair of red satin gym shorts, a feathered roach clip, tube socks, and a way-too-small 'New York is for Lovers' tee shirt. That night I take my purchases and concoct a demented street hustler look to work at The International Stud.

"Charmingly cheap," marvels Colin as I model in the mirror. We arrive shortly after one and I'm gratified to see that I am indeed the hit of the night fashion-wise, though a guy wearing plastic faux-snakeskin bellbottoms gives me a run for my money.

In no time, a raging beauty whose eyes undress what little clothing I have on, starts flirting with me. I want to swoon every time I look at his square dimpled chin, huge eyebrows, and pug nose; an erotic cartoon of a handsome face. "I've seen you before," he whispers conspiratorially, "and I want you inside me." Wow! He takes me to Avenue B where he lives in a pair of rooms, empty but for a single mattress and a small pile of angst-ridden black clothing. As we writhe in ecstasy together I imagine myself as his lover. Coming home to his lean almond-colored body would make existence a perpetual delight. And the way he screams and moans I'd guess that he likes me, too. After several consecutive bouts of carnal frenzy we lie side by side, sweaty and exhausted. He starts to run his hand up and down my right arm admiringly.

"Ooh," he swoons, "your veins, they really pop out. You could shoot up so easy. Do you like heroin?"

I'm too shocked to speak.

"Have you tried it?" he asks.

"No," I say.

"Want to?" he asks.

I briefly consider it. Back in San Francisco, Lizzie's supernaturally gorgeous boyfriend, Wilson, nodded out in our living room a couple times. Lizzie's friends all fawned over him, thinking he was the last word in cool, as he sat slumped there with his mouth half-open in a reptilian coma. What a bore, I'd thought. Still, Colin's heroes all seem to sing or write about heroin. Would he respect me if I had a drug in common with Lou Reed, Jim Carroll, William Burroughs, and Patti Smith? I decide I don't care. They all have a certain ponderous seriousness in their work that's completely at odds with my happy-go-lucky New Wave lifestyle.

"No heroin for me," I say. "I'm too wacky and superficial. But thanks."

"Too bad," he says. "Those veins..." He feathers his fingers up my arm, making it tingle deliciously.

"I better go," I say. We don't trade phone numbers.

A gaggle of African-American teens is lolling about on the stoop next door to my building looking infinitely pissed-off, chewing gum belligerently, and staring bullets at passersby. As is the custom in this great metropolis, I walk by them making no eye contact, hoping and praying to be left alone while taking careful inventory of my shoes. A deep voice bellows, "Hey, what you got on your ear, man?" I pretend not to hear, hoping my posture doesn't betray fear. "That an earring in your ear?" The voice is louder and angrier this time. I fumble with my key. "Faggot!" I hear, just I shut the door behind me. They can't get me in here, but I still don't feel safe. Inside, my grandmothers, who I feel have been spending entirely too much time hanging around lately, are waiting for me.

"Jeremy, darling, do you really feel it's wise to remain in such a dangerous city?" asks Gramma Bea. "It's one thing for the rich who can get about in cabs and live in buildings guarded by doormen, but without money you're awfully vulnerable."

Nana Leah is off on another tack entirely. "I just got back from hearing Gus Hall speak at the Extraordinary Conference of the C.P.U.S.A."

"Communist Party of the U.S.A.," I translate for Gramma Bea, who tosses her hands up and groans.

"According to Gus," continues Nana Leah, whipping out a small manifesto, "we're entering a boomless era of decline and contraction. There is now programmed into the economy a steady decline in the standard of living. Thirty million Americans are without jobs. Added to this is that even when some new job opens up, especially in the new technology industries, robots will take over an increasing number of them. For instance, the Reagan administration is projecting that by 1990, 40 percent of all assembly tasks will be performed by robots. Now, the Communist Party is not against robots..."

"Thank heavens for that," interjects Gramma Bea with a sardonic smirk.

"As long as they are not used against the workers for the sole purpose of maximizing profits," finishes Nana Leah.

"Mustn't maximize any profits," mocks Gramma Bea, agreeably.

Nana Leah continues reading. "Continuous struggle for communist standards and practices is of the utmost importance for assuring victories in the daily class struggle and for advancing socialism. A necessary and correct assessment of the work of our party can be made only if it is viewed as an integral feature and with correct evaluation of the forces, struggles, and movements of the moment."

"Gobbledy-gook," says Gramma Bea, waving her arm as if to shoo away a fly.

Nana Leah goes on. "We are going to fight this corporate blitzkrieg, fight supplyside grand larceny, fight the Maoists as they try to mobilize all the counterrevolutionary trash of the world..."

"Rhetorical drivel and sloganeering," cries Gramma Bea.

Nana Leah puts down her literature and takes my hand. "Jeremy, the point is, the Party needs you. We're in the middle of the biggest upsurge in membership since the Depression. We've consolidated our bases in many of the industrial centers, our influence is growing among intellectuals and professionals..."

Something inside me, perhaps a strong desire to avoid listening to more indecipherable communist propaganda, prompts me to speak to Nana Leah as I never have before. "Nana, I appreciate all you've done, working hard so Dad could go to school and helping unionize the garment workers, but I just don't think I'm ever going to be the communist type."

"What?" asks Nana Leah, bewildered. "What type exactly do you think you are?"

"New Wave," I say without even having to think about it.

"Isn't that the style of music you listen to?" asks Gramma Bea.

"It's not just that," I explain. "It's about not trying to be natural or normal. It's about being unpredictable and fun."

"Bourgeois individualism," says Nana Leah shaking her head.

"Not bourgeois. Bohemian," corrects Gramma Bea.

"The oppressed must rise up against the ruling class or be crushed. Being unpredictable or fun isn't going to put meat on the table, and that's the truth," says Nana Leah.

"Colin says that if you repeat the truth often enough in a pedantic or self-righteous tone it becomes a lie," I say.

"Oy, oy, oy," says Nana Leah.

Having begun, I see no reason to stop. "I also believe in being stylish. Why should things be ugly when they can be Art Deco or Atomic Modern? And all the wrong things are illegal: homosexuality, drugs, prostitution, and nudity should be OK, but sports, guns, fast food, and suburbia should be outlawed."

"So this is your philosophy?" asks Nana Leah.

"It is," I say. "It really, really is."

"I suspect he's quite serious," says Gramma Bea.

Nana Leah stares vacantly, stunned.

"And," I continue, "I believe in musicals, the way the dancing and singing and glitzy outfits make you feel good inside even when everything goes wrong and the whole world is against you."

"Escapist fantasies," spits Nana Leah.

"No, they're political too," I insist. "*My Fair Lady* is better propaganda against the class system than any manifesto."

Nana Leah lets out a horrified moan.

"I always say one ought never discuss politics or religion," admonishes Gramma Bea.

"If I had my way," I say, madly improvising, "Quentin Crisp would be president, Nina Hagen would be Secretary of State, and Joey Ramone, Chief Justice of the Supreme Court. Plus I'd give every city in America a monorail system like they have at Disneyland."

"What about the means of production? Are they to belong to the bloodsucking capitalists or the workers?" asks Nana Leah.

"There is entirely too much production going on," I intone grandly. "If only people would embrace minimalist interior design there'd be no need to produce so much junk and we could have a three day work week in no time."

Nana Leah won't be thrown off. "But who owns the land, the factories?"

I prepare for a second coming out, every bit as difficult as the first. "Workers' councils," I whisper.

Nana Leah lets out a little yelp and mutters, "No, no, no! The state, led by the vanguard party of the proletariat."

"No," I say, gaining courage. "That leads to over-centralization of power and the formation of a bureaucratic oppressor class."

Nana Leah sputters, "But, but..."

"Yes, Nana," I admit, "I have anarcho-syndicalist tendencies."

"Oh, you're not making sense," says Gramma Bea. "Either of you. You wave around some blueprint for a perfect society and accusing everyone who objects of being against paradise. But for all the fine plans and good intentions, revolutions just lead to gulags and guillotines."

"Ach," says Nana Leah, waving her hand as if to fan away a stench coming from Gramma Bea's direction.

Gramma Bea says, "Now, I'm not saying you Americans were so wrong to get rid of George the Third, but it is nice to have a monarch to set an example of poise and politesse for the common people. The world has entirely too much vulgarity and coarseness."

"Sure," I agree, "and Jackie O. would be the obvious choice. But also, I think we should abolish high school, switch the budgets of the National Endowment for the Arts and the military, put Haley Mills on the one dollar bill, and lower the drinking age to thirteen."

I'm just getting warmed up, but Nana Leah interrupts. "And how are you to get all these... reforms through while power resides with the bourgeoisie?"

"Disable them with decadence?" I suggest tentatively. The theories Colin and I come up with do sound a little crazy in the presence of others.

"And if that doesn't work?" asks Nana Leah.

Suddenly I have the answer to all the big political questions I've wrestled with since childhood. How do you balance individual rights and social responsibility? Is human nature compatible with democracy and equality? What is a just society and how do you achieve it? The answer to each is the exactly same. "How the hell should I know? I'm twenty years old. I haven't been to college. I don't even know how to drive. I can't even make spaghetti and you expect me to figure out how to bring about the millennium? Get back to me when I'm forty."

"You don't have to get huffy," says Nana Leah, disappearing uncharacteristically in a puff of smoke.

"The woman is mad," says Gramma Bea with a resigned sigh. She then arches an eyebrow. "But really, Jeremy!" And with that, she too vanishes.

Summer arrives, turning New York's chaotic streets into a non-stop fun fair. Colin and I go on a walk through the Lower East Side. We eat pickles out of a barrel served to us by an old man with an apron off Hester Street. We slurp chocolate egg creams at Dave's that make us wonder why anyone ever drinks milkshakes, and nosh on potato latkes on East Houston. At a Canal Street secondhand store I unearth a copy of *Shindig* from a stack of ancient magazines. It's for fans of the go-go era TV show and purchasing it for a dollar makes me feel like an archeologist uncovering treasure from a pharaoh's tomb, but without the curse. We walk to an unused section of the elevated West Side highway. In an uncharacteristic outburst of athleticism I climb onto a huge metal support arch and a tourist takes my picture as I wave to the Colin and the other pedestrians two stories below.

On our way home we pass a bar and Colin insists on running in to pee. A second after he goes through the door, however, he comes right back out waving a paper in my face.

"Look!" he says. It's a copy of the *New York City News*.

"What?" I ask. He opens it up to page eight and I see... my Teenage Frankenstein article!

"Colin, how'd this get in here? You did this? I'm in here!" He smiles impishly and I want to kiss him, but of course I don't dare. "I thought you didn't even like it. I thought you thought it was stupid and shallow because I should just sleep with ugly people like myself."

He shrugs. "Well, yeah, but it is funny."

My name in print is going to my head like a thousand glasses of champagne. "They must have liked it, too. They printed it."

"The guy I showed it to said you should show him your stuff from now on. But there's no money."

"No money?" I ask.

"Nope."

"I don't care about the money," I decide. "I'm just glad it's in print."

Colin sighs. "That's the trouble with you rich kids, no ambition."

It's been a full day of picture postcard perfect moments. Just what life would be like if Colin became my boyfriend, I think, half-aware of my own self-deception even as I deceive.

Right Back Where I Started From

I'm walking down the street. Everything is alive and malevolent; ordinary objects have the weird intensity of an acid vision mixed with the lunacy of a Saturday morning cartoon. Mailboxes are compact living creatures with hungrily gaping mouths. Snake-like street lamps loom menacingly, emitting a sickly yellow-green glow. Trashcans hide mysterious gnome-like beings. Wriggling microbes on the sidewalk fester and multiply, emitting multicolored vapors that swirl and eddy. I smell rotting banana. This can't be a dream because you can't smell things in dreams! Or is it that you can't taste things? I've got to find some food and see if I can taste it. If I find Colin, he'll go to a Chinese restaurant with me and we can see if the hot-and-sour soup has any flavor. But where is he? All I see are people without faces skulking behind corners. One of them starts following me. As I run away I look up; the sky is dirty and clouds resemble the profiles of dead presidents! In the street, cars are too large! Gnats buzz in my ears! To my right bricks drip goo! To my left, rats with mustaches and human ears dance in the gutter!

"Auugh!" My own scream wakes me. I jolt to an upright position, sweating, panicked.

Colin, lying on his bed in only his underpants, looks up at me. "What's with you?"

My mouth moves without my volition. "I love you, but you hate me."

"That's not true! Think of all the time I spend with you. Do you see me spending that much time with anyone else? Do I even spend that much time with Cliff?"

"No, but..."

I don't get to finish. Colin drops his magazine and folds his hands over his stomach. "You're more fun than anyone else. You're always ready to go anywhere or try anything new. You write and paint and make your own clothes. And you're a great dancer. I mean, which would you rather do, have sex or go out dancing?"

I think for a moment. "It's a toss-up."

"When you're dancing you look like you're having an orgasm. You feel the music so much it's scary. Plus you read. You think for yourself and aren't afraid of having opinions other people think are ridiculous. You argue and don't back down or change positions just to be agreeable."

"What opinions of mine are ridiculous?" I ask indignantly.

"And it's cute the way you jump all the time," says Colin.

I'm mystified. "What are you talking about?"

"Well, Jeremy, you're a little on the short side, and when you're standing in a crowd of tall people you start standing on your tiptoes, and then you just kind of... jump a little."

I realize he's right. It's a combination of perpetual excitement and nervous anxiety. I never consciously noticed because I didn't think anyone else did.

"And you never, ever use foul language," says Colin. His arched eyebrows indicate that this is funny. "I've never even heard you say damn."

The truth is, I never picked up the habit of swearing what with Gramma Bea always hanging around and reminding me to be a little gentleman. "Well, somebody has to keep a civil tongue," I say, relieved that he thinks this is an amusing eccentricity and not evidence of repression.

"However," says Colin, "there are other things you do that drive me crazy. You think it's easy for me to live with someone who's always mooning at me?"

"I don't moon!"

Colin looks at me with great saucer eyes and a pouting lip. Ugh! Do I really moon like that?

"You're my best friend, but you can't seem to get it through your head that I'm not the marrying kind, and anyway, you're not my type sexually. And you're always good for a loan..."

Before I know what's happening my body is leaping down to the floor. I throw myself at Colin, hugging him as if for dear life. My mind floats above, watching the scene. "Jeremy, what on earth are you doing!?" asks Gramma Bea. Colin laughs a little and tries to push me off, but I won't go. As we wrestle I love the feel of Colin's skin against mine. It's like the soothing relief of cold water on a burn.

"You need work," says Nana Leah. "Work will straighten you out."

"Beastly," says Gramma Bea, her voice quavering with emotion. She knows that I'm really losing control even if Colin doesn't.

Colin and I fall off his bed onto the floor, roll over several times like cowboys in a cheesy Western, and then, in a flash, he has me pinned.

I feel the flush of shame in my face as my body raptures from the physical contact. Even being pinned to the floor by Colin is better than the best sex with anyone else. "Why I put up with you, I'll never know," says Colin.

"I love you, I love you," I say as I'm gasping for air.

Gramma Bea picks a bit of ectoplasmic lint off her purple dress. "We've all noticed, dear. Believe me, we've noticed."

Some part of me knows I'm playing my big scene as I utter my lines. "Is there any hope? Are you ever going to love me? Do you even like me? Or do you just like bossing me around and borrowing money?"

Colin is shaking his head. "I just told you I like you, but no, there's no hope whatsoever in any way that I will ever be your boyfriend."

This shuts me up for a second, during which lyrics from "Tainted Love" echo in my head, "Now I know, I've got to run away, I've got to get away…"

"Colin," I say, my voice kept steady only through a huge exertion of willpower. "I'm leaving."

Colin gets up off me and sits on his bed. "Oh?"

"Yup." I get up off the floor so I can stand and face him. I should be crying. Why aren't there hot tears running down my face? Instead I feel supernaturally calm. The Plan, were it to exist physically, would lie in confetti-like shreds at my feet.

"Going back to San Francisco?" asks Colin, squinching up his face as he pronounces the name of the city we love to hate.

"I guess so," I say, experiencing a twinge of homesickness. "It wasn't so bad there. At least there I could afford my own room. And I can hardly wait to get back to the thrift stores. Plus there's The Stud and snowless winters and little cable cars that climb halfway to the stars." I don't mention that I'm also thinking of my parents. The suspicion is also lurking around the back of my head that the whole corny crusading spirit of kookdom that prevails in the Bay Area makes it a more congenial place for befuddled types like myself than connection-driven, careerist New York.

Nana Leah, never a big smiler, is grinning like a jack-o-lantern. "You'll make something of yourself. Serve the people. It's such a relief to hear you finally talk sense. You've been worrying me sick for I don't know how long." Her ghostly form starts to fade. "Perhaps all of this couldn't be helped. *Der gleichster veg is ful mit schtainer.*" I shoot her a questioning look and she translates, "The smoothest way is sometimes full of rocks."

"I can't spend anymore time waiting for you," I say to Colin.

"I never told you to wait for me," he replies.

"Well, I'm not anymore," I say.

"Good then," he says.

"Now I can get some rest," says Nana Leah, her voice barely audible as she recedes into the ether. "I'm going now. Be good, Jeremy; don't forget The People, don't forget The Revolution!" Is she gone for good?

Colin tries to exonerate himself. "I mean, you follow me here like a puppy dog and tag along with me everywhere... it wasn't my idea."

I stare at the facial imprint on the wall. I imagine a drag queen coming home after a night of cruising the piers and making a record of her youthful visage. See, I looked like this. This was me. My little essay from the *New York City News* was my impression. Now that I've made my mark, I can go.

"I'll give you this month's rent, and I'll be out sometime in the next few weeks."

"But New York is the center of the universe," states Colin.

Is he trying to get me to stay or make me feel bad while I'm leaving? Do I care? "My mind's made up," I say.

"You don't want to be with me anymore?" Colin seems perplexed. "I thought we were having fun."

"I'm not accomplishing anything here," Surprisingly, I'm standing my ground. "One mustn't shirk one's duties."

"My little gentleman," says Gramma Bea. "I always knew you'd get some backbone and turn out well. I have to admit, though, that at times you really had me worried. I must be leaving, too. Good-bye, dear." She trundles over and kisses me on the cheek, then her form dissolves rather cinematically as she smiles both comforted and comfortingly.

It looks like I'm losing not only Colin, but my grandmothers, too. And I never even said good-bye or asked what the afterworld is like. I sort of almost feel a little bit like weeping.

Colin walks over to the window and looks out. In the bright afternoon light he looks really bad. His skin is yellowish and his eyes sport heavy black baggage. How long has he looked like this?

I casually stroll over to the mirror and peek at myself. I don't look any better. Jaundice, they call this.

"Well, all right, go back," sniffs Colin, "but I'm going with you."

I'm stunned. "What? What about Cliff? What about New York?"

"I love Cliff, but he'll never leave Barry. And whoever said you have to live in the center of the universe? I'll go with you."

"I knew you'd come," I lie.

"Pretty sure of yourself. Maybe I should stay here. You've got your pay-rents waiting for you in California. What do I have?"

"Me," I say. "Obviously."

Colin smiles a funny little smile that reminds me of the end of *City Lights*, but not so much the beautiful flower girl as the little tramp.

The next day I go to the bank to close out my account. Just for kicks, I try and cash Leopold's check which has been sitting in my wallet. To my astonishment it clears. He must have thought he'd waited long enough that I'd have thrown away the check by now. Ha! I think. Ha and double Ha!

Sheila traipses into the café looking, possibly for the first time ever, brilliantly beautiful. Love agrees with her. After she finishes telling me about the new Hayzi Fantayzi album I simply must have, I spill my guts. "I came to New York because I was in love with Colin. I thought I could make him fall in love with me by being his best friend, but I failed. So now we're both moving back to California."

Sheila is incredulous. "You're leaving New York?"

"I had to get away from Colin."

"But I thought you said he was going with you."

"He is."

Sheila rolls her eyes. "OK, fine." Pause. "Did you know you look kind of yellow? And didn't you used to weigh about twenty more pounds more? Are you sick?"

"Not especially," I say.

"I'll miss you," says Sheila, "but you have to do what you have to do. Say hello to Lizzie for me. Tell her to come visit."

"I will," I say, suddenly missing Lizzie. "And I'll miss you, Sheila."

"Oh, we'll see each other again soon," she says, her tone so offhand I don't believe her for a moment.

Neither of us being the hugging type, we give each other little waves as we say bye.

Cliff looks like he's about to cry as we load our suitcases into the trunk of the taxi. Though Barry is watching from the stoop, Colin leans over and kisses him on the lips. I'm pretty misty-eyed myself. Have I destroyed Colin's one chance at finding true love? As the cab winds its way to the bus station Colin and I stare silently out the window at the busyness we love so much. On the airport shuttle we sink into the seats in the very back and sit quietly until the uncharacteristic silence between us takes on a voice of its own, silently taunting "You're quitting! You lost! Losers! Ha, ha, ha!" Then all the harshness, discomfort, fear, poverty, disease, and cold I've zoned out of my consciousness for the past year surfaces in my memory and I feel less like I'm retreating from a battle than escaping a prison.

"Hey Colin, look." I nod my head towards the hazy towers of the Manhattan skyline receding in the distance.

With his usual telepathy, Colin understands my point instantly. "What... a... dump," he says a la Bette Davis. We cackle as the mocking voice of our silence fades to nothing.

We're standing in a crowd outside the airport check-in counter when Colin excuses himself and rushes off into the crowd. For a few terrible minutes I imagine that I'll never see him again, that he's gone back to Cliff and Manhattan which is, after all, the throbbing center of the universe. I feel ridiculously alone. Then I catch sight of Colin pushing his way through the crowd, back to me. He flashes a crooked little smile and holds up two "I ♥ NY" buttons he's purchased at a trinket stand. We laugh as we pin them on our jackets. In no time we're soaring into the heavens, together.

Acknowledgments

Thanks all the people who've aided and abetted my literary aspirations: my dream team of advance readers, Jennifer Blowdryer, Mark Ewert, Malcolm Hamilton Kevin Killian and Andrea Lawlor; writing workshop guru Dodie Bellamy; world's best boss Kate Rosenberger and the gang at Dog Eared Books; my brilliant editor Jennifer Joseph; and the plethora of people who've offered advice, encouragement, and/or publicity, including Brian Bouldrey, Lynn Breedlove, Clint Catalyst, Justin Chin, Sherilyn Connelly, Erin Cullerton, Robbie D., Deena Davenport, Alexandra D'Italia, Art De Brix and Richard, Philip R. Ford, Marc Geller, Trebor Healey, Tyler Inglolia, Katrina James, Jennifer Jazz, Tara Jepson, Miss Judy, Shawna Kenney, Bruce LaBruce, Miss Bambi Lake, Jon Longhi, Richard Loranger, Brontez Purnell, Kirk Read, Matthue Roth, Alexis Scott, Jeff Simpson, Karl Soehnlein, Timmy Spence, Horehound Stillpoint, Michelle Tea, Alex Robertson Textor, Joan Valencia, Joe Westmoreland, and Molly Zuckerman. Heartfelt appreciation also goes out to everyone who took the trouble to write fan mail or mention my books on their websites (believe me, it helps). I'd also like to express my undying gratitude to my sister Ann and brother Bo, without whom I would be powerless before these infernal computing machines.

Last but not least, I'd like to extend a very special thank you to the inimitable, impossible, and unrepeatable Michael Joseph Collins.

Manic D Press Books

I Married An Earthling. Alvin Orloff. $13.95
The Beautiful: Collected Poems. Michelle Tea. $13.95
In Me Own Words: The Autobiography of Bigfoot. Graham Roumieu. $12.95
Molotov Mouths: Explosive New Writing. James Tracy et al. $13.95
Splinter Factory. Jeffrey McDaniel. $13.95
Walking Barefoot in the Glassblowers Museum. Ellyn Maybe. $13.95
In the Small of My Backyard. Matt Cook. $13.95
Monster Fashion. Jarret Keene. $13.95
Concrete Dreams: Manic D Press Early Works. Jennifer Joseph, editor. $15
The Civil Disobedience Handbook. James Tracy, editor. $10
This Too Can Be Yours. Beth Lisick. $13.95
Devil Babe's Big Book of Postcards. Isabel Samaras. $11.95
Harmless Medicine. Justin Chin. $13.95
Depending on the Light. Thea Hillman. $13.95
Escape from Houdini Mountain. Pleasant Gehman. $13.95
Poetry Slam: the competitive art of performance poetry. Gary Glazner, ed. $15
I Married An Earthling. Alvin Orloff. $13.95
Cottonmouth Kisses. Clint Catalyst. $12.95
Fear of A Black Marker. Keith Knight. $11.95
Red Wine Moan. Jeri Cain Rossi. $11.95
Dirty Money and other stories. Ayn Imperato. $11.95
Sorry We're Close. J. Tarin Towers. $11.95
Po Man's Child: a novel. Marci Blackman. $12.95
The Underground Guide to Los Angeles. Pleasant Gehman, ed. $14.95
The Underground Guide to San Francisco. Jennifer Joseph, ed. $14.95
Flashbacks and Premonitions. Jon Longhi. $11.95
The Forgiveness Parade. Jeffrey McDaniel. $11.95
The Sofa Surfing Handbook. Juliette Torrez, ed. $11.95
Abolishing Christianity and other short pieces. Jonathan Swift. $11.95
Growing Up Free In America. Bruce Jackson. $11.95
Devil Babe's Big Book of Fun! Isabel Samaras. $11.95
Dances With Sheep. Keith Knight. $11.95
Monkey Girl. Beth Lisick. $11.95
Bite Hard. Justin Chin. $11.95
Next Stop: Troubletown. Lloyd Dangle. $10.95
The Hashish Man and other stories. Lord Dunsany. $11.95
Forty Ouncer. Kurt Zapata. $11.95
The Unsinkable Bambi Lake. Bambi Lake with Alvin Orloff. $11.95
Hell Soup: the collected writings of Sparrow 13 LaughingWand. $8.95
The Ghastly Ones & Other Fiendish Frolics. Richard Sala. $9.95
King of the Roadkills. Bucky Sinister. $9.95
Alibi School. Jeffrey McDaniel. $11.95
Signs of Life: channel-surfing through '90s culture. Joseph, ed. $12.95
Beyond Definition. Blackman & Healey, eds. $10.95

Please add $4 to all orders for postage and handling.

Manic D Press • Box 410804 • San Francisco CA 94141 USA

info@manicdpress.com   www.manicdpress.com